AGAIN AND AGAIN

MISTY MALONE

Published by Blushing Books
An Imprint of
ABCD Graphics and Design, Inc.
A Virginia Corporation
977 Seminole Trail #233
Charlottesville, VA 22901

Misty Malone
Again and Again

eBook ISBN: 978-1-64563-649-6
Print ISBN: 978-1-64563-651-9
v1

Chapter 1

Jasmine Montgomery pinned her nametag on her uniform shirt as she walked to the front of the gas station-convenience store to relieve the night shift cashier. She hadn't even made it behind the counter yet when her co-worker, who looked exhausted, sighed. "Boy, am I glad to see you, Jazz. I thought this shift would never end."

"What's the matter, Ella; rough night?"

"Not rough really, just busy. You should be slow today because I think everyone in the state of Tennessee stopped in last night and filled their vehicle up, then got some snacks before they left."

Jasmine couldn't help but laugh. "Good. Then maybe I'll have time to study for a test I have tonight."

"Yeah, I don't know about that. Good luck with the test, though."

"Thanks. Anything I need to know before you leave?"

Ella perked back up and turned to face her friend and co-worker. "Yes, there is. I'm glad you asked. Tom said to watch out for a guy that's been shortchanging stores like this. He gives the cashier a fifty-dollar bill, but wants change for a hundred, swearing that's what he gave them. We're keeping all the hundred dollar bills under the drawer so there's no hundreds in the register, just in case he comes in and tries to pull that."

"So are we keeping them in the drawer, but under the tray of money, or dropping them in the slot where we put any checks and credit card receipts?"

Tom Hardin, the store manager, walked over when he heard their conversation. "Slip them in the slot," he answered. "That way there are no hundred dollar bills anywhere in the register that he can claim is the one he gave you."

Jasmine nodded. "Okay. Has he come in here before?"

"Not that I know of, but the sheriff called me and said there's a man that's tried it several places around this area, so just watch out for him. The sheriff says he's well dressed and very nice looking. He always wears a suit, and he gets away with it sometimes because he looks like an honest guy and someone that would have hundred dollar bills in his wallet."

Jasmine chuckled. "Or if he's good looking, maybe the cashier's flirting with him and not paying attention to the money."

"Could be," Tom agreed. "'But watch for him."

"Will do." Jasmine exchanged her cash drawer with Ella's and told her friend good-bye, just as another customer came to the counter.

Her morning was pretty routine - not slow enough that she could get any studying in, but not busy, either. Early in the afternoon a man came in the store. He had clothes on that looked dirty and had rips in them, and after coming into the store he simply walked about aimlessly. He wasn't looking at anything in particular, but kept watching the other people in the store. She waited on everyone as they came to the counter, but kept an eye on this man. He was really starting to creep her out, especially since he was the only one still in the store with her. She hit the button under her counter which alerted Tom or whoever was in the office that something was going on out front.

She felt relieved when Tom came walking out, looking around, taking in everyone that was in the store. After a quick perusal of everyone there, his attention became focused on the man she was feeling uncomfortable about. He went to the counter next to Jasmine and started playing with paperwork there, appearing to be looking for something.

She looked at the man in question and quietly told Tom, "He just creeps me out."

"Been here long?"

"Longer than normal. At least ten minutes."

Tom nodded and looked around. No one else was in the store at the moment, and he approached the man. "Anything I can help you find?"

"No. I'm good."

Tom glanced at Jasmine, who was subtly shaking her head, and he turned back to the man. "So there's nothing you're looking for?"

The man sighed, and looked nervous. "Look, I'm not going to steal anything. I'm homeless, but I'm not a thief. I got a job and I start today. A man that works there said he'd pick me up here and take me in since I don't have a car. I know I look bad, but this is a labor job and they said to wear old clothes. Now that I have a job I hope to be able to get some better clothes. If I offend you I'll wait outside. I was afraid if I was standing around outside people wouldn't feel comfortable getting their gas."

He started for the door, but Tom quickly said, "No, no, I'm sorry. You're welcome to stay inside here. We just wondered what you were doing, but now that we know, you're fine waiting inside. I'm sorry if I offended you. Good luck with your new job." He quickly went back to his office, but not before giving Jasmine a bit of a glare.

She knew he wasn't happy with her, but how was she supposed to know this man's story? She assumed he'd yell at her before she went home today, and that thought bothered her. Part of her job description was being alert and reporting anything suspicious. That's all she was trying to do. She tried to turn her attention to something else, but she couldn't get his glare out of her mind. The more she thought about it the more she knew he'd yell at her for it, and the more upset she became.

She was getting pretty agitated when a gentleman walked up to the register to pay for $30 worth of gas and a bottle of water. She watched as he thumbed through his wallet, and saw he had two fifty-dollar bills. He thumbed through his wallet a bit more before handing her a bill. She counted out change for a fifty and gave it to him.

He looked a little anxious as he looked at her and at his hand. "I'm sorry, Miss, but I gave you a hundred dollar bill. You gave me change for a fifty."

She was upset as she looked up at the man to argue, but she stopped when she saw what he was wearing. He was a very good-looking man, tall and muscular with dark blond hair and gorgeous blue eyes, and he had on a suit. Not just any suit, but a very nice suit. This had to be the man Ella warned her about. She casually hit the button under the counter again, thinking Tom might be upset with her for calling him again right away, but she was sure he'd be happy with her when they caught the guy.

She plastered a smile on her face before answering. "I'm sorry, sir, but I gave you the correct change. You gave me a fifty dollar bill, and that's what I gave you change for."

She saw Tom come around the corner, not looking too happy. She wasn't surprised, and assumed he was upset about being called back out again. He apparently heard what she said as he rounded the corner, though, because when he looked at the man and saw the nice suit, he seemed to be instantly on high alert.

The customer returned her smile, but shook his head. "I'm sorry, but we seem to have a misunderstanding."

Tom walked up quickly. "I'm sorry, sir, is there a problem here?"

The man looked at Tom and the nametag indicating he was the manager. He smiled as he politely said, "I don't think it'll be a problem, sir, just a misunderstanding. I gave the cashier a hundred dollar bill, and she gave me change for a fifty. I'm sure if she looks at it again she'll see it was a hundred."

Jasmine was a bit perturbed by the man's patience and manners. What a fake! No one was that polite or patient. If it would have been her and she really had given the cashier a hundred dollar bill she'd have been yelling by now. This guy was so good looking, she was sure that's how he'd been getting away with it. He'd flash a lady cashier a winning smile and look at her with his gorgeous blue eyes, and she'd be a goner. Then he'd turn on the charm and smooth talk his way right into an extra fifty bucks! Well, not with her, he wasn't.

She smiled back at him, but didn't give in. "I don't have to look at it again, sir. I saw it as you were taking it out of your wallet. It was a fifty."

The customer's eyebrows rose when she emphasized the word sir, but he quickly regained his control. "Could you please just humor me, then, and show me that it's a fifty? I thought I pulled out the hundred."

Jasmine couldn't believe this guy. He wasn't giving up. Tom was standing there, as well, watching and listening. She once again pasted a smile on her face. "Once again, it was a fifty. Maybe you should take your change and leave, sir, before I call the police."

Tom and Jasmine both saw the shock on the man's face. To his credit, though, he pulled his wallet back out and thumbed through his money again. He looked at Jasmine one more time and shook his head. "I'm sorry, but I still – you won't even look at it again to be sure?"

Tom stepped in just as Jasmine was getting ready to tell the guy off. "Jasmine, can you show me which bill it was he gave you?" He looked down at the register and froze. There on top of the stack of fifties in the register was a hundred dollar bill. When she opened her mouth to say something, he quickly caught her eyes and looked down at her stack of fifties. "Jasmine, look at your drawer before you say another word."

She followed Tom's eyes and looked down at the drawer. She paled, but quickly took out a fifty-dollar bill and handed it to the man. "Sorry," she said.

"No harm done," the patient man said with a smile. "Thank you." He looked from one of them to the other. Anyone could easily see there was obvious tension between the cashier and her boss, and he paused a moment. "No harm done at all. You two have a good day."

After he left Tom looked around to be sure they were alone. "Jasmine, did you even look at the money when he gave it to you?"

She couldn't stop glaring at Tom. She was still angry that he was upset earlier. "Obviously, I thought it was a fifty. He didn't seem to be upset about it, so let's just drop it."

She turned to walk away, but his words stopped her. "No, I won't just drop it. You obviously weren't paying attention to what you were doing, and if you upset the customers we'll be losing business. That's the second person you've upset today."

"How was I supposed to know what that first guy today was doing?"

"I don't know. Maybe you could ask?"

Jasmine was beyond controlling her temper now. "You think you can do it so much better than me? Fine. Show me how. I'll sit here and watch the expert in action. Maybe I'll learn something."

"I don't have time to train you again, Jasmine. If you can't do it now, and do it right, maybe you just shouldn't be doing this job."

Jasmine couldn't believe what she was hearing. She didn't think she deserved to be fired, but isn't that what he was saying? Her temper and pride sure wouldn't allow her to beg for her job, though, and she knew it, so she'd save him the trouble. She got up and walked out before she had a chance to say something she might really regret.

She went straight home, sat down on her sofa and cried. She needed a job, but decided to worry about that later. She had a big test in her class tonight, so first things first. She studied for her test, cooked some Raman noodles for dinner and went to class.

After taking her test she went to the student lounge to get some coffee and unwind before going home. Linda, a lady she'd seen in her class, came and joined her. After talking about the test and how rough it was, Jasmine told Linda about her awful day. "You don't know of any jobs, do you?"

"Actually, there's a restaurant around the corner that has a 'waitress wanted' sign in their front window. I don't know anything about it, but I've seen the sign."

"Thanks. I'll go there first thing in the morning."

Two days later Jasmine made her debut as a waitress. It was a lot harder work than she thought it would be, but the tips were good. She'd been able to work her hours around her classes, and although she'd be getting roughly the same number of hours, she thought it might actually give her a little more money, which would be nice.

Her third day on the job was a Friday, and she was working over the lunch hour. She hadn't worked over lunch before, so she didn't know if lunch was always this busy or if this was unusual, but it seemed packed. She was carefully picking her way between tables, dodging people, which took more time. Try as she might, she had a couple of people complain about her service. She tried to get back to her tables with more coffee, but she just didn't seem to have enough time to do everything. The more behind she got the more frustrated she got.

She was walking carefully past a table while carrying a tray full of water, Cokes and iced tea, when a little boy jumped up right in front of her. She jumped, trying to avoid the boy. Unfortunately, the tray of drinks toppled into the lap of the man sitting at the table beside her. He immediately jumped up, and she quickly grabbed napkins. The owner of the restaurant heard the commotion and came out to see what had happened. He apologized to the man, who of course was wearing a now very wet and sticky suit.

Jasmine went in the kitchen and grabbed some towels, but when she went back out to help the poor man who'd been drenched, for the first time she looked at his face and found herself staring into his eyes. She was shocked to be looking into the same gorgeous blue eyes of the man that told her a few days ago that he'd given her a hundred dollar bill and not a fifty. "Oh, no, it's you again. I'm so sorry."

The owner took the towels from her and sighed. "You've done enough here. I don't think you were meant to be a waitress."

Jasmine was so embarrassed she turned and ran into the kitchen, and straight out the back door. He'd said that in front of the entire dining room, where of course everyone was already staring at her. She got in her car and drove home, tears running down her cheeks. She was still upset when she went to bed that night, and had a hard time falling asleep. Besides being embarrassed, she knew she would have to start a new job search right away.

———

Wednesday when she got home from her classes she collapsed onto her couch. She'd spent three days looking for a job, with no luck. She was a senior, would be graduating, receiving her degree this year, but she needed a job now. She had living expenses. She laid her head onto the back of the couch and closed her eyes. She was exhausted. Looking for a job was harder than any actual job she'd ever had.

She had about fallen asleep when her phone rang. It wasn't a number she recognized, but she'd given her number out so many times over the last few days while applying for jobs, she knew she couldn't ignore it. Someone could be calling to offer her a job, or at least an interview.

She answered, trying to sound much more pleasant than she felt. "Hello?"

"Hello, is this Jasmine Montgomery?"

"Yes."

"This is Trent Douglas."

"I'm sorry; who?"

"Trent Douglas. Please don't hang up on me until you hear me out. I'm the man at the restaurant the other day, and at the gas station last week. You ran out before I had a chance to talk to you Friday."

She was quiet for several moments, then took a deep breath. "I really am sorry. I didn't get a chance to tell you that Friday, but I mean it, I really am sorry. I'll be happy to have your suit cleaned. I know it must be a mess."

"Thank you for your concern, Ms. Montgomery, but I'm not worried about my suit, and I don't want you to be, either.

I'm much more concerned about you than my suit. I understand you lost your job because of that, and that's not right. What happened wasn't your fault. I'd like to offer you a job to replace that one."

"You'd like to – a job doing what?"

"Well, I'm not sure exactly. I'd like to have dinner with you so we can discuss it. Are you free tonight?" After an extended silence he sounded concerned. "Ms. Montgomery?"

"Sorry, I'm still here. I'm a little confused. Who are you, and how do you know who I am?"

"My name is Trent Douglas, as I said, and I found your name by asking the people you worked with. I'll be happy to answer any questions you have over dinner, while we talk about what kind of job you may be looking for. Are you free tonight?"

"Are you serious about giving me a job?"

"Of course I am. I know you don't know me yet, but when you get to know me you'll see that I don't say things I don't mean. Now, can we talk more over dinner? Tonight?"

"Umm, yeah, I guess I'm free, but how do I know I can trust you?"

"Would you feel better if we met at the restaurant, or if I were to pick you up somewhere other than at your apartment?"

"How did you get my phone number?"

"Ella at the gas station. She wouldn't give it to me until I told her I want to get in contact with you so I can offer you a job. We spoke for quite some time before she agreed. By the way, she said if you were hesitant to have dinner with me I should tell you that it's okay, I buy three Tic Tacs, and you can trust me."

Jasmine giggled. "Okay, good. Now I believe you. With that kind of recommendation, I'll have dinner with you."

"Good. Maybe over dinner you can explain to me what that means. Is it okay if I pick you up at your home?"

"Yes. If she trusts you I can, too. Do you know where I live?"

"No."

"112 North Lincoln Street, Apartment 2B."

"I know just about where that is. Can you be ready in half an hour?"

"Sure."

An hour later Jasmine and Trent sat down in a booth at a family restaurant. He reached over and patted her hand. "Thank you for agreeing to have dinner with me. I've got to ask, what was that all about when Ella said you can trust me because I buy three Tic Tacs?"

"Ella and I are good friends, and we both noticed the price of the Tic Tac mints. They're so much each, or three for so much, which was actually cheaper than buying two. It was always a joke between us that people that bought two packs didn't pay much attention to things that should be fairly important, like prices, and we didn't think we could trust them. But people who bought three were smart, alert, knew what was happening around them. They had to be the kind of people you could trust. So when she told me you buy three Tic Tacs, that was her way of telling me she thinks you're someone we can trust. You must have spent some time with her, though, because she wouldn't have told me that if she didn't truly trust you."

Trent threw his head back and laughed. "I wondered what buying mints had to do with trusting me."

"Basically it was her way of telling me to give you a chance, hear you out."

"Well, I'll have to thank her the next time I see her. I am glad you agreed to meet with me. I intend to offer you a job, but I'd like to know more about you so we can see what kind of job would suit you best."

"What do you mean you intend to offer me a job? What kind of job is available, and how can you offer it to me? Oh, wait, are you like some kind of personnel manager somewhere that hires and fires people? I mean, I'll appreciate it if you can get me an interview for a job somewhere, but can you really just flat out offer me a job?"

"Boy, you have a lot of questions," he said with a smile. "And they're all good ones. Let me explain. I have a company and it's doing rather well. We're expanding and we've been hiring additional people on a fairly regular basis. Therefore, I'm sure we can find a job for you somewhere. But I'd like to get to know you better so we can match you up with the job that would be the best fit for you."

"Wait a minute. When you say you have a company, do you mean the company you work for?"

"Yes and no. It is the company where I work, but I don't want to mislead you. I own it, so to answer one of your questions, yes, I can offer you a job, not just an interview."

Jasmine's eyes grew huge. "You own a company?"

Trent chuckled. "Yes, but don't get too excited. It's not like General Motors or IBM. It's just a fairly small, local manufacturing company."

"Wow." She froze suddenly, and slowly looked at him carefully. "Did you say your name is Trent Douglas, as in Douglas Manufacturing?"

His smile reached to and included his eyes. "You've heard of my company?"

"Duh. Everyone around here has. I've heard it's the best place around here to work. You own that?"

"You've heard that, really?"

"Of course. Everyone says you're very fair to work for, and you pay more than other places around."

"That's wonderful to hear," he said, deep in thought. She could tell his words were sincere.

"How can you do that? I mean, if you pay more than other places, won't your profit be lower?"

"I don't think so, no. When I started this company I told everyone that I believe if you treat people right they'll treat you right. I know how I want my business to run, but I can't do it all myself. I can't make it, sell it, ship it, collect the money, put it in the bank, and pay the bills all myself. So that means I have to rely on a lot of other people."

"I'm with you so far."

"If I want them to care about this business and do the best job they can for the company, the best way I know to do that is to treat them fairly. The longer someone works for me, the more they know about the company and the more they care about it, and the better job they do. So if I want them to stay there and have that longevity, I have to treat them right. That's been my philosophy from day one, and I've been really happy with how it's been working."

"Wow. I'm impressed."

"It's not really that impressive. It's just treating people the way I'd want to be treated myself. Now, about that job."

"You're serious? You'd offer me a job, knowing I just got fired from my last two jobs?"

"The last one wasn't your fault, and in my opinion the owner had no business firing you. The kids at that table behind me were not at all behaved. They kept jumping up and running around the restaurant. It was much too busy for them to be doing that. In my opinion the owner would have been a lot better off kicking them out and keeping you in his employ. But since it was already done and I couldn't do anything to stop it, I have to admit I was happy that it gave me a chance to meet you."

"Why would you want a chance to meet me after the way I treated you at the gas station?"

"Besides the fact that you're a beautiful young lady, Ella told me you'd been warned to be on the lookout for someone in a suit trying to pass off fifties and saying they're hundreds. I understand what happened."

She looked up at him, a smile forming. "So you wouldn't have fired me for what I did?"

"Fired you? No."

Her smile grew. "Thank you."

"I might have taken you into my office at the end of the day and given you a good spanking, but I wouldn't have fired you."

Jasmine about choked on the water she'd taken a sip of. "You'd what?"

Trent chuckled, and changed the subject. "So, tell me about yourself. What do you like, what do you not like? What would be your ideal job?"

"Now or once I get my degree?"

"Both. What kind of degree are you aiming for, and how close are you to getting it?"

"I just started my last year. It's taken me six years because I haven't had the money to go full time, but I've taken at least two or three classes every semester, and I hope to get my degree in May. It'll be a degree in business management."

"And what kind of job will you be looking for once you graduate?"

She shrugged her shoulders. "This is going to sound weird, but I'm not real sure. I really like business; all of it. At first I thought I'd like to be a human resources manager or personnel manager. But then I studied purchasing, like to be the manager of a purchasing department. I love shopping and looking for bargains, and I think I'd like that kind of job. I don't buy anything until I'm sure it's the best deal I can find, so

I think I'd be great at it. Tell me what you need and I'll find a good deal on it and buy it. Besides, what could be bad about getting paid to spend other people's money?" She giggled, and he laughed as well, loving her smile.

"So you'd like to work in purchasing some day?"

She shrugged her shoulders again. "I think I'd like that, yeah. But I also think I'd like working in personnel. I took a few classes in sales and marketing, but I don't think I'd like that as well. The same way with accounting. I took a couple of classes so I can read financial statements and know what they're saying, but I wouldn't want to be in accounting."

Trent was nodding as he listened carefully. "Okay, I think I have a little bit of an idea what kinds of jobs you might like when you graduate. How about now? Since you were working at a gas station and as a waitress, can I assume you're willing to do, how should I word this? Maybe, less glamorous jobs until you get your degree?"

"I'm willing to do about anything." She blushed as she quickly looked up and clarified her statement a bit. "Well, anything legal and moral."

Trent laughed at the little lady sitting across the booth from him. "I hear you, and I appreciate the clarification. Just so you know, I'd never ask you to do anything that wasn't within your comfort level."

Trent thought she looked adorable when she blushed. "I'm sorry. I didn't think you would."

He put his hand over hers and tried to get her to relax. "I know. Now, I know a little about what you want to do professionally. Tell me about yourself. Did you grow up locally, do you have family nearby?"

She wasn't real forthcoming about her family and growing up, but when she changed the subject slightly, he allowed it. They soon discovered conversation flowed easily between them, and they enjoyed their meal. He took her home, and after they talked for another hour, he convinced her to have dinner with him again on Friday. He gave her a gentlemanly kiss on her cheek before thanking her for having dinner with him and saying goodnight.

He thought about Jasmine as he drove home that evening. In fact, he couldn't seem to get her out of his mind, and was glad she'd agreed to have dinner with him again. There was something about her that grabbed his attention the first time he'd met her at the gas station. She was very genuine, and he admired that.

She may have been small in stature, but she was big in likability. She was confident in her opinions and words and obviously comfortable in her skin, which he also admired. He couldn't help notice her long light brown hair, with even lighter highlights that caught the light perfectly, telling him her hair color was not from a bottle. In fact, she was a beautiful young lady, but he didn't think she realized it. She wore little makeup, just enough to accentuate what he considered her best assets, which made her breathtaking in his opinion. But what he liked was that she seemed totally unaware of her beauty. She had natural grace and charm, and enough self-confidence to be herself. All of that put together, the whole package was something he was anxious to get to know better.

Chapter 2

Trent called his personnel manager into his office the morning after meeting Jasmine. He talked with him regarding any open spots in the company right now, along with any openings they expected may become available in the future. He spent time over the next couple of days thinking about Jasmine and what job he would ultimately offer her.

Jasmine spent the following day trying to study, but having a difficult time. Her mind kept going back to her dinner with Trent. There was a lot to consider. First, there was the fact that he was so handsome. He had gorgeous dark blond hair, thick with just enough wave in it to make her want to run her fingers through it. His blue eyes were not only gorgeous, but so inviting, so easy to get lost in. His physique was what she personally considered perfect. At just under six feet he was fairly tall, but not too tall. He was very muscular, which she liked, but not too much, like one of these overgrown hulks. He had an air of confidence about him, which she really liked, but not so much that he was arrogant. The whole package together made him perfect – not overdone, just incredibly sexy.

She was surprised to learn Douglas Manufacturing was his company. When she first encountered him she hadn't thought he was more than a year or two older than herself, but that didn't seem possible. If she would have gotten through college in four years she would have graduated two years ago. Even if he was two years older than her and one of these geniuses that made it through school in three years, he would only be five years out of college. Could he have started a company and made it this successful in five years? She tried to think back, but couldn't remember how long it had been around.

She couldn't believe he was going to offer her a job, and had to wonder why he would do that? She also had to wonder about him taking her out to dinner. Was it just so he could offer her a job, or was that like a date? She shook her head at that thought. He was extremely hot and sexy, and owned his own company. Why would he take her out on a date after seeing her lose her last two jobs?

And then there was that weird comment he made about taking her to his office after work for a good spanking after she'd messed up. Surely he was only kidding, but what would make him say such a thing? There were so many mysteries about him, many of which were the exact things that drew her to him, and she'd love to get to know him better. That idea was absurd, though, and she had to stop thinking of him as anything other than a potential employer. While that thought made perfect sense to her, she knew it would be easier said than done.

Ella called her while she was deep in thought, and she jumped, before managing to grab her phone to answer it. "So, did you go out with him? Did he offer you a job? Was it strictly business, or did he ask you out again?"

"Whoa, slow down," Jasmine laughed. "And thank you for the tip with the Tic Tacs."

"He seemed really sincere about wanting to offer you a job. What was that all about? Why is he offering you a job? And what kind of job?"

"Again, slow down." The two friends spent the next half hour talking on the phone. Jasmine shared much about last night, and some of the questions she'd been wondering about. The only thing she didn't mention was the comment about spanking. She was still assuming he'd been just kidding around.

Not long after her phone call with Ella, Jasmine's doorbell rang. She opened the door and was shocked to see a beautiful bouquet of flowers. After double-checking to be sure they were in fact for her, she took them inside and read the card. 'Thank you for dinner last night. I enjoyed it immensely and am looking forward to Friday. Trent.'

Jasmine read it twice. Did that mean last night was a date? He was taking her out again this Friday, but was that just for the job, or would he ask her out again? She didn't want to get her hopes up, but it was hard not to.

She found herself thinking back to other men she'd dated. Manners were important to her, and something that she noticed about a man right away. Unfortunately, manners didn't seem to be too important to many men these days. Of the ones who at least tried to be mannerly, it seemed to her that many of them were simply going through the motions, making an obvious attempt to appear mannerly. It didn't take long to see through their often rather feeble attempts, which was always disappointing.

Trent, however, seemed different. He seemed genuine, like a true gentleman, which was why it didn't surprise her all that much when he called her Thursday night. Unlike most of the men she'd dated, his actions with regards to manners were very natural, which could only mean they were very real. She was looking forward to dinner Friday evening, but was also a little worried. She didn't want to do or say anything stupid. He seemed more refined, and she was more spur of the moment. She was determined to mind her p's and q's.

He told her on Thursday that he'd pick her up Friday at 6:00. She started getting ready two hours early, not sure what she wanted to wear, and not wanting to be late. She changed her outfit seven times, but finally decided on a skirt and blouse that several of her friends said fit her great and was a good color on her. Knowing she often got compliments when she wore it, it always made her feel confident, which was just what she needed at the moment. She hoped it would help settle her nerves.

It was also no surprise to her when he rang her doorbell Friday evening at precisely 6:00. She was ready, having convinced herself she looked presentable. When she opened the door the smile on his face was real, which made her return his smile. "You look fantastic, Jasmine. Are you ready to go?"

"I am. I didn't think to ask where we were going, so I wasn't sure what I should wear."

"That's perfect," he assured her. Once he'd helped her into his car and they were on their way, he started the conversation. "Do you like seafood?"

"I love it."

"Good. I do, too. Have you been to Taylor's Seafood?"

Her eyes grew huge as she looked at him. "I've been there once, and I loved it, but it's expensive."

He ignored her comment as to the prices. "I really like it, too. What did you like about it?"

"Well, the food is amazing, but it's not just the food; it feels like an experience. I love how every table has privacy. It's decorated so that each table feels like it's in its own room somehow. It's so cozy, and the chairs were so soft and cushy, you couldn't help but be relaxed and comfortable. I loved it."

Trent loved her enthusiasm. "I know what you're saying about the privacy. That's one of the reasons I picked there for tonight. I want to be able to talk to you so I can get to know you better while I tell you about your new job."

"You really are going to give me a job?"

He frowned momentarily. "Jasmine, I told you, I don't say things I don't mean. Hopefully after a few more dinners and evenings spent together you'll start to believe me."

Jasmine couldn't stop the huge smile that appeared on her face after his last comment. She tried to hide her excitement a bit, but knew she was probably failing miserably. "Maybe. We'll see."

He pulled into the parking lot and turned to look at her. "Wait right there." He was out of the car before she had a chance to question why, and he appeared at her door, holding out his hand to help her out. He also led her in with a gentle hand on her back. She'd never been treated like that, but she liked it. She liked it a lot.

Once they were seated and given menus, he offered his assistance. "I don't know what kind of seafood you like, but I've tried several things here. If you want any suggestions, I'll help if I can."

"I've only had scallops a couple of times, but I loved them. The other time I was here I had the crab-stuffed flounder. I loved the stuffing, but I'm not real big on fish."

"Do you like shrimp?"

"Love it."

"Then you might like combo number six. It has scallops fixed three different ways, and crab-stuffed shrimp. The shrimp are huge and they're stuffed with the same crab filling they put in their flounder."

"Oh, that sounds wonderful. I want to try that."

Trent again loved the big smile on her face. When the waitress came to take their order he ordered for both of them, another first for her. Once the waitress left he asked a couple of questions and they were soon talking easily again.

He never mentioned a job for her, and she never thought about it until they were driving home. "Trent, I loved dinner. The food was fantastic, and I had a great time. But I thought you were going to talk to me about a job."

"We'll talk about that when we get to your apartment, okay?"

"Okay. I never thought about it during dinner, I was having such a good time."

"I'm glad to hear that. How are your classes going this semester?"

They talked about her classes until they got to her place. Again he told her, "Wait right there."

This time she knew why, and had no problem waiting. He seemed to watch out for her, or take care of her even, and although it was new to her, she was starting to like it real well. Not only was he giving her a job when she needed it, but little things like helping her decide what she wanted for dinner, and suggesting she might want a coat for later since they were calling for it to cool off. She could get used to that.

He helped her out of the car and into her apartment. He went to the kitchen with her and opened a bottle of wine he'd brought with him. She poured them each a glass, which they took into the living room.

Once they were comfortably seated on the couch and each had a sip of wine, he turned toward her. "Ready to hear about your job?"

"Absolutely. I still can't believe you're actually willing to give me a job, after the way I treated you."

"Yeah, we'll talk about that in a few minutes. First I want to tell you what I have in mind and see if you're interested."

She wasn't sure how she felt about the first part of that statement, but she put it aside for the time being. "I'm anxious to hear about it."

"What I'd like to do is have you work as an assistant in the purchasing department."

He watched her eyes light up with his words, but he also saw some trepidation. "What does an assistant in the purchasing department do? Make coffee? I mean, I will, but _"

"Let me explain our purchasing department to you. George Engels is the head of it. Each department head is responsible for letting George know what supplies they need, when, and how many. When we develop a new product the engineering department makes a detailed list of the raw materials that will be needed and how much of it will be needed, and it's up to George to find those materials at a good price. Over the years George and the purchasing department have gotten busier and busier. He now has a lady that works there part-time and helps, along with a full-time administrative assistant."

"Secretary?"

Trent grinned as he shook a finger in warning. "Be careful how you refer to them. I'm told they're no longer secretaries, they're administrative assistants."

Jasmine giggled. "Sorry. I just wanted to make sure I knew what you meant. I'll be careful now that I know. I don't want to hurt their feelings. They really do play an important role in any company."

"They do at that," Trent agreed. "But the purchasing department plays a very important role, too. Without the raw materials we need we won't be manufacturing a thing. And here's the thing. George is getting too busy again and needs more help. I need to hire someone to help him, but I want to find someone I can hire to help him now, but is willing to learn what he does so they can take over in about a year. George told me he wants to retire next year."

"What about the lady that's part-time now?"

"She works part-time and has no desire to work full-time. She has twins that started first grade this year, and she wants to be able to get them on the bus before she leaves for work, and be there when they get home in the afternoon."

"So she'd rather be a full-time mom than a full-time employee?"

"Apparently. And there's nothing wrong with that. As long as a woman does what she feels in her heart is right for her, I respect her, and her decision."

"Me, too."

"So I want to hire someone that can work part-time now and learn what they're doing. Then I'd want them to go full time, say after you graduate in May, and work closely with George so that when he retires in about a year you can step in as the manager. Are you interested?"

"Seriously?"

"You still haven't learned that what I say I mean, huh? Yes, I'm serious."

"How about my college classes?"

"They come first. We'll set your hours around your classes. We can change them as your class schedule changes."

"Trent, that sounds terrific!"

Trent could easily see how excited she was at his job proposal, and he was glad. But as much as he hated to lessen that excitement, he had to make sure she understood a couple of things. He took a deep breath and forged ahead. "I'm glad you think so, Jasmine. But there are a couple of conditions that go along with this job, and I want to be sure you're aware of those before you decide if you're interested."

She studied him for several moments. "Conditions. What do you mean by conditions?"

"Well, this job involves talking and working with people. You can't lose your temper and yell at someone or upset them when you're trying to negotiate prices."

Jasmine sat up straight. "What are you saying? You don't think I can work with people?"

"I think you can, yes, or I wouldn't be making this job offer. But I also know you've lost three jobs because of your temper, and I'm saying that having a temper tantrum is not something I will allow."

"What do you mean I lost three jobs because of my temper?"

"That's not counting the last two jobs you lost, which I already knew about. I don't feel the last job was your fault, in any event."

Jasmine glared at Trent. "How the hell do you know I lost any jobs because of my temper? You had no business checking up on me."

Trent's expression turned instantly stern. "Jasmine, watch your language, and your temper. I just got done telling you I will not allow temper tantrums. That means not only while you're working, but anytime we're together."

Sarcasm was something else she knew she needed to work on, but just like her temper, she never thought about it until after she'd already lost control. "I'm sorry, did you just say you won't allow me to have a temper tantrum?"

"That's exactly what I said, Jasmine."

She stood up and glared at him, her hands on her hips. "And who the hell do you think you are, anyway?"

Way too quickly for Jasmine to grasp what was happening, Trent stood himself, picked her up and in one fluid motion sat back down, laying her over his lap. "I'm the man that can help you break that bad habit, which will allow you to achieve your goals." He flipped her full, but fairly short skirt up over her back and pulled her panties down in one quick movement. He anticipated her objections to that act, and had his left arm around her waist, securely holding her in place, while his right arm raised. His hand came down with a swat to her bare bottom, just as she was struggling to get away.

"Oh, shit!" She struggled harder to get away. "Trent, what are you doing? That hurts! Stop this instant!"

He tightened his hold on her, a bit surprised at her strength as she fought to break free. He smacked her bottom again, which brought about more verbal complaints. "Damn it, Trent, I said that hurts! Let me up."

She put great effort into struggling to get off his lap, but he tightened his hold once again, keeping her right where she was. "Jasmine, settle down, and watch your mouth."

He settled into a pattern of spanking her left cheek, then her right, as she clearly let him know that she was not at all amused by what was happening. "You stop this right now, you jackass! You'll be sorry you ever even thought of doing this! Ow! I'm not warning you again!"

Trent had to chuckle at that. "That's a good idea, sweetheart. You stop warning me long enough for me to get a warning of my own in. You may as well settle down and listen to what I have to say, because this spanking is happening. I'm not going to stop until I feel you've learned the lesson I'm trying to teach you. The longer you keep swearing and fighting me, trying to get me to stop, trying to get off my lap, the longer it will go on, because I know you're not listening to what I'm trying to tell you. I'll keep spanking until you decide you're ready to settle down enough to hear what I'm saying. Then I'll start talking, not yelling like I have to do now so that you'll hear me, and I'll tell you what I want to say. So how long this lasts depends on you. The sooner you settle down and listen to me, the quicker it will end. It's up to you."

"Oh, I'm so mad right now!"

"I can see that," he said quietly.

She continued to yell and struggle, all to no avail. Once she realized it was getting her nowhere, she stopped fighting and started crying. When Trent saw that he stopped the spanking, but kept his hand on her warm bottom. "Are you ready to listen now?" he asked quietly.

Tears were streaming down her face and she sniffled. "Do I have any choice?"

"Yes, you do. You can keep fighting and I'll keep spanking, or you can stay like you are and we'll talk a little bit."

"Can I sit up to talk?"

"No."

She immediately started struggling again. "Damn you, Trent, let me up! I said I'd listen now!"

He started spanking her again. "And I said when you settle down we'll talk; not before. I also said to watch your mouth. I repeat, I'll continue to spank you until you decide you're ready to listen to what I have to say."

"I said I'd listen, but you won't let me up!"

"I think you'll listen to me better right where you are. I will stop the spanking while we talk, though. So you let me know when you're ready to listen."

Without saying anything else, he started spanking with gusto again. It wasn't long at all before she stopped struggling. "Okay, I'll listen," she said quietly.

"Good." He stopped the spanking, but again left his hand on her bare bottom, which was quite warm now. "Jasmine, you said I had no business checking up on you and your past jobs. Actually, I do have that right. Ella told me where you'd worked. I called them and said I was considering hiring you, and asked about your employment with them. They were very helpful. I think I see a pattern forming here. They all, every single one of your past employers, told me you were a very intelligent lady and a good worker. They had lots of good things to say about you as a person. But when I asked them why your employment with them ended, I kept hearing the same thing. It seemed to always be because of a problem with your temper."

Jasmine was quiet, listening to what he said. At the last statement, she started sobbing and slumped over his knees. He rubbed her back gently. "I can help you with that, sweetheart, if you'll let me. I think you have a lot to offer an employer, and if you learn to control your temper you'll be an asset to any company. I'd like that company to be mine."

She was quiet, and he could tell she was listening, so he continued. "But there's another thing, and I'm going to be very open and honest with you here. I'd like to have more than just an employer/employee relationship with you, Jasmine. I felt something for you the first time I saw you in the gas station. I felt it again at the restaurant. And the two dinners we've shared have confirmed it; I feel something special for you. I don't know if you feel the same way or not, but I'd really like to explore those feelings and see if anything comes of them."

Jasmine was still quiet, and had now turned quite still. She turned her head to look at him with an obvious look of confusion. "How can you say you feel something special for me when you're doing this?"

"This may be hard for you to believe right now, but if I didn't feel something special for you I would never be doing this."

"Well, aren't I lucky to be special?" she said sarcastically.

"I deserved that," he surprised her by saying. "Let me try to explain what I mean, and maybe it'll make a little more sense to you. When I heard your former employers say this, what would have been the easiest thing for me to do?"

She shrugged her shoulders, but didn't answer. He gave her a sharp swat on her bare bottom. "I hate when people simply shrug their shoulders when I ask them a question.

Think about it, Jasmine. The easiest thing for me to do would have been to say, her temper is a problem. I can't take a chance by putting someone that volatile in my company, or putting a lot of time and effort into developing a relationship with her, because a temper is something I cannot simply ignore. It ruins relationships."

Trent could tell she was listening to him, which was good. "But that's not what I want. I really feel you're a special little lady, and what I want is to get to know you better, see if we can have a relationship. When I do something I do it the best I can. When I find something I want I'm willing to put a great deal of time and effort into it. That includes relationships. I've only had a few, but I tried my best to make them work, until it was obvious to me that we weren't looking for the same things. Then we parted as friends. And I also feel that you have the potential to be a big asset to my company. But for both of those things to work we have to control your temper. I'm trying to help you do that."

"By beating my ass?"

He gave her six more swats. "You really do have an attitude, don't you? In answer to your question, I'm trying to help you do that with a spanking. Not just a spanking, but a spanking every time your temper is a problem."

"You think you're going to do this again?"

"If your temper is a problem again and you're working for me or we're in a relationship, yes, I do." Before she could object again, he held up his hand. "Let me ask you something. Your parents never spanked you, did they?"

She harrumphed. "Hardly. They were never around. But neither did any of my nannies or any of the people at any of the boarding schools."

Trent's eyebrows raised. "You had nannies and went to boarding schools?"

"Yeah. So?"

She turned around a bit and was surprised to see a sadness in his eyes. "I'm sorry, Jasmine."

She turned her head sideways to study him better. "Sorry you spanked me?"

"No, you totally deserved that. I'm sorry you had nannies and boarding schools instead of parents."

"Don't be, it could have been worse."

Trent was rubbing her back gently again, and he continued to do that. "Meaning?"

"I ran away from one of the boarding schools once and I met another girl about my age. She was walking home from school and we started talking. Her dad abandoned her and her mom, and then her mom was killed in a crash. She was living in a foster home, and they made her do all kinds of work. She sometimes didn't have her homework done for school because they didn't give her any time to work on it."

Trent saw that tears were coming down her cheeks quicker now. He pulled Jasmine up and sat her down on his lap. He wrapped his arms around her, guiding her head to rest on his broad chest.

She looked up at him, tears streaming down her cheeks. "She was real skinny and her clothes were old. I may not have felt loved by my parents, but I had good clothes and a chance to go to a good school, and I had plenty of food. I felt so sorry for her."

Trent was rubbing her arm, trying to soothe her. On a hunch, he asked, "Did you ever get to talk with that girl again?"

Her eyes brightened as she answered. "I got her address before she got home, and we've written letters ever since. One day I hope to —"

When she paused, Trent tried to encourage her. "One day you hope to what, sweetheart?"

Jasmine blushed, but she continued. "She'd like to go to

college, but she can't afford it. The day she graduated from high school she had to move out of the foster home. They didn't get paid to keep her once she was eighteen and out of high school, so she got a job and moved into a tiny apartment. She barely makes enough to pay her rent and buy food, let alone save for college."

Trent was touched by how much Jasmine cared for this other girl. After a couple of minutes where neither of them said a word, a thought occurred to him. "Jasmine, if your parents hired nannies and sent you to boarding schools, why are you working your way through school? Why aren't they paying for it?"

She sat up straighter, but dropped her head, and he heard a few sniffles. He gave her a handkerchief and a hug. "I'm sorry; that isn't any of my business."

She laid her head on his shoulder again as she wiped her eyes, still struggling to gain control of her tears. Eventually she found her voice. "Trent, I think it's my turn to be open and honest with you. I have no idea why I feel the way I feel right now. I should be really mad at you, but for some reason I feel I can trust you and open up to you. That's a strange feeling for me."

"I'm glad to hear that. Thank you for telling me, and you can trust me, Jasmine. I'm very serious about everything I said. I hope I haven't scared you off because I really would like to have a relationship with you."

"You haven't scared me off, although I truthfully have no idea why not. I feel like I should hate you right now and should be trying to run away. But for some reason, I can't. Your shoulder and your arms around me feel too good."

"I'm glad to hear that, too."

"It's comforting." After a moment or two, she added, "But I still feel like I should be running from you as fast as I can."

"Maybe you're not running because you know I really do want to help you."

She shook her head as she looked up at him. "See, I believe that, but I don't know why. I still feel like I should hate you."

He smiled down at her. "Your bottom probably does hate me right now, but I hope your head and heart tell you you can trust me."

She looked a bit embarrassed, but she managed a small smile. "Again, I don't know why, but that is what they're telling me."

"Good." He guided her head back to his shoulder, and simply held her for a couple of minutes, giving her time to settle in and feel comfortable.

"To answer your question about working my way through school, after I graduated from the last boarding school they sent me to I really wanted to get to know my parents. I hoped I could stay with them for the summer before I started college." A few tears escaped again, but she continued. "But they still didn't have time for me. They told me since I was eighteen now I didn't need a nanny, but I could stay in the house. They were going to Europe for the summer. It was going to be a mixture of work and a vacation they said they sorely needed. I asked if I could come visit them some. I told them I really wanted to get to know them. They laughed and said they were my parents, I already knew them."

Trent tightened his arms around her. "I'm sorry, Jasmine."

"Yeah, well, it told me a lot. So I stayed in their house that summer, but I got a job and saved my money. They never asked where I wanted to go to college or what I wanted to do. I was expected to go to their alma mater, so they had it all arranged. I applied and got into a cheaper college here and made my plans to go here in the fall. I got a letter from my parents one day about mid-summer, saying what day they'd be home." She fought back more tears. "They said if I had to leave before then to go to college, that they'd see me over Christmas break. So two days before they were to get home I went off to college. I found an apartment that I shared with three other girls because it was cheaper than living on campus. I got a job, and I've been going to school and working ever since. The other girls went to school full-time and didn't work, so they finished in four years. I moved into my smaller apartment and have been living alone since they graduated."

"Have your parents helped you at all?"

Tears started flowing again. When she got them contained once more she sighed. "I've never heard from them. I didn't leave them a note when I left because I really didn't know what I wanted to say. So I just left. I figured they probably wouldn't think anything was wrong until I didn't come home for Christmas that year. Then they might call the college and find out I wasn't going there. I figured if they cared and wanted to find me it wouldn't be too hard. I used my name and Social Security number at the college and every job I had, so if they wanted to find me they could have. They obviously haven't wanted to."

"Honey, they don't know what they're missing. They haven't seen the wonderful young lady you've grown into."

She smiled up at him and laid her head against his chest. He tightened his arms around her and watched, amazed, as she seemed to nestle right in against him, looking very content. He knew right then and there this lovely little lady had stolen his heart already. She was the first lady ever to achieve that, and it sure hadn't taken her long. That convinced him she was the woman he was meant to be with. Now he just had to convince her of that.

Chapter 3

Trent held Jasmine in his arms and they talked a little more about her childhood and after she left for college. He was still curious about one thing, but did quite a bit of thinking before asking her about it. "Could you finish your sentence from a moment ago? You were talking about your friend you write to and you said someday you hope to do something. What's her name, and what is it you hope to do?"

Trent watched her blush again. She was the most adorable little lady he'd ever met. She looked at him and answered slowly. "Her name's Sheila Wiles. I always thought I'd like to try to help her go to school, too. I thought once I graduated and got a job that paid better I could help her with money for tuition and books."

Trent gave her a little squeeze, touched by her thoughtfulness. Before he could say anything, though, she continued. "She deserves to be able to go to college, too. We were both working to pay our rent, but I had some advantages she didn't have. When I graduated from high school my parents gave me a car, so I had that. I also had several thousand dollars in a savings account that I had from when I was small. My grand-parents always gave me some money for my birthday and Christmas and it went into the account. Then that last summer I stayed at my parents' house without paying any rent, and I saved all the money I made working at a fast food place. That money's about gone now, but if I wouldn't have had that and my car I wouldn't have been able to go to college, either."

"Does she know you plan on helping her when you get a job?"

"No, I never told her. I didn't want her to get excited about it and then me not be able to find a good job. I thought when I have the money to pay for her first semester and books, I'll surprise her with it then."

"Have you seen her since that day you met her?"

"We've exchanged some pictures, but we've never seen each other in person again. She lives clear out in Arizona."

"Your parents sent you from eastern Tennessee clear out to Arizona to a boarding school?"

She looked down as she nodded. "I always assumed it was so I couldn't ask to come home on the weekends."

They talked ten more minutes with her tucked in against him. Finally he sighed and looked down at her. "Jasmine, I hate to break this spell because I've really enjoyed our little talk here, but I have to make sure you're okay with what happened this evening." He felt her stiffen, and he didn't like that. "After we talked I want more than ever to get to know you better, and I hope you accept my job offer. But it's important that you understand what will happen anytime your temper is a problem."

She was quiet, and he gave her time to collect her thoughts. "If you have any questions I'll answer them, and if you need time to consider my offer I understand, but I need to know your thoughts."

Again she was quiet for quite some time, and he was

patient. She was still enveloped in his arms when she looked up at him with a determined look on her face. "I'm afraid if I take much time to think about this I'll over-think it. When you spanked me all I felt was anger. Well, anger and a lot of pain. I wanted you to leave, and I never wanted to see you again. I was really angry, but then when you started talking to me, then took me in your arms and held me, I started feeling confused. I don't know why, but like I said, for some reason I feel I can trust you."

"You can trust me."

"I also feel you really do care and are trying to help me. That's a feeling I'm not used to, but it feels nice. In fact, I feel better right now than I've felt in a long time, other than my butt. It still really hurts."

"As it was meant to, to teach a lesson." He gave her a little squeeze. "Thank you for sharing some of your feelings with me, Jasmine. Are you willing to accept my job offer, or do you need more time to consider it?"

She sighed, sounding resigned. "I do have a problem with my temper occasionally, and could use some help with it. What that means is if the job offer still stands, I want to accept it, before I over-think it."

He chuckled, but hugged her tight to his chest. "I'm impressed. It takes a strong person, and I've found very few, who can or will be that honest with themselves and their feel-ings. I'm also very glad to hear you say that, sweetheart."

"Which part?"

"All of it. I'm glad you're willing to admit to yourself that you have a problem, but I'm very glad to hear you're willing to work on it, and that you're going to work for my company. I'm also really glad you feel good right now. I hope that means you feel comfortable and safe with me. I should probably tell you, I feel very protective of you, Jasmine, and my goal is that you always feel safe with me."

"I do. I think that's a lot of why I feel so good, is I feel safe and secure with your arms around me. Again, this is a new feeling to me, but although it's new, I love it."

He tightened his hold on her. "I love it, too. Having you in my arms just feels right to me." He grinned as he caught her eyes. "But just so you know, I'm also glad to hear your butt still hurts."

"Seriously? Why?"

He looked down at her. Her red face was so cute. "That means I did it right and hopefully it'll help you remember what will happen the next time your temper gets the better of you. That's the whole idea behind a spanking, you know; to convince you you don't want to do that again. Think it'll work?"

She sighed. "I sure hope so, but I can be a bit −"

"Stubborn? Willful? Unyielding? Obstinate? Impulsive? Am I getting close?"

She giggled as she hit his chest. "Maybe," she admitted.

"Don't worry," he soothed. "A few good spankings will cure all of the above."

Her eyes grew huge. "A few?"

He grinned. "Okay, several."

"Several? How about one, or maybe two?"

"That would be great. Let's aim for that."

"That's better," she said as she snuggled in against his chest again.

"It's totally up to you, you know. But just so you feel safe and secure, rest assured that I work out, so my right arm's in good shape. It'll be up to the task, no matter how many it takes."

"What?" But even as she jerked away from his chest she heard his chuckle, and when she looked into his face, she saw the smile, both on his face and in his eyes. "Oh, you!" She cuddled back in against him, thinking how lucky she was, even though her bottom might not think so at the moment.

The following Monday morning Jasmine was at Douglas Manufacturing ready to start her new job. Trent was waiting for her in the lobby, just as he'd said he would, and took her to the personnel manager. He waited while she filled out a couple of quick forms. He took her to the purchasing department then and introduced her to George, her new boss, and the part-time lady, Beth, as well as the administrative assistant, Cindy. She was shocked when he was very open and honest with them all. "I want everyone to know up front that I'm seeing Jasmine on a personal level, but that isn't how she got this job. We met when she dumped iced tea over me a couple of weeks ago at lunchtime."

George laughed out loud. "I remember that day."

"So do I." Trent laughed. "I knew right then and there she'd be better off in a purchasing department than working as a waitress." After they all enjoyed a little laugh, he continued. "She's in her last year of college, though, so I'm hoping you can train her to take over when you leave, George. That gives you close to a year. Think you can do it?"

George smiled warmly at her. "I think so. Serving iced tea isn't a requirement here, so you'll do fine, Jasmine." The rest all chuckled, but welcomed her warmly. Trent kissed the top of her head. "I'll be by to see you at lunchtime," he said, and left.

By noon she had a rough idea what she would be doing, and she was excited. The three people she'd be working with all seemed real nice and easy to work with, and the work seemed challenging. She was working hard on the first project George had given her, and didn't realize how late it was until she heard Trent's voice. "Are you free for lunch before you go to your class?"

"Oh," she said, startled. "Yes, I have time. I didn't know it was that late." He enjoyed listening to her talk about her morning while they ate. It was obvious she was happy. He was also glad to hear they'd taken her down to the break room during break time and introduced her to some of the other employees. It was important to him that she enjoyed working for his company.

The first three weeks went by smoothly and quickly. She enjoyed her work, and George was giving Trent positive reports about her work. She'd quickly gotten into a routine, working when she wasn't in class, and getting her homework done at night. Trent made sure she left enough time for the two of them, as well, suggesting they eat dinner out often, saying she'd have to take the time to eat anyway. The truth was that he enjoyed his meals so much more when they ate together, and he had become a bit concerned about her eating habits when she ate alone.

She mentioned eating Raman noodles often because they were cheap, as she put it, and that worried him. While she was taking a shower one time he took the liberty of snooping around in her kitchen, and wasn't too pleased with the lack of healthy food he found. Not wanting to upset her this early in their relationship, though, he simply told her he hoped that now that she was making a little more money she could buy more nutritious food. He then set out to assure himself she was eating properly by taking her out to eat as often as possible. At least then he knew she was getting one healthy meal a day.

Their relationship was coming along nicely, as well. There were a lot of things they found they both enjoyed, and they spent time together whenever they could.

One evening Trent took her to his house after work, and

they worked together to make dinner. Afterward, they cuddled on the couch to watch a movie. He was very observant when he was around her and had gotten to know her and her mannerisms rather well, and had a bit of a concern. "You've been kind of quiet this evening. Did you have a bad day?"

"No, it was okay."

He turned her so he could see her eyes. "Now tell me that again like you mean it." She looked confused, so he tried to explain. "I know something's wrong, honey. What is it? Anything I can help you with?"

"No. I guess I am upset, though. I'm sorry."

"What's got you upset?"

"This morning while I was going to work I got stopped for speeding." She felt Trent stiffen, but it was too late now, so she continued. "I was upset because there were three of us all going together. I was the last one. A guy came up fast behind me and whipped around all three of us and pulled away. The next thing I knew there was a cop behind me with his lights on. I pulled over, thinking he was going to pass me and stop the guy that zipped around us. He pulled in behind me, though, and said he pulled me over because I was speeding. I was furious!"

"Were you speeding?"

"Maybe, but not as much as that guy that flew right past me. And if I was, so were the other two cars."

"How fast did he say you were going?"

"I'm not even sure. I think 79 or 80."

Trent frowned. "This was on the interstate?"

"Yes."

"So that would be about ten miles over the speed limit?"

"I guess, but nobody goes 70."

"That's not the point. Were you going 79 or 80?"

"Maybe. I really don't know for sure. I was just following the other two cars. We were all going the same speed, in the middle lane. There were other cars that passed us from time to time, so we were just going along with traffic. There were cars going faster than us, some going slower."

"So you were probably going 79 or 80 in a 70 mile an hour zone. You got a ticket for going 79 or 80, and that's what you're upset about. Am I right?"

"Damn it, Trent, don't make it sound like this was all my fault. I'm upset enough as it is."

Trent quickly flipped her over and gave her a solid swat on her backside. "Watch your language and your attitude, Jasmine. That's the only warning you'll get." He turned her back over and pulled her in against him again, watching her reaction carefully.

She glared up at him, and he met her eyes and held them, with one eyebrow raised. He was happy when she backed down. "Sorry. I've been upset all day because I just don't think it's fair that I got a ticket and the other two with me, and especially the guy that flew around us all, didn't. I don't think that's fair."

"I understand why you're upset, but let me ask you something. Would you feel better if all three of you would have gotten a ticket?"

She thought for several seconds before answering, "Probably not because I don't think we should have gotten cited at all. I think he should have gone after the guy that was going faster."

"I understand. But you know how to avoid that happening again, don't you?"

"How?"

"Go the speed limit." He saw the anger on her face, but he went on. "Technically all three of you could have, and maybe should have gotten speeding tickets. If you would have been going 68 or 70 and gotten the same ticket, everything else being the same, I would have paid for us to go talk to an attorney about it. But I can't really get too upset because he gave you a ticket you deserved."

He watched her expression and had to smile when she realized he was right. "Do you have the ticket?" he asked. "Can I see it?"

She got up and retrieved her purse and handed him the ticket. He looked at it and took his phone out. Jasmine listened to his end of the conversation. "Hi, John, this is Trent. How have you been? Oh, I've been good. As a matter of fact, I've been excellent. I met a special lady. Yep, she's that special. Actually, that's kind of why I'm calling. She's been upset all evening. I asked her why, and she said she got a speeding ticket this morning. No, she admits she was doing the nine miles over the speed limit she was cited for, but is upset because the other two cars she'd been following for some time didn't get stopped, and was especially upset because a car that she says flew past all three of them didn't get stopped. I looked at her ticket, and guess who wrote it?"

He chuckled at something, and nodded his head. "No, she's paying it, not fighting it, but I was curious about it. Do you happen to remember it? Yep, that's the one." His smile disappeared and he turned to look at her, now with a frown. "She did? Ah, that's interesting. Yeah, I think I did hear something about that, now that you mention it. No, I completely understand. Thanks for explaining it to me, John. We'll have to get together soon. I'd like you and Sue to meet her. Well, I guess you've already sort of met her, but I'd like you to formally meet her. Okay. See you later, buddy."

He turned to look at Jasmine, who was now looking down at the floor. "Is there anything else about that stop you'd like to tell me, young lady?"

"You know the state patrolman that wrote this, I take it?"

"John's a good friend of mine from college. Now answer my question. Is there anything you'd like to tell me?"

He had to listen closely to hear her mumbled response. "I'm sorry, Trent. I didn't know he was a friend of yours."

He reached over with one finger to lift her chin. "That should not make a difference, Jasmine. I'd like to hear your side of what happened. Remember, I've already heard his, so this would not be a good time to lie to me or forget to mention part of it."

Jasmine swallowed, but then she met his eyes. "Okay." She took a deep breath and he could tell she was nervous. "Well, I was upset that he stopped me and not the guy he should have stopped, so I may have been a little annoyed."

"Jasmine?"

"Okay, I was a lot annoyed."

"And what happened?"

"I did everything he asked, but I may have been a little less than friendly towards him."

He was watching her with a stern expression on his unsmiling face. "Do I need to turn you over my knee to get you to answer my question?"

"No!" She looked down again, but quickly continued. "After he looked at my license and registration and insurance he said I was speeding. I was really upset that he stopped me, and that I might be late for work now, and I asked about the other guy."

"How did you ask him?"

"Okay, damn it. I said, 'How about the asshole that flew past all three of us? You don't care about him?' That's the whole story. Are you happy now? How the hell was I supposed to know you knew the guy?"

Trent didn't say a word. He simply picked her up and laid her over his lap, face down. He lifted her skirt onto her back again and was pulling her panties down when it seemed to him she came to life. "Oh, no. Not this again! Please don't, Trent. I'm sorry."

He finished lowering her panties and gave her half a dozen smacks to her bare bottom before saying a word. This time when he started talking she listened. "Jasmine, you have got to learn to control your temper. That's what got you that speeding ticket today. John said they've started a campaign to slow people down through that section in there, particularly during rush hour, because they've had three accidents there in the last month because of so many people getting on and off exit ramps. They started two days ago, and they're giving out warnings. In two weeks they're going to start writing tickets instead of warnings. John said the only reason you got a ticket this morning instead of a warning is because of your temper."

Trent was spanking steadily while he talked, but this time she was listening, and not saying anything other than letting him know the spanking hurt. She was looking at the floor, refusing to even glance at him, and he hoped it was because she was ashamed. "If you would have acted a bit more civil to him, not only would you have received a warning instead of a ticket, but he would have told you he called a description of the car that passed you on to his co-conspirator up ahead, and that officer had him stopped and was giving him a ticket, not a warning."

Jasmine glanced back at him when he said that, but looked back down quickly. Trent continued the spanking, but he was pretty sure she understood what her poor behavior had cost her. To be sure she understood how disappointed he was, there was one more thing he had to tell her. She wouldn't like it, but she had to hear it. "Jasmine, I'm disappointed that the first time my good friend met you he saw this side of you. He's a good friend, so I'm sure we'll see him and his wife fairly often, and now look at the first impression he has of you."

She started crying louder, just as he anticipated, and tears streamed down her face. "I'm sorry, Trent."

"So am I. But you're lucky this time. John's a good guy,

and he understands why you were upset. I think as he gets to know you he'll see that's not what you're normally like." He gave her a few firmer swats where he knew she would feel them, where her bottom met her thighs, as he continued the spanking. "But remember this, because at work if you have a tantrum like that while you're talking to one of our suppliers, he or she won't have the opportunity to get to know you outside of work. That's the impression they'll have of you, and how successful do you think you'll be trying to negotiate prices and work with them in the future to get exactly what we need, and at a good price?"

She became quiet and slumped across his lap. He hoped that got his message through to her. After a few more swats to her tender sit spots he paused. "Do you have anything to say for yourself, young lady?"

"I'm sorry."

He stopped the spanking, but kept his hand on her bottom. He wanted to be sure she understood why he was upset. "Anything else you want to say?"

"That's the most painful speeding ticket I've ever gotten. I can't believe I just got spanked for speeding."

"You didn't get spanked for getting a speeding ticket, Jasmine."

She twisted around to look back at him. "It sure feels like I did."

He was not smiling. "That spanking was not for you speeding. You tell me. What was that spanking you just got for? If you don't know, I guess I'll have to explain it to you again as I do it all over. Think about it. What did I just spank you for?"

She gave him the classic doe caught in the headlights look. Her eyes were huge.

"Don't just stare at me, Jasmine. Think about it. If you can't tell me what that spanking was for it obviously won't be effective."

She turned back around and was quiet. After giving her ample time he sighed. "Okay, I guess I'll have to start from the beginning."

His hand left her bottom, and she started to plead. "No, Trent, please don't. Not again."

"You seem to be saying 'not again' frequently lately. I hope you've realized that anytime you earn a spanking you will receive one. I guess I'll just have to start answering with a 'yes, again.' Now, can you tell me what that spanking was for, or do I have to do it over?" After several more silent moments he shook his head. "Okay, it looks like yes, again."

He raised his hand to begin spanking again, but she suddenly yelled out. "No. I know now. I'm sorry."

She twisted around again and saw the skeptical look on his face. "It was for losing my temper with you."

"Very good, Jasmine. That's exactly what it was for. Your little temper tantrum with me just now, and what else?"

She looked horrified for a moment, but he could tell she was thinking. She slumped back across his lap. "When I lost my temper I also swore."

"Yes, you did," he said, and accentuated each word with another swat. He laid his hand back on her bare bottom after those last three swats. "But it was for more than just losing your temper with me. You got a ticket instead of a warning this morning because you lost your temper with the officer, and now you lost your temper while telling me about the ticket. Your spanking was to cover both of those. Are you starting to see that losing your temper doesn't help anything?"

"Yes. It doesn't help, it hurts."

Trent had to smile at her words. "Yes, it does. It hurts in more ways than one."

Chapter 4

Trent gently helped Jasmine up and onto his lap. When he wrapped his arms around her she snuggled right in against his chest. "I really am sorry," she whispered.

"I know you are, sweetheart, and you're forgiven. But do you see why it's important that you learn to control that temper?"

"Yes. For the first time, I think I do see now why it's important. I feel bad that he's your friend."

"Like I said, John's a good guy. I'd like to see you apologize to him when we see him, but I think if you do he'll give you another chance to show him what you're really like."

"Good."

"But if you lose your temper with someone at work you probably won't get that second chance. You need to remember that."

She rubbed her sore bottom. "I think I'll remember."

"I hope so," he said with a chuckle. He brought her hand back around in front of her. "But no rubbing. If you rub the sting away it won't be as effective. If I catch you rubbing away some of the sting I'll have to replace it with a new, fresh sting."

"Are you serious?"

"You still haven't learned that I don't say things I don't mean? Try rubbing after a spanking sometime and see if I'm serious."

"No, I believe you." She laid her head against his chest and sighed. "You know, as much as I hate those spankings, I sure like this part afterward."

"I'm glad. Why is it you like this; you like to cuddle?"

"Yeah, I love to cuddle with you, but it's something more." He looked down at her and could tell she was thinking. "It's like I feel happy, and content. Relaxed, that's what it is. I could stay right here like this forever, I think."

He chuckled and kissed the end of her nose. "A spanking settles you down, and then the endorphins kick in."

"It settles me down?"

"Yes. You were upset about getting the ticket and hadn't been able to put it aside, stop thinking about it. This spanking helped you settle, get it off your mind. It was the same way with the first spanking. You get yourself all worked up, and a spanking helps you settle down."

After a stretch of silence she said, "Huh."

He looked down at the thoughtful look on her face and chuckled. "You thought about it, and I'm right, aren't I?"

She looked up at him and grinned. "Maybe."

He pulled her in against his chest a little tighter. "Maybe, huh? Well, maybe I'll remember that the next time you get yourself all wound up about something."

She looked up at him, a bit of concern in her eyes, but also a bit of mischief. "What are you saying? That I'll be saying 'not again' again?"

He returned her grin and look of mischief. "Again and again possibly. And I'll answer, 'yes, again' right before I help you settle. But then afterward just think how much better you'll feel, just like now."

"I do feel better," she said honestly. "All except for my butt."

They both laughed, right up until he leaned down and kissed her passionately, but yet very possessively.

The next week things were going well, both at work and with their relationship. As Trent got to know her better he was starting to see a vulnerability in her he hadn't seen before. As was his way, when she did something he was especially happy about or proud of, he praised her. It soon became clear to him that praise was something that had been missing in her life. It was a sad realization, but when he thought about it, it made sense. Her parents didn't spend much time with her, and she'd said she had numerous nannies over the years, none of them staying very long. She thought it had something to do with their having to deal with her parents.

She'd also gone to numerous boarding schools. She wasn't sure why, but they switched her from school to school, but all of them were in the western part of the country, while her home was in Eastern Tennessee. The result of being switched around so often was that she readily admitted she hadn't had any close friends growing up.

Now that he knew that, he tried to right that wrong. It was easy for him to see how well she responded to a compliment or simple praise, so he made sure she heard them regularly when she'd earned them. As he did that, he watched her thrive as a person and knew she was happier. He knew he was much happier since she'd come into his life.

They were working on her temper, and he could tell she was slowly becoming more aware of how often it actually was a problem for her, and she'd been making some headway. There were a couple of other things he patiently started working on, as well, that he knew would be beneficial for her. His next main goal was to achieve a gradual change in her diet.

He was gradually trying to introduce some healthier food into her diet, like vegetables, which she seemed to have an aversion for. He'd discovered early on that her idea of a meal did not include vegetables. Luckily, he'd found that she liked salad, so he often suggested a side salad as one of her side dishes when they went out to eat. When they cooked at home he always had lettuce so they could fix a salad.

He was slowly convincing her to try just a couple of bites of something new if they fixed it together, especially if he covered it with cheese or a special sauce. He praised her for trying it, even if it turned out she didn't like it. That praise helped convince her to try the next new taste. He was proud when she tentatively tried a very small bite of the pea salad they'd just made together, and smiled. "That's not so terrible," she admitted. He watched as she tried a little bigger bite, and looked up at him. "In fact, it's not bad."

Smiling ear to ear, he covered her hand with his. "Thank you, honey. I am so proud of you for trying these new things for me."

"It really means a lot to you for some reason," she said. "I can tell."

"Yes, it does," he confirmed. "In case you haven't noticed, I'm rather protective of you."

"I have, and I like it. I'm still not used to it, but it makes me feel special."

"You are special, Jasmine. You're very special to me and I want you to be healthy, as well as happy. No vegetables in your diet is not conducive to keeping you healthy. I know you're not a big fan of them, so I'm very proud of you for trying vegetables of any kind and giving them a chance."

She looked at him and he could tell she was considering what he'd said. She eventually smiled and nodded. "Now that I know why it's so important to you that I try them, I'll keep trying. I didn't say I'd eat them all, but I'll try them."

He smiled at her and patted her hand again before going back to eating his dinner. She ate a full serving of the pea salad, which suddenly didn't seem to taste too bad to her. It also felt like he was holding her just a little closer that evening as they watched a show on television they both liked.

After that incident, and hearing how much he watched out for her, even in what she considered little things like the way she ate in order to keep her healthy, and seeing the patience he'd shown her in trying to get her to eat healthier, she gave him and their relationship a lot of thought. She found herself doing things she wouldn't normally do, knowing he would appreciate it or be proud of her.

As a result, she found herself changing little things here and there, without him asking. She no longer grabbed a pack of Twinkies on her way out the door to eat on the way to work or school for breakfast. She still didn't take the time for a sit down breakfast, but she switched the Twinkies out for a protein bar. She'd always liked corn, but she would now also eat, and even order in restaurants, peas and even green beans as long as they had some bacon in them. She also discovered she liked asparagus, which was a true shock to both of them.

He praised her every time she ordered one of them, which she could tell was true praise and not just lip service. She found that not only did she enjoy knowing he was proud of her, but she was proud of herself. She smiled every morning when she picked up her protein bar as she hurried out the door. She could admit she was slowly changing, but although the changes made him happy, she was happy with them, as well. She was feeling better about herself than she had in a long time, and she had Trent to thank for that.

The more she thought about that, the more she wanted to thank him, so she told him she wanted to cook dinner for him on Saturday. He had some work he had to get done at the office, but assured her he would be done in plenty of time to be at her apartment by six o'clock.

She enjoyed cooking and was usually a good cook, but this would be the first meal she cooked for him, and she was nervous. By the time he got there her nerves had gotten away from her and she was a nervous wreck. He sensed this the moment he greeted her, and took her in his arms. He held her a few minutes while he asked about her day, and felt some of her stress draining from her body. He opened the bottle of wine he'd brought with him, and suggested they sit down on the couch and relax a while before dinner.

She readily agreed, and it wasn't long before he had her calmed back down. Dinner went splendidly. He was surprised by her menu, which included both a salad, which was delicious with a homemade dressing, and asparagus. He didn't want to make a big thing of it, but had to let her know he noticed it and appreciated it. "Delicious dinner, honey," he said, taking her in his arms after they finished their meal. "I appreciate all your work involved in preparing it, from planning the menu, which was wonderful, to cooking it all to perfection. Thank you."

The look he saw on her face was priceless. He could tell she was happy that he'd liked her meal, but it was easy to see the pride in her eyes, as well, and he was glad to see that. Since they'd been together he'd watched her self-confidence grow, which meant more to him than she would probably ever know. She was a beautiful, very intelligent young lady with a lot to offer, both as a caring person and as an employee. Beyond that, he had already fallen in love with her.

They went to her living room and cuddled on the couch with another glass of wine. They spent the evening there, both perfectly content to stay home, her leaning against him with his arm around her as they watched a little television, but mostly talking. They never had a problem finding something to talk about, but were equally happy leaning against each other in companionable silence.

Jasmine totally enjoyed her new job, and the following week things were going well, right up until Thursday. George had begun giving her more and more responsibility, and she was doing real well.

She had a test in a class she'd been having trouble in, and the test hadn't gone well. Trent saw her shortly after she arrived, and could tell something was wrong. When he asked about it, she denied it. "Nothing's wrong, I'm fine."

"No, you're not," he said as he gave her a quick kiss on her cheek, "and I think you'd feel better if you'd talk to me about it." She frowned and didn't say a word, and he debated, not wanting to upset her at the moment. "I'll give you a little time if you're not ready to talk about it yet. Just remember to watch your attitude, though. Whatever's bothering you, don't take it out on anyone around you."

His words bothered her at first and she looked up, angry. But she saw nothing but caring in his eyes and realized he was just trying to help her, again. "Okay," she answered with a smile.

But he went into the purchasing department later that afternoon to talk with George, and couldn't believe what he heard. Jasmine was on the phone with a supplier. "Look, I know perfectly well what you said, my hearing is just fine. Now why don't you listen to what I'm saying?" Trent went over and stood directly in front of her, arms crossed, glaring at her.

It had exactly the effect he was hoping for. She froze midway through her next sentence. She quietly started it again. "Mr. Henderson, I'm terribly sorry. I've had a horrible day today, but that's certainly not your fault. Would you mind if I take some time to calm myself down, and call you back? I'm really sorry, but you've done nothing wrong and certainly don't deserve my ranting. Thank you very much. I'll talk to you later. Bye."

She looked up at the frown on Trent's face and was glad she was the only one there at the moment. "I'm sorry," she told him.

"I'll venture to say you're not as sorry as you're going to be." Her shoulders slumped and Trent thought she looked resigned to her fate. He was real glad to see that and hoped it meant she could admit now that his spankings help her. "It sounds to me like you need some help settling down."

"Oh, no. Not again."

To his surprise, she didn't look as upset as he expected. "Yes, again," he responded, and was surprised when she moved closer to him and leaned against his chest. His eyebrows raised, and noticing no one else was around, he pulled her in for a quick hug. "Ready to talk now?"

"Yes," she answered humbly. "I should trust you more. You were right. I was upset and if I would have talked to you about it you probably would have been able to help me settle down." She saw a hint of a grin on his face and added, "Just by talking."

"Oh, I'll still help settle you down," he promised with more of a grin.

"I know," she said in a resigned way, rubbing her bottom.

"Let's go to my office and talk. Just talk," he added when he saw her frightened look. "You can tell me what has you upset and we'll see if we can talk you through it and get you settled enough to call Mr. Henderson back."

"Thank you." They waited until George came back from the restroom so someone was in the purchasing department, then Trent took her to his office.

They had a talk, and she opened up to him about the class she'd been having trouble with. "Why didn't you tell me you were having a hard time with that class? I could have been helping you with it."

"You have enough to do without having to help me with my classes."

"Honey, I want to help you any way I can. I thought you knew that by now. I like spending as much time with you as possible. I've been trying to make sure I give you enough time to get your homework and studying done. If I can help you with that it gives me a reason to spend more time with you. Besides, I took that same class. It was four years ago, but I had the same prof you have. He can't have changed that much in four years. I'll help you get through it."

She threw her arms around him. "Thank you, Trent. I should have talked to you sooner."

"Yes, you should have. But I'm glad you did now at least." After holding her a few minutes he looked down at her. "You seem settled again. Do you think you can make that call to Mr. Henderson now?"

"I'm okay now. Thanks."

"I'm glad I could help. But I have to warn you, tonight when we get back to your place —"

"I know. Not again."

"Yes, again," he said with a chuckle. "The best way to get you past this bad habit is with consistency. Lucky for you, I can be very consistent."

"Yeah, lucky for me," she murmured as he chuckled.

"I promise you that I care enough about you to be as

consistent as I need to be to help you get control of your temper." He kissed her forehead before turning her and giving her a light swat on her bottom to get her headed out his door and back to her office.

Jasmine thought about Trent's promise as she made her way back to her office. Although he chuckled, she knew he was very serious. She would be receiving a spanking tonight. She realized, though, that for the first time that thought didn't scare her so much. Oh, she knew it would hurt a lot and she wouldn't like it a bit. But this time she also knew in her heart that he wouldn't do it unless he cared a great deal for her. Now she knew why she always felt so good cuddled in his arms afterward. Having someone care that much for her was an awesome feeling, especially when it was Trent, and she returned his feelings.

Trent sat down at his desk after Jasmine left his office. He was shaking his head, wondering how to get through to her. As he thought about her, he realized he'd forgotten to tell her he had a meeting over lunch, but would take her out for dinner this evening. He wanted to let her know that so she wouldn't wait for him for lunch, but could go ahead and get some lunch and go to her afternoon class, so he left his office and headed for hers.

When Jasmine got back to the purchasing department she sat at her desk, and stared at her phone. Before she called Mr. Henderson back, she wanted to go over the conversation they'd had, so it was fresh in her mind. As she went back over it, his words in response to something she'd said struck her. She had a sinking feeling the more she thought about his words. After a few moments, she was sure – she'd mistaken what he'd been trying to tell her. She felt terrible, but did what she knew she had to do.

She called him back and as soon as he answered, she apologized. "Mr. Henderson, I owe you a big apology."

"Everyone has a bad day from time to time," he said.

"True, but that's no excuse, especially now. You see, I took some time to cool off, and then I went back over our conversation. When I did that, I now see that I mistook what you said, and I am so sorry. What I said was inexcusable, but especially in light of what I now see was a misinterpretation on my part of what you were trying to tell me."

Trent had reached her office, but hearing her voice, he paused, not wanting to interrupt her. He heard her apologize to Mr. Henderson, and turned around and went back to his office. He could talk to her later. As he walked back, he went over what he'd just heard. He knew Jasmine well enough to know he'd just witnessed a sincere apology, but Mr. Henderson didn't know her that well. He could only hope it was received as such by him.

As Trent went back to his office, Jasmine waited nervously. There was a moment of silence before Mr. Henderson responded. "Are you saying when I told you I didn't want to sell you the amount you were asking about, you thought I was trying to push you into buying more of the same thing?"

"Yes, and I feel terrible about that. Now I see you were trying to tell me you have something you think would be more cost effective for us and were suggesting we try some of each and see which works better for us, weren't you?"

"Yes, I was. As you described what you would be using them for, my mind went to a new product we have. We haven't advertised it yet, so I can understand your confusion. I think it may be perfect for what you want, though, and if you're interested I'll be happy to explain it to you."

"Even now, after I was so rude to you? You're still willing to work with me?"

"Absolutely," he said with a sense of seriousness. "You've been honest with me, so let me be totally honest with you. I was upset with your demeanor earlier, but you got my attention when you stopped, said you were having a bad day and asked for a chance to calm down and call me back. I've seen and heard a lot of people have a bad day and fly off the handle, but this is the first time I can remember someone taking responsibility for it and asking for a chance to correct it. You had my respect then. Now when you called and said you'd gone back over everything and now see where the mistake was made, I completely understand how you could have done that, and it's probably my fault as much as yours for not telling you I was talking about a new product we have. How would you have known about it?"

"Thank you, Mr. Henderson, for giving me another chance. I would love to hear about the product you think might help us." They spent the next ten minutes on the phone, ending with her placing a revised order. She'd asked Mr. Henderson to hold her order for one hour before processing it to give her time to okay it with her boss, and assured him she would call him back within the hour if there were any problem. With that in mind, she immediately went to talk to George. He nodded his head in agreement, but thought it would be a good idea to run it past the engineering department to be sure. They approved it, as well, saying Jasmine had done a good job.

After work that evening Trent took Jasmine out for dinner, but she was very quiet. He suspected it was because of the upcoming spanking he'd promised her when they got home, but he tried his best to get her to relax and enjoy dinner.

Word had gotten back to Trent later that day that Jasmine had made an exceptional purchase, and he brought it up in the conversation, hoping to cheer her up some. From what he'd learned, the purchase she'd made had the engineering department and cost department both thinking it would save Douglas Manufacturing a fairly good amount of money. He expected to see that proud look on her face he generally saw when he praised her for her work, but it wasn't there this time. He reached over and took her hand in his. "What's wrong, Jasmine? Why aren't you proud of what you did for the company?"

She sighed, but met his eyes. "That was how my phone call with Mr. Henderson turned out. I've been thinking about it all afternoon. I almost blew that chance for us because of another temper tantrum. I'm so sorry, Trent."

Things quickly fit into place for him and he understood her somber mood. It was in fact a great outcome, but she was honest enough to admit to herself that if he hadn't walked in when he did while she was talking to Mr. Henderson she probably would not have gotten that result. He hoped that would help her see how important it is for her to get control of her temper.

But for right this moment, he could easily see that she was full of guilt. He knew exactly how to rid her of that guilt, and saw no reason to postpone it now that he'd seen how much it was affecting her. "We'll talk about it more when we get home, Jasmine, but you still deserve credit. Yes, you made a mistake, and you'll be paying for that shortly, but you still were able to call him back, I assume apologize, and you made a good decision. Don't cut yourself short. Are you finished with dinner?"

"Yes," she said with a nod and another sigh.

"Then let's go get this over with so we can enjoy the rest of our evening together." It was a quiet ride home, but he reached over to squeeze her hand a couple of times, hoping to reassure her.

When they got to her house he locked the door behind

him, took her coat, and led her directly to her living room. He closed the curtains before going to the couch and sitting down. He directed her to a spot directly in front of him. "Okay, I'd like to hear what happened when you called Mr. Henderson back."

His request surprised her, and she stood still, not responding for several moments. "Jasmine?"

"Sorry. I thought you were going to go straight to the spanking, and I was ready for that."

"We'll get to that, but I want to know exactly what happened before I do this."

"Why? Will it make a difference?"

"It might. Not answering me when I ask you a question will for sure."

"Okay, okay." She explained how she'd stopped to go over the conversation in her mind before she called him back and realized she'd misunderstood. She was crying by the time she'd finished her explanation. "I apologized and told him what I'd done, he very graciously accepted my offer. Afterwards I sat at my desk and wanted to cry. I was so excited when you gave me a job, and I wanted to make you proud of me. Instead, I almost screwed up really bad."

"Let me ask you something, and I want an honest answer. Do you see now why it's so important that you get your temper under control?"

"Yes," she said as tears streamed down her cheeks. "I'm so sorry, Trent."

He was glad her version of what happened coincided with what he'd overheard. More importantly, though, when she broke down, it told him she understood now the seriousness of her temper at work, which was what he was hoping would happen. He moved her over to his side and a quick tug on her wrist had her over his lap in one fluid movement. He had her dress draped over her back and her panties down, and she hadn't said a word. That spoke to how bad she was feeling. Now he just had to help her deal with her guilt and make sure she remembered it.

"Let's see if we can't give you another reason to want to control that temper of yours," he said, patting her bare backside. "While I do this, I want you to think about what could have happened today, and how you would feel if it had. Then remind yourself that anytime you lose your temper, you can look forward to this same thing again."

Without any further words, he started the spanking. Again, she didn't start fighting and wriggling around trying to avoid the spanking, like she usually did. He hoped that meant she was admitting to herself that she needed to change, and was accepting this spanking with that in mind. He didn't disappoint, using firm swats that were intended to make a lasting impression.

After several minutes of solid spanking, he asked her a couple of questions. "Jasmine, do you see the importance now of not losing your temper?"

"Yes," she sobbed. "I'm sorry."

"Do you think you'll remember this the next time you decide it's okay to have a temper tantrum?"

"Y- yes," she managed between sobs and hiccups. "I sure h-hope so."

That brought a smile to his face, but he was glad she didn't see it. She needed to see him being firm with her. "I do, too," he said with a couple of harder swats right before pulling her up and onto his lap. "Because otherwise we'll be right back here again." He let her settle in against his chest, and immediately wrapped his arms around her so she would have that protective feeling that she'd talked about having after a spanking. He wondered if she would be surprised to know that the same cuddling that gave her the safe, protective feeling she had afterwards was just as important to him. He needed to feel her snuggling up against him afterwards, letting him know all was good with them.

He held her tightly against him, whispering words of encouragement in her ear and reminding her how special she was and how much she meant to him, while she finished crying and calmed down. Once she'd managed that, he kissed the top of her head. "Okay now?"

"Yes, I am now," she murmured, sounding half asleep. He smiled a bit again, and rubbed her arm. She'd worried so much about what almost happened that she'd worn herself out. Once the guilt was gone, she was exhausted. He held her in his arms, talking softly as she fell asleep. Afterwards he held her a while longer, not ready yet to let her go.

He let her sleep against his chest for over half an hour before picking her up and carrying her to her bedroom. He laid her down on her bed, covered her with the quilt she kept at the foot of her bed, and leaned down and gave her a kiss. He turned her light off, along with the rest of them in her apartment, and locked her door as he left.

Chapter 5

Trent was true to his word, spending two or three nights a week at Jasmine's house helping her with her economics class. This was the second and last one she needed to graduate with her business degree. Unfortunately, economics was not a subject that came naturally to her and she struggled through the first class, never really understanding several of the concepts. Since this class began with the information gained from the first class and not only expanded on it, but also put it to use in practical ways, it was proving to be nearly impossible for her.

This became very evident to Trent the first night they started studying together. "Honey, you're right, you never really did get a good grasp on many of the concepts in the first class. To be honest, I'm rather surprised you passed the class with a C. I think we need to go back to the material in the first class and go over that again. I think until you have a handle on that, this class is not only going to be very difficult for you, I think it will be virtually impossible."

"I agree. I didn't understand most of it last semester."

"Did you ever talk to the prof about it?"

Jasmine's face turned red, which had Trent curious. He watched and waited for her to explain. "I did," she said a bit hesitantly. "He asked me out."

"The professor asked you out?"

"I know. I didn't think that was allowed, and I asked him about it. He stammered a few times, then tried to tell me he didn't mean it as a date. When I told him I didn't think I'd feel right about having dinner with one of my professors he said he totally understood. Then he said there wasn't any reason for me to mention this to administration, and told me not to worry too much about this class, that he thought I'd do okay in it."

Trent's eyes grew huge. "So he asked you out, and when you turned him down he basically gave you a C for not telling administration about it?"

"That's what I assume," she admitted. "I didn't deserve a C in that class, but I asked for help once, and I didn't know what else to do. I didn't plan on looking for a job that would have required any kind of expertise in economics, so I didn't say anything to anyone. If I would have had to take the class over I would have had to go another semester before graduating and looking for a job, and money is already an issue. Besides, to be able to take the class again I would have had to explain to administration why I wanted to retake a class I got a C in. I didn't want to get him in trouble. I didn't know how lost I would be in this class, or what to do about it."

Trent took a moment to digest what she said before slowly shaking his head. "It's a real shame it happened, but I understand the position that put you in," he finally said. "I think the best way to approach this is for me to go back and help you understand what you missed in the first class. I think once you have those basic skills you'll be fine in this class. It'll take us some time and effort, but if you're willing to put in the time, so am I."

"I am, and thank you, both for helping me, but also for understanding. I didn't feel right about it when it happened, but I didn't know what I could do."

Trent patted her hand and picked up her economics book. They spent two hours studying that night, and several nights a week from that point on. He was impressed with her determination. She listened as he explained things, and stopped him if she had a question. She often asked for an example, or suggested an example to him, to make sure she understood what he was explaining. It didn't take long for him to see that using examples was how she learned best, and started offering more as he explained things. As a result, the pace of her tutoring stepped up a bit, and eventually she was caught up with the class.

During this time they'd been studying together, their relationship grew stronger. She was working on her temper and caught herself a couple of times, only earning one additional spanking. Afterward, as she snuggled his lap and they talked quietly, he started thinking. Holding her in his arms and feeling the love between them, he came up with an idea. The more he thought about it the more he liked it. Now he just had to tweak the details of his plan before she had her next temper tantrum.

After work one day they ate dinner out, then were going to her apartment to do a little studying. She picked up her mail before going inside, and was leafing through it as they headed for the living room. "Oh, I got a letter from Sheila." Without waiting for a response, she flopped down on her couch and tore the letter open. She read it quickly, then went back to the beginning, reading slower.

"Is everything okay with her?"

"Yes and no. She's okay, but she has to find a new apartment. The building she was in has been sold and they're tearing it down to make a parking lot. She's having a hard time finding one for the same price. I sure hope she finds one soon. I know money's pretty tight with her."

"Have you two ever considered her moving out here? You could share an apartment."

"Of course we've thought about it, silly. I'd love it, but she doesn't have the money to make the move. I mean, she doesn't have a car, so she would have to pack everything up and rent a U-Haul truck, or just bring what she could take on a bus. But either way, she would need money to live until she found a job out here because unfortunately, I would have to get a bigger apartment, which would obviously cost more, and I don't have the money to do that myself."

She was frowning and he knew how disappointing that was for her, but she smiled and went on. "When I told you once I graduate and get a full-time job and help her with college, that's part of my plan. I want to get that bigger apartment and pay to have her moved out here. Then she can try to find a part-time job here while she goes to school. If I have a better job then and can pay the rent and utilities, along with her tuition, a part-time job should be all she would need while she goes to school."

"Sounds like a good plan," he said, loving the big smile on her face. "And you're getting close to being able to carry out that plan. Do you think she'll be okay with moving out here to Tennessee?"

"I think so. She doesn't have anything keeping her there, other than the fact that she doesn't have the money to move anywhere else."

He got a phone call, and when he finished with it she had her economics book out and he started quizzing her for her upcoming test. He felt she was ready for this test and would do real well, but he knew she was worried about it. She insisted a B or even a low A wasn't good enough. After the way she did at the beginning of the semester, she felt she had to get solid

As on all her tests from here on out if she had any chance of getting a B in the class.

"Honey, I know you like to do the best you can, and I admire that. But in this case, it's not worth you getting so upset over getting less than a B in this class. Considering what happened last year in economics and where you started off at the beginning of this class, getting a B on a test now and a C for the course is something to be proud of. I know how much hard work you put into it, and I'm proud of you."

"Thanks, Trent. I never would have been able to pass if you hadn't helped me."

"So to get a B on this test is something to be proud of."

"It is," she conceded, "but an A would be nicer yet."

"You really are a little overachiever, aren't you?" He laughed and pulled her in close for a kiss. "But you're my little overachiever, and I love you."

Her test was the next morning, and Trent was anxiously waiting for her when she came in for work the next afternoon. Unfortunately, he could tell from her expression it hadn't gone as she'd hoped. "Well, honey, how was it?"

"It was awful," she said, trying to brush past him and into the purchasing department.

"Wait a minute, Jasmine. I'd like to talk to you a minute before you start working." Trent turned to George. "Can you do without her a few minutes? I need to talk to her, but I'll try to keep it quick."

"Sure, no problem," George said. "We don't have anything pushing this afternoon, so take your time."

"Thanks." Trent led her to his office, and closed his door after them.

"What was so important we had to talk before I went to work?" she asked, obviously nonplussed about being there.

"You are," he answered, "and your attitude. What happened with the test? You knew the material. If you don't think you did very well, there has to be a reason. I repeat, what happened?"

"My attitude? Again? Really?"

"Yes, Jasmine, again, really. Think back a minute. The last time I knew you were upset about something before you started work ended with your conversation with Mr. Henderson. I don't want that to happen again, so today I'm going to address it before you start working."

She cut in before he finished his thought. "You're going to address it?"

"That's right; one way or another I'll address it. I planned on talking to you; see what's wrong and talking it out, which is usually all it takes. However, with your attitude right now I'm getting close to addressing it over my knee. At this point it's actually your choice. Talk to me in a civil manner so we discuss it, or you'll find yourself staring at the carpet while I get your attention and see if I can't improve your attitude that way. Which is it going to be?"

She started to argue, puffed her chest out, then looked at the unflinching but not unkind look on his face, and reconsidered. She didn't say anything for several moments, and he willingly gave her that time to think. "Okay, maybe you're right," she said eventually. "I do feel better after we talk."

"Thank you for thinking that through, and you're right, you do always feel better after we talk. I just wish I could get you to see that and talk to me about your problems more often, before you lose your temper. Now, please answer my question. You knew the material in your economics class, but I assume you're not happy with how the test went. Why?"

"Because he put a stupid question in there just to trip us up."

"What do you mean?"

"I thought I did pretty good on the test, but then I was talking to a guy afterwards, and he said he misunderstood that question until he read it again carefully. He explained why, and if he's right, then I got that whole question wrong. It was an essay type, where you explain what you would do and why, so if I misunderstood his question, then my answer is all wrong."

"So are you saying you think your answer is good for the question you thought he was asking, but it's possible you misunderstood the question, and if so, your answer isn't what you would have said had you understood the question differently?"

"Yes. I don't think it's fair to ask a trick question like that."

"How do you know he meant it as a trick question?" She looked a little doubtful, so he continued. "I know Professor Leighty, I had him for several classes, and I can't really see him purposely putting a question in a test designed to trip you up. I would suggest you send him an email and explain what you just told me, though in a nicer way. Tell him you felt good about the test until you talked to another student, and now you're wondering about the meaning of his question. Explain to him how you took his question, and that you stand by your answer if that is the question. However, this other student thinks the question was asking something different. If that's what he was indeed referring to, your answer wouldn't be the same. See what he responds."

"Do you think it would matter?"

"Yes, I do think it would matter to him. If you explain what you think he was asking, but what the other person thought he was asking, I think he would go back and read the question again. If he agrees it could be interpreted two ways he would read the answers carefully before grading them, in case other people interpreted it differently, as well, and grade them accordingly."

"Do you really think he would?"

"I do. Besides, how do you know it was you who may have

misunderstood what he was asking? It may have been the other person you talked to. Have you talked to anyone else?"

Her expression told him she hadn't even considered that. "No, I haven't, and I guess you could be right," she said after reflecting on that thought. "So you actually think I should email him?"

"Not only do I think you should email him, I think you should do it right now. Use my computer if you want, and let me read it over before you send it. Be courteous, but let him know you talked to someone else and are now concerned. Professor Leighty will appreciate that you're concerned because that will show you care about his class."

He'd guided her over to his desk while he talked, and she looked at him, nodded and sat down. A few minutes later she motioned him over and pointed to the screen. "How does that sound?"

He leaned down and read what she'd written, and nodded. "It sounds perfect. Give him your email address, though, or he'll answer on mine. Let me know what he responds, but I have a feeling it won't be the cut and dried 'too bad for you' response you thought you'd get. He doesn't seem like a bad guy to me."

"I hope you're right," she said as she hit the send button.

"Me, too. Now, we both need to get to work, if you're feeling better?"

"I am," she said a bit sheepishly. "Sorry, but thank you."

"You're welcome," he said sincerely. "But please remember this. If you feel bad, come talk to me, especially before you go to work. We've both seen what a temper tantrum can do here at work, and it's something I can't and won't put up with. You need to learn that."

She nodded as she leaned up to kiss his cheek. "I know." He led her to the door and gave her a quick kiss before opening it so she could go back to the purchasing department.

Later that afternoon he wondered if she'd heard back from the professor yet, and wandered down to purchasing to ask. As he neared the door to her office he heard her mumbling, rather loudly. "Come on, Professor, this is ridiculous. How long does it take to check your emails?"

Trent frowned. Apparently she hadn't heard back from him yet, and it didn't sound like she was handling it well. He'd realized she learned by example, so he'd thought maybe he could use that to help her avoid a temper tantrum. Now would be the perfect opportunity to put his plan into action, if he could just figure out a way to do it. After a moment of quick thinking, he knocked on her open door and walked in. "I've got good news and bad," he said with a smile.

She was instantly concerned. "Bad news?"

"Well, not terrible, but when I'm anxious or worried about something, I do something to get my mind off the negative and onto something positive. I was getting pretty anxious waiting to hear if you heard from your prof yet, so I started thinking about us, and planning our weekend. That got my mind off of that and onto something I like to think about. So the good news is I've come up with a good idea for us for this weekend, but the bad news is if you haven't heard from him yet I'll have to come up with something else positive to think about."

She smiled, but he could tell she was thinking about his words, too. "Does that usually work?"

"It keeps me from doing something I know I'll regret later, yes. Thinking about you, or us, is one example. I've also tried thinking about the last vacation I took, or immersed myself in a project, especially at work." He could tell she was thinking about what he'd said, so he gave her a couple of moments, but didn't mention it again. No use to upset her. "So, have you gotten a response from him yet?"

"No, not yet," she said. "I've been getting pretty antsy about it, too."

"Well, I guess we'll both have to find a project or something to do. Do you have something to work on that will get your mind off waiting for him to return your email?"

She thought a moment before answering. "Nothing's pushing right now, but we did have a supplier that was late on his last two deliveries, and had a price increase at the same time. George and I were thinking in our spare time we'd start looking around for other suppliers that could furnish the same things and check their prices. Maybe while he doesn't need my help for the every day things too much right now, this would be a good time to jump into that project and see what I can find. I'm looking at it sort of like a challenge. If they're going to up their prices and be late on shipments, it's up to me to find someplace that can supply us what we need at lower prices and with better service."

"There you go," he said with a smile. "That sounds like a good challenge, and something that should keep you occupied for a while. Go get 'em, tiger!" He checked to be sure no one was around before leaning down to give her a quick kiss on her cheek.

He turned to leave, but she stopped him with a hand on his arm as she stood up. "Thank you, Trent. I see what you did there, and I appreciate it. You said when we were studying together that examples help me learn, and you're right, they do. Not only did that example help just now, but you're the best example I could have in my life, and I'm learning a lot from you."

He turned around further so he was looking into her eyes and reached up to take her face in his hands. "What a compliment. Thank you, Jasmine. I think we're good for each other, because I've learned a lot from you, too, and your generous heart." He gave her a kiss that was rather short, considering where they were, but was long on feeling.

She looked at him with a smile on her face, but also a look of confusion. "My generous heart?"

"I'll tell you more about that this weekend," he said as he gave her another quick kiss on the tip of her nose and turned again to leave.

"What are we doing this weekend?"

"I told you, I was thinking about it earlier this afternoon, and now I have our weekend planned out. I'll tell you more about it later. Good luck on your project this afternoon. Let yourself get absorbed in it so your mind is on it and not on waiting for a reply email."

"I hear what you're saying, and thanks again, for saving me."

"Saving you?" he asked with his eyebrows raised.

"Yes, saving me," she admitted. "I wasn't handling the waiting real well, but your example got me on the right track again. That's why I thanked you."

"You're welcome," he said with a silly grin. "Besides, that was as much for me as for you." He went back over closer to her and leaned down so he was close to her ear. "I have a spot on my hand that's a little sore this afternoon. No need to irritate it further."

He was grinning again as he left her office as she was growling.

It was a few minutes after five o'clock, quitting time, when Trent heard a knock on his open door and looked up to see a bubbling Jasmine, barely containing herself. "You busy?" she asked.

"Never too busy for you," he said as he stood and started

over to meet her, a big smile on his face. She practically ran to him and into his open arms. "Did you by chance get a reply back from your professor?"

"How did you know?" Without giving him time to respond, she continued. "He thanked me for sending the email and said he went back and read the question again. He said he meant the question the way I understood it, but admitted he could understand how the other person interpreted it, as well. He went through several of the tests, reading just that answer, and said some of the answers make much more sense if you interpret them the way the other student did. He assured me he hadn't meant it to be tricky or confusing, so he's going to grade the question according to either interpretation."

"That's wonderful, honey."

"Wait, there's more," she said, still bouncing a bit in his arms. "He said the answer I gave was exactly what he was looking for, and he was impressed. He graded my whole test before replying to my email so he could tell me how I did."

"And how did you do?" Trent asked, pretty sure he already knew the answer, but wanting to give her a chance to say it out loud.

"I got an A! He said he didn't know what I was doing differently from the beginning of the class, but whatever it was, it's sure working. I told him you've been helping me study and you're a good tutor. He said he didn't doubt that one bit, since you were a good student and have obviously put what you learned in school to good use in your business. He said to tell you hello, by the way."

"This calls for a celebration. Let's go out for dinner some-where special, and I'll tell you what my plans are for this weekend."

"That sounds perfect! I've been trying to figure out what you could have planned, but I haven't come up with anything."

"I'll tell you about it over dinner. You go home and change if you want, and I'll pick you up around 6:30. That's kind of early, I know, but I want to have time that we can talk a little when we get back to your place."

She instantly looked concerned. "Talk? About what?"

"You'll find out at dinner, but don't worry. It's all good, or at least I think you'll like it."

"Okay, I'll trust you."

"Good. Now go home and get ready." He gave her a quick kiss and watched as she left. He loved seeing her so happy. He hoped the news he had for her would make her happy, as well.

Chapter 6

Trent was surprised when he went to pick Jasmine up that evening. She had apparently gone home and taken a shower and changed, and had obviously spent extra time on her hair and makeup. "Jasmine, you look fantastic," he said as he leaned down to give her a kiss. "I like your hair like that."

"Thank you," she said, twirling around so he could see the back, as well. "I wanted to try something a little different. I know you like my hair down, though, so I left most of it down. I was hoping you'd be okay with it."

"I'm more than okay with it. Your hair, your dress; you look stunning." He pulled her in closer to him for a kiss meant to show his appreciation. By the look on her face after the kiss, it must have worked. "Are you ready for dinner?"

"I am, but I'm especially ready to hear about our weekend. You said you have it all planned out, and I can't imagine what that could mean."

"I'll tell you over dinner. Let's go."

"Oh, come on. Can't you at least give me a hint now?"

"Okay, one hint. I'll bet it's nothing you've planned, and will be a total surprise."

He turned them toward the door, but she stopped. "That's it? That's not a hint. A hint is like a clue, something I can use to help figure out the mystery."

He laughed as he started them toward the door again. "Maybe on the way there you better explain to me what exactly a hint would be comprised of."

"Oh," she said, slapping his arm a little. "You're just stalling, trying to placate me until we get to the restaurant."

"Is it working?" He chuckled as he locked the door behind them and headed them toward his car.

After helping her in, he went to the driver's side, but had barely gotten inside before she started her explanation. "Okay, we seem to do well with examples, so since you obviously don't know what a hint is, let me give you some examples of them."

He laughed as he started the car. "Okay, honey, you give me some examples."

"Okay, say you got me a present and I was trying to guess what it was."

"So far that sounds very plausible, so it's a good example," he said with a grin.

"Funny," she said, unable to contain her own smile. "A hint would be that it's blue, or that it's something to wear, or something that would look nice with blue jeans."

"Something that would look nice with blue jeans? You call that a hint? That's practically telling you what it is."

"No, it isn't."

"What else could it be, other than some type of sweater or blouse?"

"It could be shoes, or a purse, or something to put in my hair, or a coat, or —"

"Okay, I stand corrected," he said with a chuckle. "You have a vivid imagination."

"Why would you say that? All those things would look good with jeans. So, now that you know what a hint is, can I have a hint about what we're going to do this weekend?"

"Give me a minute to think here." She nodded, and tried her best to sit patiently. Just as she was about to explode, he patted her knee. "How about this? We'll be getting our exercise in this weekend."

She looked at him, obviously thinking. "We're going hiking somewhere? That sounds like fun. No, wait. Maybe we're going for a long bike ride. That would be fun, too. Which is it?"

"I'll tell you over dinner," he said with another grin. "In the meantime, get that vivid imagination of yours working. Are there any other possibilities?"

She was quiet for a couple of minutes, but then had another thought. "Well, you did say you couldn't believe I've never been in a canoe and some day you'd show me what I've been missing. Is that it? Are we going canoeing?"

"You'll find out over dinner."

"Are we about there yet? This is maddening. Oh, I thought of something else. Are you into rock climbing?"

"Is that something you'd like to try sometime?"

"You know me. I'm willing to try about anything once. I won't guarantee I'll do it a second time, but I'd try it once, sure. It might be fun. Where are we going to do that?"

They'd reached the restaurant, and he parked the car and came around to her side to help her out. "I'll explain it all during dinner," he said with another smile.

Once they had been seated and ordered, she leaned in. "Okay, all that's finally done. Now, where are we going rock climbing? Have you ever done it before? Is it hard?"

"Whoa, honey, back up," he said with a laugh. "I never said we're going rock climbing. Now that I know you're interested, though, we may try it sometime."

"But not this weekend?"

"Nope."

"Then what are we going to be doing?"

"Well, this is all dependent upon you. If you like the idea, we'll go with it, but don't feel you have to say yes just because I have it all planned."

"Now I'm really curious. What did you plan for us to do this weekend?"

"Move you into a new apartment."

Jasmine stared at him a few moments. "Are you serious?" When he nodded, she shook her head. "Okay, I'm ready to listen now, because I'm totally confused. I haven't been looking for an apartment, and I just paid my rent ten days ago. Why would I want to move now, and where to?"

"The other day when you got a letter from Sheila I watched how excited you were when you read it."

"I'm always excited when I get a letter from her."

"I could tell. I love seeing you that excited and I'm eager to meet Sheila. I also listened carefully to your plan to graduate, get a full time job, and once you have more income you can get a larger apartment and pay to have her move out here and live with you. I love your plan to pay for her tuition so she can go to college. That's what I meant when I said I learned a lot from you and your huge heart. I think it's great that you want to help her like that, and I might be able to help that happen a little sooner than you thought."

She looked reservedly happy. "How? You've done so much for me, Trent, and I appreciate all of it, but I won't take money from you. I've told you that, and I mean it."

"I know that, honey, and I respect that. I'm not offering you money. I'd love to see you be able to move Sheila out here to live with you. Although I'm more than willing to help you do that, I knew you'd never accept money from me because of your pride. Although it can be frustrating at times, it's also one of the things I admire about you, so I get it."

"Thank you. But if you're not offering me any money, how am I going to move? I'm not following this."

"A friend of mine is an engineer that works with a company that makes large pieces of industrial equipment. He had a big part in developing a particular piece of equipment a company in Germany contracted with them to build. It's finished now and he's going to go to Germany for possibly a couple of years while they install this equipment and get it running. He has a condo in a gated community that he really likes. It's not real big, but is perfect for him, with two bedrooms and two baths. He doesn't want to lose it while he's over there, and is afraid if he lets it set empty he may come home to a disaster."

"How so?"

"If people see no one's living there they could break in and steal what they want, and do who knows what kind of damage to it. People are even stealing the copper piping out of homes now because the price of copper is so high."

"But if it's a condo, wouldn't other people in the building see people taking things out?"

"It's a condo, but they're all separate buildings. They pay a condo fee and that covers all the common areas, like the pool and tennis courts, and the pavilion with grills. They even have people that mow all the lawns. They're all separate houses, though, not all in one big building. That's why he doesn't want to lose it. He loves the fact that he doesn't have any mainte-nance, but he still has the privacy of a stand-alone home."

"I don't blame him. Sounds perfect to me."

"But he's afraid with no one living there it will be vandal-ized. Even if it's not, something could happen to it, like the furnace could go out. If that happened the pipes could freeze and cause a huge mess. He decided he'd rather rent it out to be sure someone was living there, so he'd know if there was a problem. He wouldn't have to worry about paying rent in Germany, plus utilities and insurance on his house here."

"I'm sure he could rent that out for quite a bit of money," Jasmine said. "How does this relate to me?"

"He would rather rent it for a smaller amount, but to someone he could be very particular about. He wants someone he can feel confident will take care of it and not trash it, will pay the utility bills on time, and won't have wild parties or something else that will upset his neighbors or the condo board. That's where you come in, honey."

"Trent, I really can't pay any more than I'm paying now, though."

"Which is what I told him and why he was fine with that. He's looking to have someone he can trust in his condo so he knows it will still be there, in good shape, when he returns. That's part of why he's willing to rent cheap, is because it will only be for a couple of years, or however long he's over there. Most people want to find a place they like and can stay there. If he can cover the cost of his utilities, condo fees and insurance, he'll be happy. That's really all he's looking for. He added all them up and it comes up to just under what you're paying now for your rent."

She looked up at him with hope in her eyes. "So he would accept what I'm paying now?"

"He will," Trent assured her. "Another engineer at his company was planning on going to Germany to oversee this project, but he backed out at the last minute. They just found out his wife is pregnant and they'd rather stay here. So this move came up pretty suddenly for him. He moved his clothes and personal things to his brother's house to store, and left the furniture there. He had a cleaning service come in and empty the refrigerator and clean it all up good, so it's ready to go. He asked me if I might happen to know of someone trustworthy he could rent it to quickly."

"So this is for real? Do I have to fill out an application for it right away, or what?"

"I told him about you and how you'd love to have your pen pal come stay with you. After we talked a few minutes he says it's yours if you want it. Interested?"

"Are you kidding? Yes, I'm interested."

The waitress brought their food, and they discussed it more as they ate. There was one more aspect of this that he wanted to talk to her about, but he'd rather do that when they were at home, so he steered the conversation in another direction while they finished their meal.

Once they were back at her house, sitting on her couch, with her leaning against him, he approached the other part of this he wanted to talk about. "Honey, since you'll have an apartment with two bedrooms, is there anything preventing you from calling Sheila and asking if she wants to move out here?"

"Just the money it would take to get her moved out. She doesn't have a car, so she would either have to rent a U-Haul, or bring only what she could bring on a bus. I'll have to check and see how much that would cost."

"Does she have a driver's license?"

"She does. The last family she stayed with before she turned eighteen helped her get her license so she could take their kids places they wanted to go. She said she's been saving money to buy a car, but she doesn't have one yet. She's been taking the bus to work."

"Jasmine, I know you don't want to take money from me, but if Sheila is interested in moving out here, I'd really like to pay her way so she can come soon."

"I don't want a handout, Trent. I thought you understood my need to make my own way and pay my own bills."

"I do, honey, and I appreciate it, but listen to me a minute. I would love to see Sheila move here. I love seeing how happy getting a letter from her makes you. I love the story of how you two met and have kept in touch ever since. I love that you want to help her. I love the idea of being able to help out someone who's a good person, but hasn't been as fortunate in life. But to be totally honest, I also like the idea of you not living alone."

His last words surprised her, and she looked up at him. "You never mentioned anything about that before. I've been living alone for several years now."

"I know, and I understand why, and I'm not upset about it. I'm extremely proud of what you've done since you left home. But that doesn't mean I wouldn't feel better if you had a roommate. I feel that all single women would be better off with a roommate, for safety's sake. It's safer with two ladies living together, keeping an eye on each other, knowing where they are. But the feeling is stronger with you because I love you. Call it that protective instinct in me if you want, but I would feel a little better, breathe a little easier if there was someone else there with you."

"I didn't know you felt that way," she said quietly. After a few moments, she looked up at him. "That makes me feel special, like I should thank you for caring that much. It feels nice."

"I do care that much, and you don't have to thank me for it. But that brings us back to Sheila. It's a wonderful story of how you two met and became friends, and I really want to see you two together. Will you please allow me to help you make that happen?"

She was quiet, and Trent could tell she was thinking things through. "If I move into that condo, she'll have a place to live. She can start looking for a job right away, and hopefully she'll find something before too long. I think I can probably handle groceries for both of us while she's looking. Maybe she could find something full time until next fall, but I should be working full time by then and I'd love to be able to cover her tuition by then so she can go to college, at last part time. Maybe she could find a part-time job then. Hopefully I'll be able to handle everything except her personal things. I don't think I've forgotten anything, have I? This could actually work, and I can try to call her tonight and ask if she'll move out here, or am I missing something?"

"I think it'll work fine. Please remember that I'm here, too, Jasmine, and I won't let you fall. If something comes up and you're running short on funds, I'll help. Call it a loan if you won't allow me to simply help you once in a while, but I'm certainly not going to let you or Sheila go without something you need."

"I know," she said quietly, "and I don't think you can know how much that means to me. I'm just determined to prove I can do it on my own."

"And you have," he said quickly, reaching out to squeeze one of her hands. "From your background, I can't begin to tell you how impressive what you've done is, starting with making the decision to move out and support yourself and pay for college on your own. That speaks volumes to you as a person, and why I love you like I do. You've proven you can make it on your own. Now you want to prove you can help someone else, which is fantastic. And along the way, while you were proving to yourself and the world what you're made of, you've picked up a man that loves you dearly and wants to help you just as much as you want to help Sheila. All I'm asking is that you don't push me away if I can help you somewhere along the line."

Her eyes turned misty as she looked into his eyes. "I'm sorry, Trent. I never looked at it that way, but you're right. You're trying to help me like I'm trying to help Sheila."

"I am, except that you don't need the same kind of help. You've proven you're capable. All I want you to do is know that I'll be here and willing to help if you need it. I want you to feel confident about inviting Sheila here. I don't want you to be worrying about it. It's a wonderful thing you're doing for her, and I want you to hold your head high with confidence that you'll both do just fine. If something comes up along the way, know you have someone standing by, willing to help."

She lost her battle she'd been waging to hold back her tears, and they started flowing. She turned to face him and he wrapped her in his arms as she leaned into his chest. "Honey, are you okay? Did I say something to hurt you?"

"No," she managed through her tears. "I love you, Trent. Thank you."

He held her as she cried out her emotions. He knew she was touched by his words, but he also felt some of the tears were from the emotions she must be feeling about being able to finally put her long-time dream into motion. He was anxious to witness this reunion, as well, and he didn't even know Sheila.

When she got her tears under control, she sat back into the couch, leaning against him again. When he felt she was ready to talk he looked down at her. "Do you have her phone number so you can call her?"

"I can't call her because she doesn't have a phone. She used to, but they got real expensive out there, so she gave it up so she could start saving money for a car. I have the number for a roommate, though, and I can call her. Before I do, though, do you think she'll have much trouble finding a job out here? I know she'll ask me that."

"I know she won't have a problem if you let me hire her at the company," he said with his eyebrow raised.

"But —"

"And before you say anything, since you've been working

there, how many new people have you seen? It's a growing company and we're constantly hiring people. The kind of people I look for are people who are good, solid citizens and will show up at work. Can you tell me she doesn't fit that description?"

"No, I admit she'd be good, but she doesn't have any special training. She's worked as a clerk in a grocery store, and a waitress, and in a day care."

"We hire people that don't have special training, both in the office and the factory."

"But would she be able to work full time until she starts school in the fall?"

"Honey, we'll have to talk to her. She may not want to go to college. If she does, we'll certainly see what kind of jobs she'd like. We'll do whatever we can to find a spot for her, both now and when she's ready to start school, if you'll let me. You may recall someone else we hired under similar circumstances. She'd been a clerk in a convenient store and a waitress, and we work around her schedule."

Trent was unprepared when she flung her arms around him, and it knocked him backwards. He was laughing as he found himself lying on his back on her couch with her on top of him and his arms holding her tightly. Seeing no reason to waste a good opportunity, he leaned up and captured her lips with his. His hand moved behind her head as the kiss deepened. Eventually he relaxed his hold and helped them both up, both of them gasping for a breath, but both smiling ear to ear. "And I still appreciate you hiring me and working around my schedule."

"So you'll let me offer her a job then?" he asked with a grin on his face.

"What? Oh, yeah, Sheila," she said as her face blushed such a pretty shade of red. "Yes, I would appreciate that help. Thank you."

"No problem," he said with a wink that had her blushing again. He gave her a few minutes as he watched her take a couple of deep breaths and pull herself together. "Do you want to call her roommate and see if she's there? If she's willing to move here, I assume it will take her some time to give notice where she works and make arrangements."

"Yeah, you're right. Let's call her and talk to her, see if she's interested in moving out here and going to college. I think she'll be ecstatic."

"I hope she is, but can I mention one thing first, before you call?"

"Sure. What is it?"

"I don't want you to get too excited and then be disappointed. Have you considered the possibility that she may have created a life for herself out there and may not want to move? Maybe she has a job she likes and some good friends, maybe even a boyfriend."

"She doesn't," Jasmine said quickly. "I mean, she has a couple of friends, like her roommate, but they're not that close, and she doesn't have a boyfriend or she would have told me."

"What if she's proud like someone else I know," he said with a raised eyebrow, "and won't accept help from you? You're offering her a place to live and to pay her tuition. Even though I know why you're offering it and I know your heart, if someone would have offered you the same thing, would you have taken it?"

She paused a couple of moments to think. "I hear what you're saying, and it's a good point. My situation is different than hers, though. I had to prove to myself and my parents that I could make it without their money, especially once I realized they didn't care about me and were only giving me money so they looked good to their friends, and it kept me away. If a good friend had offered to help, I would have at least listened to their offer. I think once she knows I've had this planned for quite a while and have been working toward being able to offer it to her, she'll see how important it is to me and accept it accordingly, if that makes any sense."

"It does," he assured her. "I hope so. I don't want you to be disappointed if she doesn't, though. One thing that might help her is if she realizes you won't be paying all her tuition, so you might want to mention that."

She looked totally confused when she looked at him. "What do you mean? If she's just working part time so she has time to go to classes and study, I don't expect her to pay part of it herself."

"I mean the company. If she's working there, the company will reimburse part of it after the class is finished, just like they'll be doing for yours this semester. You can use that refund to pay part of hers, and the refund from those classes can go towards her next ones."

She was still baffled. "What are you talking about? I'm getting part of mine reimbursed?"

"Of course. Didn't I explain that to you?"

"No." She narrowed her eyes a bit. "I told you I don't want any special favors, Mr. CEO."

"It isn't a special favor," he insisted. "You didn't listen very well when the HR department told you about our policies, and you didn't read the welcome booklet, did you?"

She looked a little sheepish. "I may have skimmed through it. I was ecstatic to have a real job, and it was so fantastic, I guess I didn't pay a whole lot of attention. What did I miss?"

"I have always believed in someone trying to better themselves. If someone is going to put forth the effort to take college courses that will make him or her a more valuable employee to my company, I want to help. My policy is, and has been since I started the company, after you take a class that will benefit you in a job you want at the company, show us how you did in that class. If you get a C in the class we will pay fifty percent of the tuition. If you get a B we will pay seventy-five percent of the tuition, and if you get an A in the class we will reimburse you for one hundred percent of the tuition."

"That's for everyone, no matter what their job is?"

"It is. However, notice I said a class that will benefit the company. Political science classes aren't necessarily going to benefit someone working for our company, so they probably won't be paid for. The same is true with classes to become a history teacher. But if someone working for me now tells me they want to be qualified to hold a certain job in my company and they are taking classes toward that goal, I want to help them."

"I didn't know you did that, but I'm impressed. That's very generous."

"Well, keep in mind, I'm not handing them a degree. They still have to put forth the effort to go to class, not on company time, and do the work. They also have to pay for the books, which is a substantial investment. But if you do that, I will reimburse you for your tuition once I see you did the work. I think it's a benefit to our company."

"So I'll get some of my tuition reimbursed?"

"Absolutely. That's why I said you could use that reimbursement for part of the tuition you intend to pay for Sheila. If Sheila is reluctant to accept your help, point that out to her."

"I must not have been paying attention to what HR was telling me, because I don't remember anything about tuition repayment. That might help, though, if she doesn't want to accept my help."

"Good. Now, are you ready to give her a call?"

Chapter 7

An hour later Trent and Jasmine were both excited as they made plans. She'd called Sheila's roommate, who gave the phone to Sheila. Jasmine put the phone on speaker so they could all talk. Trent introduced himself, and Sheila quickly told him it was nice to meet him since she'd heard about him in Jasmine's letters. The more they talked, the easier it was for him to see why she and his Jasmine had become such good friends, and the better he felt about offering her a job.

They could both tell Sheila was fighting back tears when Jasmine invited her to move to Tennessee and live with her. She explained her plan, including Trent's offer of a job. She was hesitant to accept it, saying it wasn't fair for Jasmine to spend her money on her, but when her best friend explained the company tuition reimbursement, Sheila didn't seem quite as hesitant. They eventually talked her into it, once she convinced Jasmine she would rather consider it a loan that she would pay back to Jasmine once she graduated and had a job. By the time they ended the call all three of them were looking forward to the move. Sheila promised to give her notice at work the next day, and to call them to keep them informed.

Meanwhile, Trent showed Jasmine pictures of the condo, and promised to take her the next day to see it in person. She said she was sure it would be fine, and after seeing the pictures she felt like she'd won a lottery and was moving into a castle. It looked much nicer than the apartments she'd been used to. They made plans to move her into her new condo over the weekend, as he'd said earlier in the evening. Trent felt better with her living in a safer part of town, in a gated community closer to his house, and she was ecstatic. Not only did it look fantastic, but Sheila would be joining her soon.

When he took her to see it the next evening, her excitement grew. "I can't believe I can really live here," she said as she ran her hand over the marble counter top in the kitchen. "Is he renting it to me so cheap just because of you?"

"Yes, in a way, but not how you think. He really wanted someone living here, house sitting, if you will. He was afraid it would be hard to find someone that he felt comfortable with that could move in fairly soon, that he could trust to take care of it, while not upsetting his neighbors or the condo association, but would be willing to move out when he knew he'd be coming home. My thinking on that last part is that you'll be making more then and should be able to afford to pay more rent than you are now. Unless of course," he said with a sly grin on his face, "we're planning a wedding by then."

Her eyes opened wide in obvious shock. "Unless we're doing what?"

"I would love our relationship to grow to that, and you can't be surprised to hear me say it. I'd be willing to get married now, but that wouldn't be fair to you. Or us, if I'm completely honest with myself. We need time to get to know each other better and make sure our relationship is real and lasting. But some day I hope we're at the point where we can make it a permanent thing. I thought you knew that."

She walked into his open, inviting arms and laid her head against his chest. She always felt so warm and safe when she did that, and she swore she could feel his love for her coming through his arms, and she willingly absorbed it. "I knew in my heart that's what I was hoping would happen one day, but I think I was afraid to actually think about it or wish for it. It's sure nice hearing you say it, though. Thank you."

"Thank you for letting me know you feel the same way," he said with a kiss to the top of her head. He held her there, neither of them wanting to move, for several minutes. "So, does this condo pass your inspection? Do you think you and Sheila will be okay here, and should I line up some friends to help us move you in Saturday?"

"Yes, I love it, and I'm sure we'll do just fine here, but I don't think you need any friends to help us move. I don't have much stuff. All I have is my clothes, a few towels and sheets, and just a few things for cooking. I have one skillet, two pans and a set of dishes for four. I think I can probably fit all of that in my car."

"Between our two vehicles, then, we should be fine. We'll start packing tonight when I take you home. If we pack tonight and tomorrow night, we should be able to finish it up and move you Saturday. We can go shopping Sunday for anything you might need for your new place."

"What will I need? I hope not much, because my checking account isn't going to support much."

"I want to get you a housewarming gift, so we'll see what you need. To begin with, I've already ordered you a couple of sets of sheets and a new bedspread, because I know you don't have king-sized sheets for the bed in what will be your bedroom. Your sheets will probably fit Sheila's bed, but we'll have to check and be sure. I'm thinking we should get you some new towels since there'll be two of you living there now, but I didn't want to pick them out. You can do that when we go shopping Sunday."

"Trent, thank you, but you shouldn't have to pay for things like that for me."

"Honey, I want to, because these are things you'll need because of you moving into that condo, and moving you in there was my idea. I won't even try and deny that I'll feel better with you living closer to me, with a roommate and in a better area, but I love the idea of bringing you and Sheila together. I get to witness you realizing your dream. You're almost done with your schooling, so I'll get to see you graduate and start your career, and now I'll get to see you and Sheila reuniting and starting to build a future for her, as well. Those are both something special, and I feel honored to be able to watch them happen."

Looking up at him, she saw the sincerity in his eyes. He meant every word he'd said. "I love you, Trent. Thank you."

"I love you, too, Jasmine." After a deep kiss that proved their words to each other were true, he pulled back and smiled. "Ready to start packing?"

The packing and subsequent move didn't take long. Jasmine was right; their two vehicles were able to handle everything. He was surprised at how little she had to move, and that discovery was upsetting to him. It hit him then how much of a change in lifestyle she'd given up when she moved out of her parents' embrace. She was living in a meager apartment, with not much to her name, and yet she was happy and had a sense of self-pride. As he thought about that, she had every reason to be proud of herself. He certainly was proud of her.

At the same time, he couldn't help but wonder what her

parents would think if they could see her now. Sadly, he had a feeling seeing her prove herself and living like this with her own money wouldn't make them as proud of her as she deserved. Somewhere along the way during her life, someone or something had made enough of an impact on her to give her the determination to be her own person and stand on her own two feet. In his mind, she'd grown into someone that far surpassed either of her parents, and had most definitely earned his respect. She was certainly a special person, and he knew she would do well in life.

By Saturday evening they had everything moved to the new apartment and put away. Her bed was made, using the new sheets and bedspread he'd bought. "Are you sure you like this bedspread?" he asked.

"I love it, and everything you got me. I still don't think you should have spent that much money on me, but it's exactly what I would have looked for. It's my favorite color and matches this room perfectly."

"That's why I bought it," he said with a bit of a grin. "I was going to let you pick something out when we went shopping, but I wanted you to have it when we moved you in so you'd have it for your first night in your new place. When I saw this one it, jumped out at me. I was pretty sure it was your color and would look good in here. They didn't have it in a king size, though, so I had to have them order it in. I thought you'd like it."

"I love it, and I love you for knowing that I'd love it," she said, going to him and reaching up to kiss his cheek. His eyebrows were squinted together a bit as he looked at her, so she explained what she meant. "You pay attention to what I say. I mean, I've said that pink is probably my favorite color, but one time I also said that I think dark pink, sort of a mauve, and navy are beautiful together. Since this bedroom is navy, I would have looked for something in a mauve or dark pink. The fact that you found one that has both colors in it tells me how much you listen to what I say. That's what I was thanking you for."

"Ah," he said, nodding his head. "I do listen to what you say, sweetheart, because it's important to me. How else would I have known this was the perfect bedspread for you when I saw it?"

She laughed, but snuggled into his arms, which had brought her in closer to him. "I do appreciate it."

"Good. Now, tomorrow we're going to go shopping and pick up a few more things. Let's make a list of things to look at so we don't forget anything."

"I don't know of anything else I need. You said probably some more towels since there will be two of us, but I'm not sure I'll need them. I have two sets I've been using, and since there's a washing machine here, which is fantastic, we can wash them and reuse them. Besides, she may have some she'll bring with her. We should be fine. You already bought me my new sheets and bedspread, which I appreciate. You've spent enough."

"And hearing you thank me, and knowing how sincere you are about it made it worth every cent I paid for them, plus some. Now, please let me get you a few more things. It was my idea for you to move in here, so let me get you a few things for a house warming gift that will let you enjoy living here more."

"But what more do I need?"

"Some towel sets that will match these bathrooms, to start with. Then a few things to make this your home, like a couple of pillows for your couch. I know how much you liked the pillows on your couch, and I thought they were yours. When you said they stay with the apartment, I want you to pick out some you like for this couch."

"I do like couch pillows," she admitted.

"As do I. I'd also like to see you pick out a few new things to set around the apartment, tchotchkes, or knickknacks, or whatever you want to call them. I love seeing the things you had, but this apartment's bigger, so you need a few more."

"I'd rather wait for them," she said in a determined voice. "The best things like that are things that have a special meaning, like if you go someplace special and you get a little memento of your trip, or something like that. If there's a story behind it it makes it special. Then it's fun to look at them every time you dust them."

He laughed, but nodded. "I certainly can't argue with that logic. We'll just have to keep our eyes open when we go places for things that would fit that bill. Finally, I want to get a few things for your kitchen that I want. It's things I want, so you don't need to worry about me spending my money on them. I will ask you if I can keep them here, though."

"Huh?" She looked up at him totally confused. "You want to buy things for you, but keep them here?"

"Yes. Cooking dinner for us at your place is, well, a bit challenging for me because you make do without some things I have. I respect you for it, but I'm used to having them and it's harder for me to cook without them. I enjoy when we make dinner together, and want to be able to do it here. So call me selfish, but it's some things I want."

She looked up to meet his eyes, and couldn't help laughing. "Really? You look like you're ashamed or something."

"Well, I guess in a way I am. You've found a way to cook without them, and I've tried, but I haven't been able to adjust. I'm used to certain things, and I guess I'm spoiled. I want what I'm used to."

Still laughing, she nodded. "I understand, but what things are we talking about?"

"Like a mixer," he said quickly. "You have a hand mixer with a single speed. One speed! I have a stand mixer, which I will admit I've never actually used, but my hand mixer, which I do use, has ten speeds."

"Have you used all ten speeds?" she asked, not able to hold back a giggle.

He paused as he looked at her, grinning. "Proud of that, aren't you?" She nodded, a bit sheepishly. "Okay, Miss Smarty Pants, no, I probably haven't used all of them, but a low, medium, and high would be nice."

Laughing outright now and not even trying to hide it, she nodded again. "Okay, I'll give you that one. What else don't I have?"

"Wooden spoons. How can you cook without wooden spoons?"

"I guess I'll give you that one, too. After using your wooden spoons I will admit it is much nicer stirring things on the stove with a spoon that doesn't conduct the heat and get hot while you're stirring."

"Thank you. And while I'm on a roll, let's talk about your measuring cups, or lack thereof."

"I have a measuring cup," she insisted.

"Yes, you do. You have one measuring cup for half a cup. Where's the rest of the set?"

"Hey, I make do. I got that at a garage sale for ten cents. If you need a quarter cup of something, just fill it about half full. Fill it twice for a cup. What's so hard about that?"

"When I needed three cups of water I lost count and had to start over three times!"

"Maybe you have ADD. It's not my fault you can't concentrate."

"Oh, you're wrong there, young lady," he said with a laugh. "It's totally your fault that I can't concentrate on counting out six containers of water when you're in the room with me, moving your sexy little body around like you do."

"What are you talking about, moving my body around like I do?" she asked, turning to face him and putting her hands she'd balled up into fists on her hips in a challenging pose he always found adorable.

"See? There you go, you're doing it again!" He took her cute little fists in his hands and pulled her close for a kiss as they both laughed. When he managed to pull back he looked down at her, still smiling. "So are you ready to go shopping?"

They had a wonderful time gathering up things he felt she needed. She gave up trying to convince him he was spending too much when he leaned down to whisper in her ear. "Jasmine, I'm doing this because I want to, and I'm enjoying it a great deal. If you argue with me about this one more time, young lady, we'll go home and settle this with you over my lap."

Although she was a bit upset with his high handedness, she could also see in his eyes how sincere he was, so she allowed herself to simply accept it and enjoy their time together. Once she did that, she had to admit she'd enjoyed the afternoon immensely.

She was browsing in the kitchen supplies store when she started laughing. Her laughter drew him to her and he looked to see what she was looking at. He laughed, as well, when he saw the decorative motif on the cookie jar. A lady was using a rather large mixer, and the kitchen was a mess. Particles of whatever she was mixing were flying all over the kitchen. A man stood at the door, some of the batter from the bowl in his hair, and a frown on his face as he looked toward the lady, who looked pretty impish. "See what happens when you try to use more mixer than you need?" she laughed.

"He looks upset," he agreed, "but it looks to me like he's telling her she should have asked for help. He's holding a wooden spoon in his hand. I'll bet he's about to show her what else a wooden spoon can be used for."

He could tell the moment she realized what he was suggesting, when she turned to him, her eyes wide. "No," was all she managed to say.

"Oh, it works wonderfully," he whispered with a laugh. He picked up the cookie jar and put it in their basket.

"What are you doing?"

"You said extra little things around a house are better if there's a special moment or memory attached to it. I see what you mean now, and you're right. After our talk about mixers, this is perfect. We have to have it." She smiled, knowing he was right. She would remember this day and value her cookie jar forever.

Over the next couple of days Jasmine was becoming more accustomed to her new surroundings, and loved every minute of it. "I still can't believe I actually live here," she told Trent one evening while they were cuddled on the couch watching television after the dinner they'd cooked together. "I can't wait for Sheila to get here and see this apartment. I know she'll love it, too."

"Speaking of Sheila, have you decided how she's going to get here yet? My offer to loan her enough to buy a used car is still good."

"I know that would be your preference, and I appreciate that, but I'm not sure yet. I did some checking into prices from here, and she was going to check some prices there, then call me. I don't know what she found, but what I found was rather discouraging. To rent a U-Haul will be rather expensive, and I don't think she needs anything that large, anyway. I looked into renting a vehicle, and that, too, would be rather expensive, especially since she doesn't have any car insurance now. She would have to get some from the rental place, and it's more expensive if you don't have any valid insurance on a vehicle at the time. That seems rather ridiculous to me. If she had a vehicle she was insuring why would she have to rent a vehicle to move? Anyway, I checked on moving by bus, too, and that was the cheapest, but you're allowed one suitcase for the standard rate. Anything beyond that one suitcase is rather expensive. In fact, I'm thinking it might be cheaper to leave some of her clothes and sheets, towels, and kitchen things and go to a second-hand store when she gets here and buy different ones."

"On the other hand," Trent said, "if she allowed me to send her enough money to buy a used car, she could bring everything with her, and would then have a vehicle to use for going to work and school."

"I know, and to be honest," Jasmine said with a little sigh, "I'm tending to lean toward suggesting she accept that offer. I have a little saved up I can give her, but it's not enough to pay for any of these other options. That's disappointing, because I hoped I had enough to send to her to pay for her move."

"You know I said I'm here and I'll help."

"I know. In fact, I didn't say anything about maybe having to wait longer to bring her here, because I knew you'd help me get her here if I asked. But I'm thinking, if we have to ask you to borrow money, it makes more sense to borrow it for a car, which she can keep and use after her move, than for a bus ticket or car rental."

"I agree completely with that, and it sounds like something someone who's getting As in economics would say," he added with a grin. "Why don't you call her roommate? If you can talk to Sheila, suggest she start looking for a good used vehicle."

She nodded and picked up her phone. She put it on

speaker so they could all talk, but Trent let her do most of the talking. He loved hearing the two of them, and the excitement they had. Listening to them, it was hard to believe it had been so many years since they'd seen each other. He hoped they got along this well in person.

Over the next few days it was easy to see Jasmine loved her new apartment, which made him happy, as well. He felt better having her in a better section of town, and closer to his house. With a nicer kitchen, they often cooked dinner there after work, then relaxed in front of the television. They utilized the tennis courts frequently, where she surprised him. She said she'd only played tennis a couple of times, but he soon found she was quite athletic, and picked the game up quickly. What used to be a fun, lazy way to spend a little time had become quite a match. She was competitive, and their tennis matches had become extremely challenging, something they both enjoyed.

They were watching television one evening when Sheila called, excited. "Jasmine, is the offer to borrow money for a used car still good?"

"Absolutely," Trent answered quickly. "Did you find a car you like?"

"Yes, I think so. I told the people at work that I'm looking for a good used car, and one of the ladies I work with told me she had one for sale. It had belonged to her grandfather, her mother's father. My friend was an only child, and so was her mother, so his estate went to the two of them. She said he was meticulous about everything he owned, including his car, and took real good care of it. She said they would sell it to me for three thousand dollars. I looked it up in the Blue Book and the retail on it is closer to four thousand. I told her that and she said they knew, but they'd rather sell it for less to someone they know and that needs a car. Besides, she said, since he's no longer here to tell us what all it's had done to it, they can't really say it's in good working order. They feel better selling it for less, with the understanding that they haven't driven it, other than her mom took it to work the other day to be sure there wasn't anything obvious that was wrong with it."

"That sounds promising," Jasmine said.

"He was a retired mechanic, so since he took care of everything he owned, I have to assume if his car needed something done to it he did it," Sheila went on to explain.

"That sounds like a good recommendation," Trent said. "I sent four thousand dollars so you would have it when you found the car you wanted. Will that give you enough for the car, the sales tax, and to get insurance on it, or do you want a little more? Make sure you have enough money to buy gas and meals during your trip and to pay for a motel for a night."

"No, I made sure that would cover it all. I said I don't want to borrow any more than that, and I was serious. I called about insurance, and figured up the taxes. Four thousand will cover it all. Thank you again for loaning the money to me."

"You're more than welcome, Sheila. Jasmine can't wait to see you again, and she's got me excited to meet you now, too."

"I can't remember the last time I was this excited about anything," Sheila said. "I never had a family, so Christmas was never a big thing for me, but I think now I know what the excitement about Christmas must be like."

Trent laughed, but noticed Jasmine was nodding her head in understanding. He determined right then and there that he would make sure both these ladies had a Christmas to remember this year. "Well, go ahead and get the car and drive it a few days before you leave, just in case you notice something that doesn't sound right. If you do, have it looked at before you leave. If you need more money for your trip out, just let me know," Trent said.

"I will, and thank you again."

After the conversation ended, Jasmine got out her dreaded economics books and they spent a little time going over that before he left for the night.

Chapter 8

Several days later Sheila called again, very excited. "I feel like I've hit the lottery," she told them. "I got the car and I'm very happy with it. It's a Ford Focus, and it seems to run real good. Obviously I'm not a mechanic, but it runs smooth and I don't hear any weird noises or anything like that. It gets good gas mileage, too, which will help on the trip."

"That's good," Jasmine said.

"But wait till you hear the best part. I was washing it real good, inside and out, and I found an envelope under the seat. I opened it up and it had a thousand dollars in it. I couldn't believe it. As I thought about it, though, it wasn't my money. I took it back to the girl I bought it from and gave it to her and told her where I'd found it. She and her mom said it was my car now, that they'd sold it as is. I told her that money should be theirs, and they finally offered a compromise. We split it."

"That sounds fair," Jasmine said. Trent agreed. As the two ladies talked, he thought back on that. He was impressed that Sheila gave the money back, knowing how much that amount of money would mean to her. It told him a lot about her. He pulled his mind back to listen to the rest of their conversation, just as he heard his name.

"So Trent, I want you to know that now I have plenty of money to make it out to Tennessee."

"I'm glad to hear that," he assured her. "I was concerned you would be cutting it close, and I didn't want you to have to scrimp on meals. I can breathe easier now. When are you leaving?"

"Tomorrow morning," she said. Although he'd never met her, from the enthusiasm in her voice he could picture her bouncing up and down much like his Jasmine did. "I should be there Saturday evening sometime. And Jasmine, I took your advice and got a cell phone. I thought about what you said, and you're right, it would be better if I had a phone just in case I have any problems along the way. I'm on it now, so you can program this number in on your phone. It's my number now."

"Good. Since Trent's going to make sure you have a job once you get here, you'll be able to pay the monthly fee for it."

"That's what I thought. Thank you again, Trent. I can't believe you would do that, when you've never even met me."

"I may not have met you yet, but I've gotten an excellent recommendation," he said with a chuckle, "from someone very special to me."

"Once you meet him you'll see what I mean when I said I'm lucky I spilled iced tea all over him one day," Jasmine said, smiling as her eyes were locked with his.

"It seems I'm also lucky you spilled that iced tea on him," Sheila said, and they all laughed.

———

Trent suggested they go out for lunch on Saturday, hoping to get her mind on something other than Sheila for a while. She was so excited she was about to drive him crazy. "I better not leave. What if she gets here?"

"She told you last night she was at a motel and had six or seven more hours of driving yet. She hoped to leave between eight and nine this morning, so she won't be here before three o'clock. We have plenty of time for lunch. Besides, she said she'd call when she's about an hour away."

"Yeah, that's right. If she gets here sooner than planned, an hour will still give us plenty of time to get back home. Maybe going out would get my mind off of this for a little bit."

"That's what I'm hoping," he admitted as he led her to his car. They had a nice meal and went for a walk afterwards, but he relented and took her back home after she checked her watch four times in fifteen minutes.

"Why don't we make something for dinner," he suggested as he watched her pacing the floor. "I'm guessing once she gets here she would prefer we eat at home and not go out anywhere tonight. We can make something like lasagna, and get it ready to put in the oven now, then put it in the refrigerator. We can make a salad and some of your delicious dressing. When she gets here all we'll have to do is put the lasagna in the oven and it can bake while we visit. The salad will be ready to add the dressing, and we can eat."

"Oh, that's a good idea." They worked together, and he was able to get her mind off of her friend for a little while. While they were working Sheila called with an update. According to her Google directions she should be there in just under an hour. They finished their dinner preparations, and she called the front gate. They'd filled out all the paperwork for Sheila to live there, and she'd been approved already. She told them she should be arriving soon, and told them she would be driving a Ford Focus. She certainly wanted her to feel welcome, and not be hassled by the front gate or have a hard time there.

They were sitting out on her front porch when a blue Ford Focus pulled into the drive. Trent watched with a smile as Jasmine flew down the steps as the car stopped. The car door flew open and the two ladies were in each other's arms, dancing around in a circle. He made his way down to them, but gave them all the time they wanted. Eventually they separated and Jasmine said, "Sheila, this is Trent."

"It's nice to meet you, Sheila, and I'm glad you made it here," he said.

"I'm glad to finally meet you, too," she said. She seemed a bit shy, but after shaking his hand, she said, "Oh, what the heck," and gave him a hug, too. He chuckled as he hugged her back. "I'm sorry if that seemed a bit forward, but you've been so good to me already, I felt like I had to do something more than a handshake."

He smiled as he led the two ladies into the house. "Let's go on in. I'm sure you're ready to sit back and rest a little. While you two get caught up, I'll bring your things in, if that's all right?"

"Trent, you don't have to do that."

"It's fine. I'm sure you two have a lot to talk about."

Once they were settled on the couch he went back to her car to retrieve her belongings. Once again, he was a little saddened by how little there was, but he understood why the two had gotten along so well for so long. He could tell they were both proud ladies, and although they didn't have much, they had what they needed, and they'd gotten it all themselves. He had a sense of pride for both of them, just thinking about them.

Once he had all her boxes and one suitcase in her room, he joined them in the living room, sitting next to Jasmine on the sofa. He sat back, his arm around Jasmine, who snuggled up next to him. He relaxed and mostly just listened to them. He interjected comments from time to time, but for the most part he was totally content to simply watch and listen to the two of them. Seeing how happy they both were was worth a pile of gold to him.

The day after Sheila arrived, Jasmine suggested they go for a drive so Sheila could see the area and get an idea where things were, like the grocery store. Sheila agreed, and suggested she drive so she could show Jasmine her new car. While they were stopped at a red light the ladies heard a noise coming from the car that concerned them. "What was that?" Jasmine asked.

"I have no idea. I've never heard it before," Sheila said. The light turned green and she pressed on the gas pedal, and they heard the sound again. "I don't like it, though."

"Maybe we better go back home. We can ask Trent to drive it and see if he has any idea what it could be."

"That might be a good idea," Sheila agreed, as they heard it again. "It doesn't sound too healthy."

"I'm glad it happened now instead of while you were coming here."

"So am I. I'm going to turn around here and head back." Sheila pulled into a parking lot, but before she could get it turned around, they saw steam coming from under the hood.

"You better just park it back here in the corner of the lot," Jasmine said. "I'll call Trent. Maybe he can come look at it."

"I hate to bother him, but I don't know what else to do." She backed it into a parking spot in a far corner and turned the key off. They both got out and lifted the hood and were surprised at how much smoke came rolling out.

"Yep, I'm calling Trent," Jasmine said as she took her

phone out. She explained to Trent where they were and what had happened.

"Okay, you two wait there and I'll be there shortly. Don't try to start it again until I get there."

They talked while they waited for Trent to get there. "I don't know what could be wrong," Sheila said. "The car seemed to run real well the whole way here, which was a relief. I hate that it's a problem now, but at least it made it here."

"You said the previous owner took good care of it?" Jasmine asked.

"That's what they said. She told me about her grandfather, and he seemed like the type that would take very good care of it, especially since he was a mechanic. It was hard for her to talk about him a whole lot."

"Because she missed him?"

"Yes, but also because of the way he died."

Jasmine turned toward her. "What do you mean? Was he sick a long time?"

"He wasn't sick at all. Someone shot him, and they still have no idea who it was, or why."

Jasmine's eyes grew huge. "Someone shot him?"

"Yes. The police said it must have been a burglary because his house was ransacked. He wasn't rich, and he didn't live in a real nice house, but the house was all torn apart. It was strange, though, because there were a couple of things that were fairly nice, but they didn't take them. The police asked Mom if she could come up with a list of things that were stolen, but she couldn't. She didn't really know of anything he had that was worth a good amount of money. He had a sixty-inch television that he was real proud of, but it was still there. She couldn't think of anything that had actually been stolen."

"But they think it was a burglary?"

"They think maybe it was supposed to be a burglary, but when they didn't see much to take, they tore the house apart looking for something of value. The police said older people will sometimes have a stash of money someplace, and maybe they were looking for something like that, and that's why they tore the house apart." She was quiet a few moments before adding, "They said they might even have shot him because they couldn't find anything valuable to take."

"That's terrible," Jasmine said.

"It is," Sheila agreed, "but they said that happens sometimes. She said after he died the police told them not to touch anything for a while so they could look for fingerprints and things. After that they took another week or two before going over to his house because they weren't ready to face it yet."

"I can certainly understand that. That would be terrible."

They were still talking about it when Trent pulled up beside them. He looked at the car and quickly found the problem. "A water hose split," he explained. "Do you know, Sheila, if this car sat for a while without being driven?"

She took a moment to think before answering. "I'm not sure, but I'd say there's a good chance it could have. It was her grandfather's car, and she said he didn't drive too much any more. He lived close to the grocery store and she said he generally walked there because he thought it was good exercise for him."

"Good for him," Jasmine said.

"To answer your question, Trent, yes, I guess it could have sat for a while. When they were finally ready to go back to his house they cleaned the house up before they even thought about his car, so as I'm thinking about it, yes, it could have sat there for more than a month. I don't have any idea how long it had been since he'd driven it before he died."

"I'm going to call my mechanic and have him come get your car and take it to his shop. I'll have him go over the whole car and check it out. This hose that broke looks like it had some dry rot, which can happen when a car sets without being driven. If one hose was like that there's a good chance it's not the only one."

Sheila's face paled. "But how much will that cost?"

"I don't know, but don't worry about it, I'm going to pay for it."

"But you shouldn't have to pay for my –"

"Sheila, going over the whole car isn't something that needs to be done. The only thing that needs done right now is replacing the one hose, which wouldn't be a big expense. He could bring a hose here and replace it for not much money. However, I'll feel better if he goes over the whole thing, since we don't know what all it's had done to it or how long it sat. That's something I want, for my peace of mind, so I'll pay for it. I'll feel better knowing you, and sometimes Jasmine, are riding in a car that's in good shape."

"But –"

Trent held up his hand to stop her. "Jasmine can vouch for me when I tell you I tend to be protective of the people I care about. I feel responsible for bringing you here, so you're stuck with my protectiveness, whether you like it or not. Sorry, but that's just the way it is."

Jasmine started laughing, and turned to her friend. "He's right. Trust me, just say thank you and appreciate what he's doing, because he's going to do it anyway."

Sheila looked between the two of them and smiled. He had his arm around her waist and they were both looking at each other, smiling. "Okay," she said with a smile of her own. "Thank you. I really do appreciate it, but I still feel bad about you spending money on my car."

"Well, don't, because it's my choice." He made a phone call, then suggested they go to the coffee shop next door and get breakfast while they waited for the tow truck.

Once the car was on its way to the repair shop, Trent took Jasmine and Sheila to his house, rather than theirs. "Jasmine, I know you drove my car when yours was in for repairs, so you're comfortable with it. I don't care which of you borrows my car and which one drives yours, so you two talk about it and decide, and when you're ready to go back home, take my car. I'll drive my other one."

"You have an extra car?" Sheila asked.

"Yes, he does," Jasmine answered before he had a chance, "and once again, you may as well just say thank you and appreciate it because he's going to insist we do this so we each have a car to drive."

"She's right," Trent confirmed, "because you both need a car. You need to be able to get to work and back, and she needs to get to her classes, work and back. So you two decide who wants to drive what, and I'm fine with it."

They quickly decided Jasmine would drive Trent's since she'd driven it before. She drove it home later, and had Sheila drive her car to be sure she felt comfortable with it.

As Trent expected, Sheila settled into her new home quickly. She was anxious to get a job and start working, but Trent suggested she take a few days to rest and get acquainted with her new home and community. He asked what type of job she would like to have some day, but she had no idea. She admitted she hadn't given it much thought, thinking she'd never be able to afford to go to college.

He suggested she give that some thought, and he promised to check with his personnel manager to see what openings they had presently. He didn't tell her that if there was nothing suitable open at the time, he would make one. They hired people regularly, so he was sure they would come up with something for her. He hoped if she had an idea what she might like to do eventually, they would be able to find something that would prove interesting for her.

They sat down to discuss it a few days later, but she hadn't really come up with anything. "I know I'm not really interested in doing something like teaching. I'm more interested in business, but I'm not sure what kind."

"That's not a problem at all," he assured her. "Once you start taking business classes something will probably grab your attention. Until then we'll see what we can find. Maybe we'll move you around to a couple of different jobs to see if you find an area you like. In fact, I may have a good job for you to start out with, until your classes start this fall."

"I'll take anything you have."

"We have a mailroom. All the mail goes there, and Lisa sorts it and delivers it to each department. As she delivers their mail she picks up whatever they have to be mailed out. When she gets back to the mailroom she puts postage on all of it, weighing the larger things to get the right amount. Lately we've been thinking it would be good to add to that, but Lisa is already getting too busy to handle everything herself. We often have memos and other paperwork that go from one department to the other, and we get deliveries sporadically throughout the day. Rather than everyone having to hand deliver all of them, it would be more efficient to have one person make a trip to every department, much like the lady in the mailroom does every morning once the mail is sorted. We want someone to make several trips a day to deliver mail and deliveries, drop off things from other departments, and pick up mail that needs to go out."

"I could do that," Sheila said.

"You would be visiting every department in the company, both in the office and in the factory. It might give you a bit of insight into the different departments."

"And might help me decide if I think I'd like working in different areas. That sounds perfect."

"Then whenever you're ready to start, I'll take you in and get you set up with Lisa, the lady in the mailroom. She'll be happy to have some help. She can take you around with her for a couple of days while you get to know your way around the company."

"I'm ready to go tomorrow. That sounds like fun, and I'm eager to start making some money so I can pay you back."

Two weeks later Sheila had settled in at work and was enjoying her new job. She and Jasmine were getting along real well in their new apartment, and Trent was enjoying watching their friendship reignite and grow.

He was also impressed with Sheila as a person, and could easily see why Jasmine had latched onto her and stayed friends through letters. It didn't surprise him much that she quickly turned into a very good employee. She easily caught on to the routine, even learning Lisa's job so she could help her on days she was busier than most, and it didn't take long for her to make friends in nearly every department. When Lisa was sick a couple of days, Sheila willingly jumped in and did both jobs. She was tired at the end of the day, but Trent could see pride in her eyes at having been able to handle both jobs. He found himself hoping that whatever she decided she'd like to study in college, it was something she could do while working at Douglas Manufacturing. He would certainly find a position for her if she decided she'd like to stay there.

Sheila loved her new job, but felt embarrassed about her wardrobe. At her other jobs she'd had she hadn't needed to worry about having appropriate clothes. She either had uniforms that were provided by the company, or she worked behind the scenes in blue jeans and tee shirts. This was her first job in an office, and she felt out of place. She was a little taller than Jasmine, but close enough to her size other than that to be able to able to borrow a couple of her dresses. Jasmine had taken her to their local second hand shop the first week and she'd been able to find a couple of outfits that were suitable, as well, but four outfits was a meager wardrobe.

The girls were talking about her lack of clothes one evening while the three of them were fixing dinner together. Jasmine suggested they go on a shopping trip over the weekend, but Sheila was concerned about the money. "But once you've had a couple of paychecks you'll have enough to buy a few outfits," Jasmine reasoned.

"But I'll need that money. I want to pay my way here, plus I owe Trent money. I want to start paying that back. Plus there's the expense for my car repairs. It's been in the shop for a while now, so I know that's going to be expensive."

"Sheila, I'm going to pay for your car repairs. I wanted my mechanic to give it a good once over to be sure it's in good shape, and that's why he's not done with it yet. That was my idea, for my peace of mind, so I'm paying for it. He found something that he feels could fail shortly, so I told him to go ahead and replace it now. He's waiting for the part to come in. He expects it to come in shortly and he'll have it ready for you next week."

"You shouldn't have to pay for repairs for my car, Trent."

"I requested he do it, so yes, I'm paying for them. It'll give me peace of mind. He should have it for you next week sometime."

"Good. I've felt like someone's been following me a couple of times since I've been driving Jasmine's car, and I've decided it's probably someone who knows Jasmine and her car, and they're looking to see if it's her. I'll be glad to get my car back."

Trent turned to her with a serious expression. "You feel like you're being followed?"

"It's probably nothing, just one of those weird feelings you get sometimes. Sometimes it seems like someone in a car will be watching me. Like I said, I figure it's probably someone who knows Jasmine and her car, and they're looking to see if it's her, or why someone else is driving her car."

"Maybe," Jasmine said. "I know a lot of people from college that know my car and always waive when they see me."

Sheila nodded, and turned to Trent. "I still feel I should pay you back, though, before I start buying new clothes and things."

"I'm not in any hurry for you to pay me back," Trent assured her. "I completely understand that this job requires a different wardrobe than you're used to, so take your first few paychecks and get what you need. You're doing a wonderful job at work and I don't want you to feel inadequate, because you certainly aren't. I think you should take Jasmine's suggestion and take your paycheck and go shopping, and get what you need to make you feel confident. Besides, I've seen you two together enough now to know that you'll both have a wonderful time and come back happy. I'd love to see that."

She debated a few moments, but eventually turned to face him. "You're sure you won't be upset if I don't start paying you back yet?"

"I'm absolutely sure. I want you to use your first several paychecks to get what you need to be comfortable here. I'm talking about clothes, but whatever else you need, as well. Once you're settled in and feel like you have what you need, then you can think about paying me back a little at a time as you have it. I'm much more concerned about making sure you feel comfortable and at home here than I am getting that money back."

"Okay, if you're sure you're okay with it, Jazz, let's go shopping!"

"Woohoo! I love shopping trips, even if I'm not shopping for me. Ask Trent, he'll tell you."

"She's right," he confirmed. "She's the only person I know that's excited to go shopping and help me find a gift for someone. Who likes to shop for gifts?"

"I do," Jasmine stated emphatically. "So, what are you looking for, Sheila? Do you want dresses and skirts, or pants?"

The two quickly decided this shopping expedition would take place on Saturday, and then got into a detailed discussion of what all they would be looking for. Trent stood back, smiling as he listened to their enthusiasm.

Friday evening, Trent took Jasmine out for dinner, then back to his house so they would have a little time alone. "I've enjoyed seeing you and Sheila renewing your friendship," he told her as they settled on the couch with her snuggling up next to him. "It's nice to have you to myself tonight, though. I've missed our alone time."

"Me, too. I love having Sheila here, and I can't thank you enough for doing that for me, but I've missed being alone with you, too."

"Let's enjoy tonight. Tomorrow you'll be with her shopping, but call me when you get back home and I'll come over to see how you made out. Afterward maybe we can all have dinner together, then I can steal you away for a little time alone again. How does that sound?"

"It sounds perfect." They enjoyed their time alone, before he reluctantly kissed her goodnight at her door and returned to his house.

He called her the next morning before they left, which didn't surprise her. "Good morning, honey. Are you ready for your big day of shopping?"

"I am. We were just getting our coats."

"Okay. You two have fun today, and I'll see you this evening. I'll go to the grocery store and get something we can fix for dinner. If you call me when you're ready to leave for home I'll meet you there."

"That sounds like a good plan. I'll see you this evening."

"Okay. Be careful, and remember to call me when you're done and ready to head for home."

"Will do. Sheila can remind me."

"Okay. I'm counting on you, Sheila," he said. "Make sure she remembers to call before you leave. I don't want her talking on the phone while she's driving."

"Got it," Sheila said with a giggle.

After hanging up, Trent went to the office to finish up a few things before going to the grocery. When he got back home he put things in the refrigerator, leaving them in the bag so they'd be ready to take to Jasmine's when she called. He took a shower, then sat down to watch TV while he waited for the call. He flipped through channels looking for something of interest. He settled on a game, and sat back to relax a while.

Chapter 9

Jasmine drove them to their local mall, and the two went inside, eager to start shopping. They knew how much she had from her two paychecks, and set an amount she felt comfortable spending. They looked at it as a challenge, to see how many new outfits they could find for that amount, so they went from store to store, looking at everything, and making mental notes as to a pair of pants they liked here, and a blouse they liked there.

They got some lunch and reviewed what they'd found. They did some calculations and came up with what they thought would be their best choices, and set out to do their purchasing. It was an experience unlike either of them had ever had, and with each stop they picked up another item that would fit in perfectly with what they'd already gotten. They bought blouses and sweaters or jackets, which they could pair with skirts and pants interchangeably, giving her numerous options.

An hour later they were in their car, proud of what they'd accomplished, and ready to head for home. "I better call

Trent and let him know we're on our way. He'll be surprised we're done this early." She punched in his number and waited.

"You're done already?" he asked as his way of answering the phone, and both ladies giggled.

"I have my phone on speaker and Sheila heard that," Jasmine explained. "I told her you'd be surprised that we're done this soon."

"I am. Did you find what you were looking for?"

"We did. That's why we're done so early. We found a lot of things that look great together, so she has lots of options to mix and match. I can't wait to show them to you."

Trent laughed. "That's my Jasmine. You bought things for Sheila, but you're just as excited as she is. You be careful coming home and I'll be over at your house waiting to see what all wonderful things you found."

"Okay. We're leaving now, so I'll see you in about forty minutes or so."

"Okay. I love you."

"Love you, too," Jasmine said as she hung up. They were talking about how well everything they got matched, and the different combinations she could use, when a car passed them. There were two men in it and both of them were turned, looking straight at them. They got even with them and stayed there for a few seconds, looking at them, before going on around them and pulling back in, in front of them. "I wonder what their problem is," Jasmine said.

"I don't know, but I don't like it," Sheila said, which made Jasmine look over at her friend.

"Sheila, what's wrong? You look real pale."

"I'm pretty sure that's the car I saw a couple of times when I said I felt like someone was following me."

Jasmine turned to look at Sheila again. "What? Are you saying it was one car you kept seeing that you thought was following you?"

"Yes."

"I thought you meant it was different people. You should have said something."

"Why? I didn't know for sure they were following me. I never saw who was in it or anything. I haven't had a car, so driving is not something I'm used to. I thought I was being paranoid, or it was just someone you knew and they were looking to see if they knew me since I was in your car."

"I hope we're both being paranoid now, but I'll be glad when we get home. I don't like this, either. Let's just stay behind them and hope they turn off somewhere. If they don't, maybe I will. It'll take longer to get home, but I don't care. There's an intersection up here. If they go straight, I'll turn. I'm not sure where it goes, but we can use our phones to find another route home."

"Good idea." They were both quiet as they came up onto the intersection. Jasmine kept her speed constant, showing no sign of turning off. When the other car went straight, she quickly slowed and turned off. They both heaved a sigh of relief.

"I feel better," Jasmine said. "I don't know if that was anything to worry about or not, but when we get home we're going to tell Trent about it."

"I think that's a good idea. That was creepy, with them looking at us like that. Who does that?"

"Not anyone I want to meet. Now, can you ask your phone to take us home? I'm not sure where we're headed."

"Yeah, sure."

She got her phone out of her purse, but Jasmine said, "Use my phone instead and call Trent quick. Tell him we're being followed. They must have turned around, and they're coming up on us quick."

Sheila grabbed Jasmine's phone and quickly hit redial.

Then she hit speaker. "Hey, honey, what's wrong? You aren't driving while on your phone, are you?"

"Trent, we're being followed. I think it's a black SUV," she said quickly. "They were behind us and were real creepy looking when they passed us. We turned off of 92 onto 27 to lose them, but they turned around and are coming up behind us fast. Oh, no."

Before she had a chance to say anything else, the SUV rammed into them and knocked them sideways. Jasmine tried to keep control of the car, but it was spinning and sliding. The phone was knocked out of Sheila's hand, and she twisted in her seat to look for it in the back seat. She saw the SUV behind them, coming toward them again.

Trent was instantly on alert. "Oh, no what, honey?" Instead of hearing Jasmine, the next thing he heard sounded like a crash. "Jasmine, what happened? Sheila?" There was silence for several seconds, then he heard a man's voice, but he couldn't make out what was being said. Instead of saying anything, he tried to listen, but what he heard was fuzzy. Something was happening, but he couldn't tell what. It sounded like a car door shut, then another. Then more silence. "Jasmine? Sheila?" He tried several times, but got no response.

He ran to his car and quickly headed in that direction, trying to think as he drove. Should he end the call and call someone for help, or keep the line open in case she tried to talk to him again? Maybe he should call John. Being a state patrolman, he might be able to help. But did he want to end this call? He decided it would be more helpful to end the call and call John.

He quickly explained what had happened, and that he was heading in that direction.

"Okay, let me know what you find. In the meantime, I'll let my supervisor know, too. I'm sure he'll send a car over that way, too," John said. "I'm going into the patrol post so I can talk to him, and we'll figure this out. I'll also have her phone number traced and get a location for it."

John called him back ten minutes later. "I'm at the post now, and I called this in on my way here. They were able to pinpoint where the phone is. It's not moving, so we've got an officer on their way there now. You may get there first, though. If you do, wait for the car to arrive. We also have someone checking that area to see if they know of any cameras around. When the patrol car gets there, they can check for any cameras on houses in the area that may have picked up on something."

"Okay, I'm about at the road she turned off onto now."

"Good. Let me know if you see anything."

"Oh, no. John, I see her car up ahead. It's been wrecked."

"See if they're in it and if they need an ambulance. I'll hang on while you look. I can call for one if you need it."

"Okay." John assumed Trent put his phone in his pocket, as everything was muted. He heard a car door, and Trent yelling for Jasmine and Sheila. "John, they're not here. Her phone's in the back seat, and her purse is, too, and lots of bags from their shopping trip. She wouldn't have left her phone and purse here. What's happened to her?"

"Trent, try to calm down," John urged. "Our car is almost there. Don't touch anything else. I'll send an evidence team and tow truck out, and they'll tow it in and collect any evidence from the scene and also from the car that may help us. Are you okay to drive?"

"Yes, I'm fine, but what can I do? I have to find them."

"Trent, listen to me. You need to calm down. You're not going to be able to help them if you lose it. Take a couple of deep breaths, and when you're calm enough to drive, come in here to the station. The captain and I have a bunch of questions for you, and we'll get to the bottom of it. We'll find them, Trent."

"I don't know what's going on, though. How can I answer questions when I don't know any more than you do?"

"I'm talking about questions about the girls themselves. Maybe we can find a clue that will at least tell us where to start looking. I'll explain it further when you get here. Is there a patrol car coming yet?"

"Yes, I see the lights down the road, heading this way."

"Good. Tell one of them I need to talk to them right away, before you leave."

"Okay, here's one of them now. I'll give him my phone."

"John, this is Ted Lawson. What's up?"

"Trent's a good guy and friend of mine, but he sounds hysterical. There were two ladies in the car that's been wrecked. One of them, Jasmine, is his girlfriend, and her friend, Sheila. I need him back here to answer questions to see if we can find them, but I don't know if he can drive right now. See what you think. If he's not good to drive, keep him there a few minutes. There are a couple of more cars headed to you. When one of them gets there, have someone bring him in to the post, okay? I've got more officers on their way to you."

"I understand and will do. Do you want to talk to him again?"

"Yes. Thanks."

"John, what was that all about?" Trent asked a moment later.

"I need you back here to help us at this end of this, but I don't want you driving if you're too upset. There are other officers on their way, and they can drive you back."

"No, I need to do something to help. Standing here looking at an empty car isn't helping anyone, especially me. I'll come to the post."

"Trent, are you sure you're calm enough?"

"I'll be fine. See you soon."

He ended the call and headed for his car, only to be stopped by the officer who had been talking to John. "Trent, wait a minute."

"Why?"

"Can you tell me what's going on? How did you know something was wrong and you should come here? I need something to go on. I'm Officer Ted Lawson, by the way."

"Trent Douglas. Nice to meet you." Trent quickly explained the call he'd received from Jasmine. "That's all I know. John says he needs me at the station, so I'll be there, unless there's anything else I can do here?"

"No, but are you sure you're okay to drive? Another officer will be here shortly and they can –"

"No, I'm fine. I'm not waiting around here looking at the car she should be in and isn't. I know John was concerned, but I've had a few minutes to come to grips with it now, and I'll be okay."

Ted studied him a couple of moments, and nodded. "Okay, Trent, you do seem calmer than when we got here. Be careful, though, and don't let your mind focus on this while you're driving."

"Okay. Thanks." He went to his car and was soon headed to the station. He tried to keep Ted's words in mind and focus completely on his driving, but it was difficult. He finally made it to the station. He ran inside and John came out to the front to meet him. He led him back to an office. "Trent, this is my supervisor, Captain Jim Thorpe."

"Hi, Trent. Let me fill you in on what's happening so far, then we'll ask you some questions. First, a tow truck is loading her car up now, and they'll bring it back here to be processed. An evidence crew is there now, as well. They'll help the officers search the area for anything that may help. A couple of more officers just arrived, and they're going to check with homes in the area and see if anyone saw or heard anything, or have cameras on their homes that may have caught something."

"You said her car will be processed. What exactly does that mean?"

"They'll go over the car looking for clues as to what may have happened or where they might be. They'll look for finger-prints, or anything someone may have dropped in the car that may help us find them."

"Where could she be, and who was in the black SUV?"

"That's what I want to know," John said, "and why was he following them?"

Captain Thorpe agreed, and continued his explanation. "The officer there said it looked to him like the car had been rammed from the rear, and the side. He thinks someone hit it from behind, in the driver's side corner. It was enough to make the car spin, heading toward the ditch."

"So they'd lose control and have to stop," John said, thinking out loud.

"Exactly," Captain Thorpe confirmed, "so they could kidnap the ladies."

"Kidnap?" Trent's eyes were wide. "Why would someone want to kidnap them?"

"That's what we have to find out," Captain Thorpe said. "I put a BOLO out for any black SUV with front end damage. That's pretty vague, but maybe we'll get lucky and find them before they get far. We alerted all our officers out there to watch for it as a possible kidnapping in progress. We're hoping if they're all watching for it someone will see it. In the mean-time, let's sit down and talk. I've got a bunch of questions to ask about them, and maybe we can come up with something."

"I'll tell you everything I can, but I don't really know much about Sheila. She just got here a couple of weeks ago."

"Let's start there then." They sat down and Captain Thorpe and John both took out paper and pens to take notes.

"The men will tell me about anything they find, but while they're doing that, tell us what you know about Sheila. Where did she move from and why?"

Trent relayed the story of their long-time pen pal relationship, and answered any questions he could about her. He also answered all the questions he could about Jasmine.

After listening carefully to everything they said, both men were shaking their heads. "I don't see anything that jumps out at me," John said, "but I think we need to look into Sheila's history a bit more. Nothing about Jasmine seems remarkable. I'm not saying there is anything questionable about Sheila, but we don't know much about her so we can't really rule her out as a possible target."

"I agree," Captain Thorpe said. "It's a pretty big coincidence that this happened shortly after she arrived, so I think we at least need to look into her a little more before we can rule that out, as well."

"How do we do that?" Trent asked.

"If she's working for you I assume you have her Social Security number. We can start there. It should tell us where she's been living and working. While I have someone working on that, we'll see if we can find out any more. You said she didn't have a phone, but Jasmine called her on her roommate's phone. Do you have that number? Maybe we can talk to her roommate and see if she's aware of anything that might help us."

"I can get her Social Security number from work, but I don't have her old roommate's phone number. If you have Jasmine's phone, though, it should be on there."

"We can get someone working on that, as well," the captain said.

Trent called his personnel manager, who happened to be at the office finishing a report, and she gave him Sheila's Social Security number. Captain Thorpe instructed someone on what to look for with that, and had the evidence people looking at Jasmine's phone for any number registered to someone in Nevada over the last month.

"While they're working on that, let's talk about Sheila a little more. Is there anything you can think of that she or Jasmine may have mentioned that we haven't talked about? You said she bought a car to drive here. Did she have any incidents as she drove across country to get here? Her car seemed to run okay?"

"Yes, it seemed to run okay for her trip, but she had a little problem with it shortly after she got here. I had it towed to my mechanic to have it fixed, but then I asked him to go over it all to see if there's anything else that needs attention. He had to order a part for it, so it's still in the shop."

"So she hasn't been driving it?"

"No, she's been driving Jasmine's car to work, the one they were in today, and Jasmine's been driving one of mine."

John asked a couple of more questions about Sheila, and how well Trent felt he knew her. "You don't get a feeling she's hiding anything, do you?"

"No, but −" Trent stopped mid-sentence, and both men looked at him.

"What is it?" John asked.

"A couple of days ago when they decided to go shopping today, Sheila did say something that kind of threw me. She said she was anxious to get her car back because she'd felt like someone was following her or looking at her. She said she figured it was someone that knew Jasmine and thought it was her car, and they were looking at her, expecting to see Jasmine. At the time I didn't think too much of it because Jasmine said she does know a lot of people from her college that know her car and always waive at her. But maybe it wasn't Jasmine's car they were looking at, but Sheila."

"Yeah, we definitely need to look more into her background," John said.

They found a number on Jasmine's phone that she'd called or had called her a few times, all before the time Sheila got her cell phone. They checked and it was registered to someone in Nevada, so they called it. It was in fact Sheila's old roommate. She was shocked to hear what had happened, but didn't know of anything that might help. She said she hadn't had any problems of any kind, but she was able to tell them where she'd worked. John called and talked to her old boss, but he wasn't able to give them anything helpful, either.

"So now what?" Trent asked, becoming more concerned the longer they went without hearing anything from the girls.

"Jazz, wake up." Jasmine heard Sheila's voice, but couldn't quite make out what she was saying. She tried to move, but for some reason she couldn't. "Jazz, please wake up and tell me you're going to be okay." Sheila's voice sounded frightened, and Jasmine managed to get her eyes open to see what was scaring her friend. "Oh, good," Sheila said. "I was afraid they'd killed you."

That got Jasmine's eyes opened, and she looked at Sheila, then tried to look around her. Moving her head caused her head to pound, though. She tried again to move, but still had no luck. "What happened? Where are we?"

Sheila talked softly, and Jasmine had to listen closely to hear her. "The black SUV that turned around and followed us rammed into us. Two men got out and told us to get out of our car and go with them. You told them to go to hell, and they pulled guns out. They pulled us out of our car, and when you fought with the one dragging you away, he hit you on the head with his gun. You slumped over, and he carried you.

They put us in the clear back part of their SUV, tied us up, and took off."

"That explains why my head hurts so much. Do you know who they are or what they want?"

"No idea. I've never seen them before. I asked what was going on or who they were, and the one that hit you on the head said not to play dumb, and that we knew what they wanted. That's all they said, other than they talked to each other, saying they had to get us out of there before anyone came by and saw the car. They took off, and that's all I know."

"I wonder if they think we're someone else. If they think we know what they want, they must."

"Maybe," Sheila agreed. "But what do we do now?"

"I don't know, but I'd say we have to find a way to get away from them."

The car slowed, made a turn and came to a stop, ending their conversation. The two men got out of the vehicle and were almost instantly opening the door. "Oh, good, she's awake," one of the men said.

"And she'll stay that way unless she tries anything stupid again," he said, staring down at Jasmine. She shuddered, seeing his cold eyes glaring at her.

"What do you want from us?" she asked, trying to sound much braver than she felt.

"We'll talk inside. Unless you want another knot on your head, no screaming. No one will hear you anyway, but I hate that shrill sound, and I won't put up with it." Without any further instructions, the men pulled them out of the vehicle and started leading them into a house. Jasmine was a bit light-headed and woozy, but the man leading her obviously didn't care. He pushed her ahead of him, while the other man was doing the same with Sheila.

Once inside they led them through the house to a small room in the back. It looked to Jasmine like a storage room of some kind. They turned a light on as they shoved the ladies inside. Both ladies fell from the shove, and moved back as far away from the men as possible. The men stayed at the door, looking at them.

The one that had been leading Jasmine was the one that had been driving and was apparently in charge. He gave the girls an annoyed look. "Okay, now we'll talk. Are you ready to give them to us, or do you want to do this the hard way?"

"Give you what?" Jasmine asked.

"Look, I'm a busy man and I don't have time to play games, so here's how this is going to work. You're not leaving this house until we have what we want. Until then you'll stay locked in this room. One of us will be in every now and then to see if you're ready to cooperate yet. Until then, this is your new home."

"You can't keep us here," Jasmine said.

"Oh, you're wrong there," the evil-looking man said, pulling his gun out again. "I can do anything I want to do, and no one will know it. So I would suggest you give this some serious thought. No one will hear you screaming except us, and like I said, I won't put up with it. Any questions?"

"But I really don't know what it is you want," Sheila said. "You can have anything I have, but you have to tell me what it is you want."

The man in charge sighed again. "Maybe after a day in this room you'll be ready to tell us where to find them. Let's go."

He turned to leave, and Sheila paled. "What if we have to go to the bathroom?"

"Oh, yeah, I forgot," the man in charge said. "Untie them so they can get to the bathroom." The other man untied the girls, but the one in charge warned them as they did. "Don't do anything stupid like hiding behind the door and attack us as we come in. We'll be watching you on the cameras, and if you do something stupid you'll upset me. I won't be responsible for what I do if that happens." Before they could do or say anything else, the men left.

"What are we going to do?" Sheila asked.

"I don't know. What do you think they want?"

"I've been hoping you may know them, or what they want. I don't have a clue."

"Me, neither. I've never seen either of them," Jasmine said. "Let's see if we can find a way out of here."

They stood up, but Jasmine felt dizzy and a little nauseous and leaned against the wall. "Are you okay?"

"I think I will be, but I got dizzy when I stood up."

Sheila was at her side instantly. "Do you want to sit back down?"

"No, I want to see where we are. Maybe if I go slow I'll be okay." She tried standing on her own again, with Sheila next to her, ready to grab her if she got dizzy again. "That's better. I'll just move slow and I think I'll be fine."

The girls slowly made their way to the door at the end of the small room, and found a bathroom, which was the smallest bathroom either of them had ever seen. It had a toilet and small sink, and absolutely nothing else. "Well, nothing here's going to help us," Jasmine said.

"Let's look better out here," Sheila said as they returned to the first room. It was a small room with nothing but cabinets along two of the walls. They opened the cabinets, but found very little. "It looks like someone emptied everything out. Again, there's nothing that might help us. Now what are we going to do?"

"I don't know," Jasmine said, sitting back down on the floor and looking around. "This is a strange room. It's small, but look how tall the ceilings are. There's only one window and it's up so high there's no way we'd be able to get to it. We can't even reach it, let alone crawl through it. Even if we could get to it, I'm not sure we'd fit through it anyway, as small as it is. Why would they put a small window up that high in such a small room?"

"It is strange. Right now my guess is they did that to make the perfect room to put someone you kidnapped in. There's no way out of here."

"Then I guess we'll just have to think of some way of tricking them into letting us out," Jasmine said. "First we need to find out who they are and what they want from us. Then maybe we can come up with some kind of plan to get out of here."

Chapter 10

Trent was becoming extremely frustrated. "John, it's been three hours since they disappeared, and we have no idea who was in that black SUV or where they are."

"I know, and I'm sorry. It may not seem like it to you, but there are a lot of officers working on this. All of them on the road are looking for any black SUV with any damage to the front, even slight. While they're doing that, we've had people looking into both Jasmine and Sheila's background."

"Jasmine?" Trent asked, standing up, obviously not happy.

"Calm down, Trent. Yes, Jasmine, too. We don't expect to find anything, but if we're going to have any chance of finding out what's going on, we have to do a thorough job. We're concentrating more on Sheila because you don't know much about her, either. We're hoping to find some clue, no matter how small, that may lead us to something that might give us a place to start. Surely you understand that."

"Yes, and I'm sorry," Trent said, running his hand through his hair yet again. "No one's found anything yet?"

"No, but Captain Thorpe and I have an idea, if you'll agree to it."

"What's that?"

"I don't want to upset you, but I'm being totally honest with you. We wondered if possibly you would receive a ransom note."

Trent's eyes were huge. "A ransom note? Why would anyone take them for ransom?"

"Think about it a minute. Everyone knows you two are seeing each other, and you do own a successful manufacturing company. Someone could have thought that would be an easy way of getting a little money. They may have figured someone that owns a whole company will surely be able to come up with a ransom to get his lady back."

"Do you think? So when will they contact me and how? Should I be at home by the phone?"

"Slow down. Generally if someone is after a ransom they will have a way of communicating. Meaning, they'll either get your cell phone number from someone, or they could call you at work. However they do it, it's generally done fairly quickly. After all, they don't want to keep this person, or in this case, people, any longer than necessary. The fact that you haven't heard anything yet is making us think maybe that's not it. I wanted you to be aware of the possibility, though, in case you do get a call."

"So if I get a call, what do I do?"

"Keep them on the phone as long as you can. We've already put tracers on all your phones; cell, home, and at work. If anyone calls, listen carefully to what they say, but keep them talking if you can."

"Okay. But if you don't think it's that now, that means we're back to no clues?"

"We think at this point we need to look further, try to

come up with something to go on. To do that we want to go to their apartment and search through their things for anything we might find to help us."

"What sort of things are you looking for?"

"We won't know until we find it," John said. "Look, I know it may be invading their privacy, and if you tell us no, we won't, at least not yet, but we're trying to find anything that might help."

Trent sighed, but nodded his head. "I'm assuming you aren't going to leave their apartment a mess?"

"No, of course not. What we want to do is go through any desks they have, anyplace they may have some kind of paperwork. You never know when we'll find something helpful."

An hour later the three men were inside Jasmine's apartment, after using the key she'd given Trent. The two officers were going through dresser and desk drawers, looking for anything that might help. John found the title to her car and pulled it out. "Trent, according to the title to Sheila's car, she bought it right before she left, like a day or two before."

"Yes. She didn't have a car, so I sent her some money and she bought it for her trip out here. You've got a look on your face that tells me there's something there. What is it?"

"Well, I don't know, maybe nothing. Nothing stands out on this, but the mere fact that she just got it before she left, and now she's been kidnapped has to make me question it."

"Good point," Captain Thorpe said. "I think it's definitely worth looking into. Let me call this in and get someone looking into it."

"Trent, do you know anything about how she got the car? Did she buy it from a friend, or from a used car dealer? Anything you may be able to tell us may help."

"If I'm remembering right, she bought it from a co-worker. It had been her grandfather's, but he died and they sold the car to her. He'd been a mechanic, so she thought the car would probably be in pretty sound condition and would make it out here."

"Nothing about that sounds suspicious, but I don't want to overlook anything, so we'll get someone on it and see if they can dig anything up. In the meantime, let's keep looking."

Half an hour later Captain Thorpe came across a letter in Sheila's things that was more than a little alarming to him. "Trent, have you heard either of the girls mention a Chad Lexford?"

"Chad Lexford?"

"Apparently it was a man Sheila had seen." When it didn't appear Trent was recalling the name, Captain Thorpe showed him a letter. "It sounds like she dated him, and broke off the relationship, but he wasn't too happy about her breaking it off."

"Oh, yes, Jasmine did say she'd had dinner with someone a couple of times, but he seemed real pushy, which she didn't like. She turned him down the next time he asked her out, and he wasn't happy about it."

"Can you remember anything else about him?"

"Boy, I wish I would have paid more attention to what she said. This happened before she decided to move out here, and I didn't listen as closely as I should have." His eyes lit up, and he headed toward Jasmine's room. "Sheila told Jasmine about him in a letter, though, so if you can find that letter she sent to Jasmine, you'll know as much as I do. As I remember, he didn't want to accept her refusal to see him again."

"Would Jasmine have kept that letter, do you think?"

"I'm sure of it. She kept all of Sheila's letters. They may not have seen each other, but they were very close. She cherished every letter she got from her."

"I saw a stack of letters from Sheila in her drawer," John

said, "but I didn't have any reason to believe we would get anything from them, so I didn't bother with them, trying to preserve her privacy. I'll get the stack out, and Trent, why don't you read through them and see if you can find anything about him while we keep looking through other things?"

"Sure, I can do that. I'll at least feel like I'm doing something that might help." He started with the latest letters and went backwards. He smiled a couple of times when he read things the girls had obviously confided to each other, some about him. It didn't take him long to find the one which talked about Chad, and he turned it over to John and the captain. They read the letter, then called it in so someone could start checking into Chad Lexford and see if they could find anything about him.

By ten o'clock that evening Trent was beside himself. They still hadn't heard anything from them or their kidnappers, and they hadn't found anything else in their apartment that might be helpful. "Go home and try to get some sleep, Trent," John said. "Before you object, I know that's not what you want to hear and you probably won't sleep real well, but try. If we find something tomorrow, you won't be of much help if you haven't had any sleep."

"I know that makes sense, but I don't anticipate being able to sleep much," Trent said, running his hand through his hair yet again.

"I understand, but try," Captain Thorpe said. "We have people that will be working on this through the night, finding out everything they can about Chad Lexford and the man that owned the car last. All the officers on the street will be watching for a black SUV, whether it's moving or parked in a driveway. Go back into the station when you get up in the morning and we'll fill you in on anything we've found overnight."

"If you find anything important, call me, no matter what time it is," he insisted.

"We will," the captain promised.

Trent went back home, sure he wouldn't sleep and trying to think of anything either of the girls had said that might shed some light on things. Captain Thorpe and John went back to the station to see what anyone had found. They would more than likely be there most of the night, but there wasn't anything else Trent would be able to do there.

———

Trent tossed and turned all night, not really sleeping much at all. He tried going over everything that had happened and everything either Jasmine or Sheila had said lately, but wasn't able to come up with a single thing that they could even look into. Eventually he gave up trying to sleep, and at six o'clock he was up and dressed. He stopped and got a dozen donuts and some coffee before going to the patrol station.

He told the officer at the desk who he was, and John came out to meet him moments later. "I'm surprised to see you here already," Trent said. "Any news?"

"We've been here all night. We both got a couple of hours of rest on the cots in the break room, but we've been following up on things. Come on back to the captain's office and I'll fill you in on what we've learned." He led the way, and when Trent walked into Captain Thorpe's office he was a bit surprised to see not only Captain Thorpe, but the sheriff was there, as well as a city policeman and a man he didn't recognize.

"Good morning, Trent," Captain Thorpe said. "This is Sheriff Wilson, Officer Len Goldman with the city police, and Detective Brad Bittle. We've been working through the night, coordinating our efforts."

"Thank you, all of you," Trent said sincerely. "Have you come up with anything?"

"Some, yes," Captain Thorpe said. "We looked into Chad Lexford, and didn't like what we were finding. We thought we might be on to something, until we found out he was arrested two months ago. He was denied bail, so he's been in jail awaiting trial."

"I guess that rules him out," Trent said.

"Yes, it does," the captain agreed. "Everything else we checked into turned out clean, except for one thing, and we're pursuing it now."

Trent sat up straighter. "What was that?"

"Sheila's new car. You said it belonged to the grandfather of a lady Sheila worked with?"

"Yes. He died, and she and her mother inherited everything, and sold Sheila the car."

"Did she happen to say how he died?"

"Not that I can remember," Trent said. "If she did, it didn't register. The car was in pretty good shape, so I assume it wasn't from an accident in the car."

"No. We checked into that, assuming he'd died of natural causes, but we found out otherwise. He was found dead in his house. We got a copy of the police report and found out he'd been shot, and his house had been ransacked."

Trent was quiet for several moments. "So what does that mean?"

"We talked to the officer in charge of the case, which is still open. He thinks someone was looking for something."

"Did they find it?"

"They don't know. He said the house was all torn up, though. They slashed the couch and chair cushions, and every drawer in the house had been dumped out. It could be that they found it and then shot him so he couldn't identify them. The fact that everything was torn apart, though, makes him believe they never found it. Generally once they find what they're looking for they stop and leave quick, so not all of the house is in that shape."

Trent nodded, obviously thinking. "But if they didn't find what they were looking for, why shoot him? They certainly can't expect him to give it to them now."

"They may have been in the process of searching his house when he returned home and caught them."

"So they shot him," Trent said quietly, nodding. "So the police there don't know what they were looking for, or if they found it?"

"Exactly. So we thought maybe when whoever ransacked the house didn't find what they were looking for, they thought maybe it was in the car she bought."

"I have to wonder what it is they're looking for. I mean, that's going an awfully long way to look for it. It's a long way from there to here. That would mean whatever it is they're looking for must be awfully important to them."

"I know," the captain said. "We've talked about that. Like I said, we may be totally wrong on this, but until we come up with any other options, we want to keep pursuing it."

"Oh, absolutely," Trent said. "I'm just a little concerned about what may be in that car, or was. I guess it's possible something was there and Sheila already found it."

"That's a possibility that we've also talked about. How well do you know her? If she would have found a large amount of cash, do you think she would have told someone, or simply put it in the bank?"

"No, she would have contacted someone. As a matter of fact, she did." All heads turned toward him, and he continued. "I'd forgotten until you mentioned that, but she did in fact find a thousand dollars in the glove compartment. She gave it back to her co-worker, saying she bought the car, not the contents. Her co-worker and her mom said they had no idea it was in the car, and it was hers. They finally settled for splitting it. Sheila was excited because that gave her the money she'd need for gas and a motel room for her trip here."

"Well, that's good to know," Captain Thorpe said. "I think it's safe to say if she would have found something important or worth a great deal of money she would have turned it in to someone."

"I feel sure she would have," Trent agreed. "But if they thought it was there, why not break into the car and look for it? Why kidnap them?"

"You said her car is in the repair shop," John said. "How long has it been there?"

"It's been in there a couple of weeks. They had to order a part."

"If it hasn't been around for a couple of weeks they may have thought she sold the car or wrecked it, and they took the two of them in an attempt to get what they've been looking for," John said. "Maybe they think she found whatever it is they're looking for and has it someplace."

"But why take both of them?" Trent asked.

"We don't know. Maybe this was their opportunity to take Sheila and Jasmine was with her, so they had to take both. Or maybe they thought Sheila would be more likely to give it to them if she knew Jasmine was at risk, too. She wouldn't want anything to happen to her friend."

"I guess either would make sense," Trent said. "But what do we do now?"

"We're going to go look at the car, if you'll tell us where it is," Captain Thorpe said. "It's possible they've already looked in it and didn't find anything, and that's why they took the girls. If they took them because they couldn't find the car, maybe we'll find what they were looking for. If we find that, hopefully we can figure out who it is that's looking for it. If we figure out who it is, maybe we can find them."

"That sounds like a lot of ifs," Trent said.

"It is," Sheriff Wilson admitted, "but we haven't come up with anything else yet."

"It's better than sitting here doing nothing," Trent said. "Let's go."

Half an hour later Trent, John, Detective Bittle and Sheriff Wilson were talking to Larry, a rather surprised mechanic. John explained the situation and asked, "You didn't happen to look in the car at all, did you?"

"No, just under the hood," he said, "but it's right in here if you want to look at it. Maybe you'll get lucky and find something."

An hour later they had searched the car and come up empty. As they were getting ready to leave, frustrated and disappointed, Trent stood looking at the car, his head cocked to one side. "I've seen that look before, Trent," John said. "What's going through your mind?"

"It's probably nothing, but something kind of caught my attention. Look at the car in general. What's your first impression of it?"

John stood back and looked at the car again. "It's a used car, obviously not new, but it's not in bad shape. Is that what you mean?"

"Yes. Now look in the trunk, and tell me what your first thought is on that, on the trunk itself."

John looked at his friend, but opened the trunk again. This time instead of looking at what was in the trunk, he did as Trent suggested and just considered the trunk itself. "Hmm. I think I see what you're saying. Looking at the trunk itself, it looks to be in good shape." Trent nodded in agreement, and John went on. "In fact, it kind of looks nicer than the car itself. Is that what you're getting at?"

"Exactly. Why would the trunk look newer than the rest of the car?"

Sheriff Wilson, who had been listening to the conversation, stepped forward to take a closer look at the trunk area. "Now that you mentioned it, it does look to be in fairly new condition. Maybe he didn't use the trunk much."

"Could be," Detective Bittle agreed, "or maybe it's had some kind of repair done to it." He looked at it closer, inspecting the carpeting. "It has the same carpeting in it as in the car, so it's probably the original carpeting, but if you look at the edges, it looks like it may have been removed and put back in."

"Maybe we need to loosen it and see if we can find a reason it would have been taken out," Trent said. "I don't want to leave any stone unturned."

"I agree," John said. "While we're here, let's take it loose and look. I'll have my body man fix it if we can't get it back good. Let's see if Larry has some tools that can help."

Larry brought some tools and they got to work. Their eyes all widened when the carpet was pulled back to reveal plywood. "What's plywood doing in a trunk?" Detective Bittle mumbled, as he knocked on the wood. "And it sounds hollow." The men all looked at each other, a mixture of confusion and hope written on their faces.

"Larry, do you have something we can use to loosen this plywood?"

"Absolutely." A few minutes later they were all gathered around as the detective lifted the plywood, and there were several gasps as they looked down on a small stack of papers, including several photographs.

Jasmine and Sheila sat on the floor with their backs to the wall, looking around. "Well, I think we've gone over pretty much every inch of this place," Jasmine said in a frustrated tone, "and there's nothing here that can help us escape."

"I know. There's only one window and it's too small to fit through, and we can't even reach it so we can open it and try and get someone's attention." They were both silent a few minutes. "I just wish I knew who these men are and what they want."

"I know. I've been trying to figure it out, too. They act like we know what they're after, but I honestly don't have a clue."

"Neither do I," Sheila said. They were quiet another few moments, when they heard a noise. "What was that?"

"I don't know," Jasmine said very quietly. "It sounded like voices, but I couldn't make out what they were saying. Could you tell where the voices were coming from?"

"No, but let's listen. Maybe they'll say something else."

After listening for several quiet minutes, they heard the voices again.

"It sounds like it's coming from over there," Jasmine said, pointing to the other side of the room. They both scrambled over and put their ears to the wall, hoping to hear something. Eventually, they heard the voices again, but it didn't sound like it was coming from the other side of the wall, and they still couldn't make out what they were saying.

"Maybe we're hearing the voices through that vent," Sheila whispered, pointing to a heat register.

"That's possible. That storage unit is in front of it and that might be blocking some of the sound. Let's be quiet and try to move that over just a few inches so we can get to it."

"What about the camera in here? Will they see us doing it?"

"Let's hope they only check the camera before they come in, to be sure we're not ready to pounce on them," Jasmine said. "I feel like we may have to risk it. We have to try something."

Sheila agreed and they very carefully picked the piece of furniture up and moved it a few inches so the register was more visible, then moved over closer to it and leaned down to listen. Sure enough, they heard the voices again.

"I can make out a couple of words, but not enough to tell what they're talking about," Sheila said. "How about you?"

"Same here," Jasmine said. "Maybe if we could get this cover off it would help. If we can find something we can use to take the screws out, we might be able to hear better."

"It's worth a try. I'm about to go crazy just sitting here, so let's see if we can find something. What can it hurt?"

Jasmine agreed and they got up and started searching the small room again for anything that they could try to use to take the screws out of the register cover. The room was small and it didn't take long to search it, and they sat back down, frustrated again. The only thing they'd found to even try was a piece of cardboard. Although it was a good width and fit in the screw head, it wasn't sturdy enough to turn it.

They were sitting next to the vent again, trying to hear enough words to make sense of what the men were saying, when Jasmine had an idea. "Sheila, when I bought our lunch I was in a hurry and just put the change in my pocket. Maybe a coin will work." She quickly dug through her pocket and came out with three coins.

"I hope one of them works," Sheila said.

Jasmine tried the quarter and nickel, but they were too wide to fit in. The dime, however, fit perfectly. She tried to turn it, but it wouldn't budge. Sheila tried, too, with no luck. Jasmine took the dime back and tried again. "This isn't budging, but let me try the other screw. There are only two holding it on, and maybe if I can get the other one loose we can move the cover enough to jar this one loose."

"Good idea."

Jasmine worked on the other screw, and got it to move a

little. "It didn't move much, but enough to give me hope. These look old, and they're probably rusty. Since it moved a little, hopefully that knocked enough rust off to loosen it a little." She kept trying, and soon had the first screw moving. She got it unscrewed, and they worked the cover, trying to move it enough, without making noise, to put pressure on the other screw. Sheila tried moving it while Jasmine worked again on the screw.

After what seemed like hours, but was probably twenty minutes, they got the other screw loose. Jasmine unscrewed it and took the register cover off. "Oh, my gosh, look at all the dirt built up in there," she said, scrunching her nose up. "If we take that out maybe we'll be able to hear better."

"Let me see," Sheila said. She moved over closer and reached in and pulled out a bunch of dirt that resembled dryer lint. "That has to be blocking some of the sound," she whispered.

Sure enough, they heard the voices again, but could make out more of what the men were saying. They couldn't hear all of it, but enough to be able to follow their conversation. They were talking about the garage door needing to be repaired. "I don't know why you worry so much about that damn door," one man said.

"Because I'd feel better if our vehicle was out of sight," another man said.

"What makes the difference? Nobody was around when we took them, so nobody saw it. They won't have any idea what kind of vehicle they're looking for. Quit worrying so much."

"I guess maybe you're right. I'm trying not to worry, but it's hard. I mean, we basically kidnapped two ladies. We could do time for that. When I took this job I didn't know there was going to be nothing like this involved. I don't like it."

"I don't, either, but there ain't much we can do about it

now. The boss has us so deep into it now we have to see it through to make sure none of us get caught. As soon as we get those pictures back it'll be done and we'll all be safe again."

"I hope that's soon."

"Me, too. I'm going to go out and look at that garage door and see if I can get it fixed. I'd still feel better if that door would shut and they couldn't see our vehicle."

"Okay, do what you want, but I'm telling you they don't know what they're looking for anyway. It won't make no difference." They heard a man grunt, then a door closed, and it was quiet. Jasmine pointed to the other side of the room, and they both went there, as far from the register as they could get.

"Now that we can hear them, we'll listen and try to figure out what pictures they're looking for," Jasmine said in a soft whisper. "But we have to be careful. If we can hear them now, they may be able to hear us, too. Anytime we talk about this, we'll have to come over here and whisper. The rest of the time we'll have to talk in a normal tone so they don't get suspicious."

Sheila nodded. "I wonder what kind of pictures they're looking for," she whispered, "and where they think they are and why we would have them."

"I have no idea, but hopefully they'll say something that will give it away. I think we need to put that grate back on the register and see if we can still hear them, though. If they come in and find that off and we're sitting over there they may figure out we've been listening to them."

"You're right." They moved back over and replaced the grate.

They heard the door close again. "Any luck?" one man asked.

"No. The track the door slides up on is bent, and I didn't see any tools that might work to fix it. I came in here to see if there's anything I might be able to use. Aren't there a few tools in the basement?"

"I think I saw a few."

"I'm gonna go look." It was quiet again, until they heard a door creak open. "I found this. I don't know if it'll work, but I'm gonna go try. I'll be back."

Chapter 11

J asmine and Sheila heard the door close, and they went back to the other side of the small room and whispered again. "I can still hear them okay. It's not quite as loud, but as long as I can hear them, I think it's safer if we leave that cover on."

"Yeah, me, too," Sheila agreed. "I think we need to talk about something again so they don't wonder why we're so quiet and suspect something. What can we talk about?"

"Let's talk about not knowing what they want. They may not have believed us when we told them we didn't know what they want, but if they hear us talking about it, maybe they'll see we really don't know. Even if it doesn't help any, I don't see that it will hurt." Sheila nodded.

Using a normal speaking voice, Jasmine started the conversation. "Now what should we do, Sheila? I don't see anything in here that's going to be of any help to us, and I have no idea what they want."

"I know," Sheila said with a sigh. "I've been trying to figure it out, but I don't have a clue, either."

"Hopefully they'll tell us. I mean, there's nothing I have

that I wouldn't give to them, but I don't know what I have that they'd want."

"Same here. Let's hope they tell us."

They quit talking, and not too much later they heard the man return. "No luck. I guess the door's going to stay open. I hope you're right and it doesn't matter."

"Of course I am. Think about it. How would anyone know what kind of vehicle to look for? Those two disappeared. When they find their car, they won't have any idea where they went. They'll probably think they started walking to try and find some help. They won't have any reason to suspect someone took them."

"Yeah, I guess you're right there."

"Of course I am. Speaking of them, have you heard anything from them?"

"I heard them talking, but I couldn't make out what they said."

"Good. As long as they're talking, they're okay. And if you couldn't hear them, they can't hear us, either, so that's good, too. Now we just have to give them time. The boss said to wait them out until they eventually agree to tell us where they're at."

"I hope it doesn't take long. I don't like staying here. Are you going to go get us something for lunch pretty soon, or do you want me to? I'm getting hungry."

"No, I'll go. You went and got something for us last night. What do you want?"

"I don't care. A hamburger's fine with me, but I'll eat whatever you bring back. Don't forget to get something for them, too."

"It's a good thing the boss gave us money for our meals. I wouldn't be spending my money to feed them."

"Yeah, I know, but he was adamant about giving them something to eat a couple of times a day." They heard another grunt, then a door close. The girls looked at each other, sighed and leaned back against the wall.

The men gathered around Sheila's car looked down when they pulled the plywood loose. "A false bottom," Detective Bittle said. "These photos and papers must be valuable, if he went to this much trouble to hide them." He reached for the stack of papers, pulling out the photos first. They all gathered to look at them as he went through them. A man in a suit was present in all of them, and another man was with him. Most were of only those two men, but a few had others in them, as well. The two men appeared to be shaking hands in a few of them, and two of them showed the one man giving the man in the suit some money.

"Anyone recognize anyone in the pictures?" Trent asked.

"Kind of," John said. "I'm sure I've seen the man in the suit before, but I can't place where."

"I was thinking the same thing," Sheriff Wilson agreed. "The face looks familiar."

"Huh," Detective Bittle said, looking at one of the pictures closer. "I thought the man handing him the cash looked vaguely familiar, but I can't think where I may have seen him. The man in the suit's not jumping out at me, though."

"We'll see if our face recognition software brings anything up," the sheriff said. "What about the papers? Are they any help?"

"I'm not sure what all of them are," Detective Bittle said, "but I'm holding what looks to be a diary of sorts, or backup for the photos. It gives dates and where the pictures were taken. It also gives the name of someone else that was there, like maybe a witness. The photos are showing some money being exchanged, so I'm guessing it's some sort of payoff or something along those lines. We need to figure out who the people in the photos are, but I'm guessing all this is what the kidnappers were looking for."

Trent looked at the detective. "So you're saying the man that owned this car uncovered some sort of payoff scheme and got evidence of it in the form of photos, and someone else who saw it. Then the person or persons in the photo found out about it and were looking for this evidence, and that's what got him killed?"

"That's certainly a possibility," Detective Bittle confirmed. "What do you think, Sheriff?"

Sheriff Wilson nodded. "That would be my guess, as well. We definitely have to get these back to the station and find out who these people are."

"Well, if she got the car in Arizona, I say we start there," John said. "We'll look at photos of people of interest in that state, like anyone police there may be following, or politicians and business executives. If we don't find anything there, or with our face recognition software, we can check with the Arizona state police. They may be able to give us an identification."

The sheriff and detective both nodded. "Well, now that we have a plan, let's go put it in motion," the sheriff said.

"At least we have something, somewhere to start," Trent said as he and John were on their way back to the patrol station.

"If we can figure out who that is in the pictures we may at least know who we're looking for," John said. "It will at least tell us who we need to talk to."

"I feel a little better knowing at least we have a start."

"This may turn out to be nothing," John warned, "but my gut tells me this is what the men who took them were looking for. I think we're on the right track."

Jasmine and Sheila tried to keep a conversation going as much as they could to try to keep their spirits and hopes up. When they stopped talking they each found themselves deep in thought, and the more they thought about their situation the more upset they became. They decided to stay positive and encourage each other.

They assumed if they could hear the men talking, they may be able to hear them, as well, so they talked from time to time about why the men could have taken them, or what their motive was. They had no idea why, and said so frequently. They wondered if the men might have mistaken them for someone else and took the wrong ladies. They hoped if the men heard them saying that several times and trying to figure out what they could want from them, they might realize they weren't the people they meant to take.

In the meantime, they listened carefully when the men talked, hoping to get a little information from them. When they discussed what they'd heard them say, they went to the other side of the room and whispered.

They hadn't heard much from the men and were getting frustrated, when they heard a door close and the men started a conversation. After some mundane talk that didn't help them, one of the men said, "I've been thinking. Every time we take them food they ask what we want, and tell us they'll give us whatever it is, but we have to tell them. Do you think it's possible they really don't know?"

"I don't know, but I've been wondering that myself. The next time I talk to the boss I should ask him about that."

"Good idea. I mean, the stuff obviously wasn't in the old man's house, and we didn't find any evidence that he has any kind of safety deposit box or anyplace else like that he could stash it, so it almost has to be in the car. We know he's got a daughter and at least one granddaughter, so since this lady's been driving the car, she must be his granddaughter. I hoped while we followed her out here we'd have a chance to search the car, but that didn't happen. The little bitch always parked out in the public, with lights all over the place."

"Where do you suppose she hid the car?" the other man asked. "I figured she knows what's in there and that's why she hid it, but if she thought she was being smart doing that, it backfired. If she'd have left the car out and we could have searched it and found it, we wouldn't have had to take her. It would have been much easier for all of us."

"We wouldn't have had to take her, or her friend. I'd rather have taken just her, but this is the only chance we've had to get her, and since she wasn't alone we had to take them both. Now we're kind of stuck with both of them, but maybe she'll give it up sooner to protect her friend."

"I hope so, and I hope she gives in soon. I'll be happy when the boss has what he wants and this is all over with."

"You and me both." There was a pause, and they started talking about what they wanted for their next meal.

The girls made their way to the other side of the room to quietly discuss what they'd heard.

"Jasmine, I'm so sorry," Sheila said. "It's obviously me they're after, and I dragged you into it."

"Don't apologize," Jasmine said quickly. "You didn't do anything wrong. But apparently there's something in your car they want, or at least they think there is. Do you have any idea what it could be?"

"Not a clue, and I don't know where it could be, either. I went through the glove box. I told you there was a thousand dollars in there that I gave back to them, but surely that's not what they're after."

"I wouldn't think so. If they followed you clear out here,

they've spent that much following you all this time. I wonder what they think is in there?"

"Me, too. I cleaned the car out after I bought it, but other than that money in the glove box I didn't find much. There was a spare tire in the trunk and two or three tools, which wasn't surprising since he was a mechanic, but other than that, it was empty. Oh, yeah, there was a blanket and a few bottles of water, but that was all."

Jasmine sighed and took a few moments to consider what Sheila had said. "Well, now what are we going to do? They obviously think you have something. What are they going to do when they find out you don't have whatever it is they're looking for?"

"I don't know, and I don't want to think about it because it can't be good. Any suggestions?"

"Not yet, but we need to think about it. We need to come up with some kind of a plan to get out of here. I'm sure Trent's got the police looking for us, but I don't know how in the world they'll find us. I mean, why would they even think of it having something to do with your car? Even with us knowing that, we wouldn't have any idea what to look for, where to look, or who might be behind it."

"You're right," Sheila said slowly, thinking as she spoke. "I don't think we can count on anyone finding us, so we need to come up with some kind of plan. I don't have any ideas, but we've certainly got time to think."

"That's all we have, but I don't know how much of that we have left. I mean, I don't know how long they'll give us."

"I know. We better get busy thinking."

"Hey, we're two smart ladies," Jasmine said, trying to encourage both of them. "I'm sure we'll come up with something."

Once the men got back to the patrol station it didn't take them long to identify the people in the photos. The one being handed some cash was a senator from Arizona. After looking again at the paperwork they found, it became pretty clear to all of them that the owner of the car had information on this senator that would hurt his career, and had hidden it in the car for safe keeping.

They weren't sure who the man paying him was, or how the senator found out he had the evidence. He could have been trying to blackmail the senator, asking for a sum of money to keep quiet. It's possible he was trying to get something from him other than money, like a favor, or some information the senator would have. It could also be that he knew what the senator was doing was wrong and tried to get proof to take to the local law enforcement, but the senator found out about it.

Whatever the case, they determined they were going to need some help solving this and hopefully finding where Jasmine and Sheila had been taken, and rescuing them before they were harmed. They knew they had to call a law enforcement agency in Arizona, but weren't sure who to call. If this senator was taking bribes, he might have bribed law enforcement, as well. Sheriff Wilson and Captain Thorpe talked it over, made a few phone calls to other people they knew and trusted in law enforcement, and decided to call the Arizona State Patrol.

Captain Thorpe took the lead since he worked for the Tennessee State Patrol. He placed a call to the Arizona State Patrol and asked to speak to the officer in charge on duty, and was glad he was a captain, as well. Captain Thorpe told Captain Fritz he came across some things that would suggest an Arizona senator was taking bribes, and paused to hear what Captain Fritz's reaction was. Luckily, it was exactly as he'd hoped.

"Well, I'm certainly interested in what you have, and I can assure you my department will handle it with discretion. Kickbacks or bribes will not be tolerated, especially by elected politicians. I'm guessing you're at least a little reluctant to say too much, in case my office may be in on it."

Captain Thorpe had to laugh. "I will admit that thought has crossed my mind."

"It makes me more confident in your honesty in this matter, to be honest. Would it make you feel better if you were to pick one of my officers on duty right now at random, and he can join us on this call? Then he and I will be the only ones working the case, unless we find we need more to get the job done. I can let you go on line and look at the list of officers at this post, then pick one at random. If it's your choice instead of mine, hopefully you'll feel more confident in trusting me with the information you have."

"Thank you, Captain Fritz, I appreciate that offer. You wouldn't offer that if you had something going under the table with a senator, or with one of your fellow officers. You would have recommended he be included. To reciprocate and be honest with you, let me tell you there are four other law enforcement officers in my office at the moment, and we came upon this information while working another urgent case." He quickly introduced John, Patrolman Lawson, Sheriff Wilson, and Officer Len Goldman from the city police department.

"Nice to meet all of you, and if this is urgent, let's get right to it."

"It is extremely urgent," Captain Thorpe said, "but there's one other person here with us. Trent Douglas is here because the young lady he's been dating has been kidnapped, along with her close friend and roommate. While investigating the kidnapping, we came across this evidence, and we have to believe the two are related."

"So you're saying you think one of our senators is behind these young ladies being kidnapped?"

"I believe so. It's an awfully big coincidence if it isn't related."

"Agreed. Why don't you pick an officer to have in here and we'll get started?"

"After your generous offer, I feel confident," Captain Thorpe said, "so why don't I tell you what's going on, and you pick whatever officer or officers you feel would be best for this case."

"If you feel okay with that, I appreciate it."

Captain Thorpe emailed a copy of a couple of the photos to Captain Fritz, who confirmed it was Senator Kingsley. He wasn't sure who the man was handing him money, but there was no question it was indeed their senator receiving the money. Captain Thorpe then explained what had happened, what they'd found and where, with the others adding details here and there.

They discussed it some, and Captain Fritz said he was thinking about one of his officers who might be able to help. He grew up in the area and knew a lot of people. He might know who the unidentified man is, or how to find out. The Tennessee people agreed, and would keep looking on their end for any other clues relating to the kidnapping, and would await a call from Captain Fritz.

Trent was pacing when Captain Thorpe hung up. "So now what? Assuming this is what these people are looking for, what are we going to do? Knowing this is out there could easily make these people desperate to get it, which makes this a dangerous situation. We have to find them."

"I understand your concern, Trent," John said. "I'm concerned, as well. We have everyone watching for the black SUV, and hopefully someone will see it. At least we have a lead now. Captain Fritz understands the urgency, so I'm sure he'll move quickly and keep us informed."

"I know, but still, there's not much we can do but sit and wait for them. I'm not sure I can do that," John said, still pacing. "I feel like there's got to be something I can do." He busied himself looking up everything he could find about Senator Kingsley, hoping to get some kind of lead from it.

———

When one of the men brought the girls' next meal in to them, he set the food on a counter, rather than handing it to them as he'd been doing. After setting the bag of food down, he turned to face them, addressing his question specifically to Sheila. "So, are you ready to hand it over yet?"

"We've told you, if you tell us what it is you're looking for, if it's something we can give you, we will," Sheila said.

"You're still wanting to play dumb, huh? Well, okay, we can play that way, but I need to warn you, the boss is getting impatient. I'm not sure how much longer he'll let this go on, so you better give that some serious thought while you eat your meal."

Jasmine squeezed Sheila's hand before facing their captor. "We're not playing any kind of game here. She's telling you the truth. We really have no idea what it is you want that you apparently think we have. I can assure you, neither one of us has anything worth that much, but we'll gladly give you anything we have if you tell us what it is you want."

"We both know that's not true, but I'm not going to argue with you, at least not yet. I just do what the boss tells me to. I'm simply telling you, the boss isn't the most patient person I've ever met, so I wouldn't push your luck too far."

He left, closing and locking the door behind him, without giving either of them a chance to respond. Sheila had tears in her eyes as she looked at Jasmine. "I don't like the sounds of that."

"I don't, either," Jasmine agreed. "We've got to come up with some kind of plan. "I've been thinking. We've told him we don't know what he wants, and he doesn't seem to be planning on telling us. I wonder why that is."

"What do you mean?"

"Well, as I've been thinking about it I can't help but wonder why he won't just tell us what he's looking for."

"He assumes we know."

"Yes, but why not just talk about it openly? I'm wondering if maybe he's not really sure we have it. He thinks it was in your car, but he obviously doesn't know for sure."

"Why do you say obviously?"

"Well, the only way he could know for sure it was there is if he saw someone put it there, or saw it there when you bought the car. Whatever it is, he obviously wants it, so if he would have known it was there, don't you think he would have already taken it? Surely he would have had a chance to break into the car and take it before this."

"But would they follow me clear out here if they didn't know it was there?"

"Maybe. I mean, if they knew for sure it was there, they had actually seen it in your car, as they followed you here, surely they would have had a chance somewhere along the way to get it. You stopped several times along the way, and you weren't always with the car. For starters, you stayed a night at a motel. Even if they didn't feel they could break into it then without getting caught, how about when you stopped for gas or to eat or go to the restroom? You weren't with the car on those occasions, and it seems like they could have gotten to it then."

"Maybe they never had a chance when they felt it was safe.

I mean, with people around it all the time, it would have been hard to break into it."

"True, but once you got here and moved in with me, they should have had an opportunity. You drove it to work and it sat out in the parking lot, unattended. Even though it was in the garage at night, if they would have broken into the garage, they could have searched the car without worrying about being seen."

"They would have had to break into the garage, though," Sheila pointed out.

"Yes, they would have," Jasmine agreed, "but once they were inside, they would have been hidden from sight."

"That would have been a good opportunity for them to look for it," Sheila agreed.

"I've heard that breaking into a building or garage usually isn't all that difficult for people who do that sort of thing. If these guys were willing to cause an accident and kidnap us, I wouldn't think breaking into a garage should have been out of the question for them."

"That's true," Sheila said, her brows furrowed together as she thought about what Jasmine was saying.

"So that makes me think maybe they don't know for sure whatever it is they're looking for is actually in the car. They're hoping it is and we'll give in and give it to them. But in case it isn't, they're not saying what it is. That way if we would find a way to escape, we can't use it against them. Of course, they're keeping us here against our will, so we already have plenty to get them arrested."

Sheila's eyes grew. "So do you think whatever it is they think we have is even bigger than keeping us here?"

"I don't know, but I've been wondering that," Jasmine said. "If so, we could be in real trouble. It makes me think maybe we need to come up with some kind of plan to try and escape, even if it may be risky."

"Like what?"

"I don't know yet, but we need to give it some serious thought. Maybe we need to wait for him at the door and one of us can wait behind the door, and jump on him when he comes in. Maybe both of us together could subdue him long enough for us to get out the door."

Sheila fidgeted nervously. "But he would yell, and the other man would come in. Even if he didn't, how would we get past the other man to get outside, and then where would we go? Besides, he warned us not to try that."

"I know there are all kinds of problems with that idea," Jasmine assured her, "but I think we need to come up with something. Maybe if we start there we can think of some way of changing it into something we may be able to try; anything." Her shoulders slumped and she looked up at Sheila. "I'm afraid we're running out of time, and we need to at least have something we can fall back onto if things get too bad."

Sheila was quiet for several moments, before squaring her shoulders as she looked up and met Jasmine's eyes. "You're right. We don't know what they're going to do, but we have to be ready with some kind of plan, even if it's not the best, in case worse comes to worse. I'll start thinking, too, and then we'll compare thoughts and see if we can put something together. Once we have a rough plan put together, we can try to improve on it. Maybe together we'll think of something we can put into action."

Jasmine nodded and squeezed her hand again, hoping it would give them both a little encouragement.

Chapter 12

Trent was still pacing half an hour later when Captain Thorpe heard back from Captain Fritz. "We've been waiting for your call," Captain Thorpe said. "I have a roomful of people eager to hear what you have to say, so I'm going to put you on speaker. Okay, go ahead."

"When I heard two ladies have been kidnapped, we got right on this. Time is of the essence, so I brought in everyone I felt we needed. Some were looking into the photos, while others were working on other pieces of this puzzle. Everyone reported back here, which has become our central office, and here's what we've come up with. The man in the photos is Senator Charles Kingsley. Unbeknownst to me, there's an ongoing investigation by a separate department in our agency into him possibly taking kickbacks."

People in Captain Thorpe's office exchanged glances, knowing this had become something big. They all listened carefully as Captain Fritz continued. "Apparently companies and industries have paid him in exchange for a vote in the senate that would benefit them. The state police here were about ready to bring charges against him, but were looking for one more solid piece of evidence that couldn't be explained away. They didn't feel they had quite enough evidence to accuse a senator of something this serious. After looking at these photos they agreed they now have the evidence they need to file charges."

"That's good," Trent said, "but it doesn't help us find Jasmine and Sheila."

"You're right, and time is obviously of the essence here, so we've come up with a plan. Let me run it by all of you and get your reaction. If you agree with it, we'll have to act together, and quickly."

"We'll obviously do whatever we can," Sheriff Wilson assured him. "Tell us this plan."

"We looked into each of the men that work for the senator. One of them drives a black SUV, and no one around here seems to have seen him the last few days. In fact, apparently he hasn't been around much at all. One of the other men is said to be out of town on some kind of assignment. We were told the senator had him looking into something important."

"So it sounds like he and his black SUV have been here, following Sheila, thinking she has the damaging pictures," Captain Thorpe said. "And now he's got the girls, looking for the photos. Any idea how we can find him?"

"We might. We've put this plan together quickly, so listen carefully. We may have to tweak it some."

"Will do," Captain Thorpe said. "Let's hear it."

"Since time is vital we want to get this going and push them a bit. We'll have a man tailing each one of his men that we know the whereabouts of, and get a warrant, which I'm sure we can get quickly because of the kidnapping, and have the senator's phones at his office and his home bugged, as well as his cell phone. We're suggesting we take one of the pictures, maybe one that's a little blurry, not a real good shot of him, and approach him with it. We can tell him we know about the bribes and think he's behind the two missing girls in Tennessee. He'll more than likely deny it, claim it's not him in the picture or it's a fake. We'll tell him he needs to tell us now where the girls are, and if he won't, we'll go get the proof we need and we'll be back, but it'll be worse for him."

Captain Thorpe looked doubtful. "Do you think the threat will get him to talk?"

"Probably not," Captain Fritz agreed, "but one of the men will plant a small bug in his office before they leave. That way if he uses a burner phone that can't be traced, hopefully we'll at least be able to hear what he's saying."

"Can you do that?" Trent asked. "I mean, I didn't think it was legal to use a bug."

"It is in this case because of the urgency. A kidnapping is as urgent as it gets, so we can use anything that lead to information as to where they may be," Captain Fritz said. "With the search warrant we can have the phone company trace any outgoing calls right after our visit that go from his office to Tennessee. If it's on a burner, or disposable phone they won't be able to tell us what phone number they go to, but they can pinpoint the area they go to. Once we have that area, you guys will be able to pin them down closer. If we luck out and he uses his cell phone instead of a burner phone we'll be able to trace the call exactly, and we'll know who he's talking to and their exact location."

"That would be great, but I'm thinking like you, he will probably know better than to use his own phone," Captain Thorpe said. "Tracing it to an area out here will help, though, and give us a smaller area to concentrate on. Maybe we can find the black SUV."

"That would help," Sheriff Wilson agreed. "And you never

know what somebody's going to do when they get scared. He may use his own cell and lead us right to his men."

"Or on the other hand," Trent said with concern written all over his face, "he could panic and tell his men to get rid of the girls so there's nothing to connect him to the kidnapping."

"He could," Captain Fritz admitted, "but that wouldn't make sense. If they think the girls have the pictures or they're in the car, getting rid of them won't necessarily solve their problem. If they think the girls already found the pictures, they may have already turned them in to someone, or showed them to someone. At the least they would probably have put them someplace for safekeeping. Even if they were to kill the girls, the pictures would more than likely come out. If they hadn't found them and they're still in the car, they would want the car. They don't know where it is right now, and if they kill the girls they'll have no way to find it. They certainly won't want a car out there with pictures hidden that anyone could find."

"I hope you're right," Trent said.

"It is dangerous," John told him, "but I agree that it's probably our best shot at finding them. I agree they more than likely won't hurt them if they don't have the pictures. Plus, if they can trace a call to a certain area out here, that may be all we need to find the SUV. Since we know one of his men has a black SUV and he hasn't been around there, that's probably the one we're looking for. We can get that license number. That should be a big help in finding it, especially if we can pin down a smaller area."

Captain Thorpe nodded. "That's true. Plus we can put lots of cars in that smaller area and watch for any unusual activity. If the senator calls them and alerts them we're following him, these guys may do something stupid, like try to move them. With lots of men in the area watching, we'll find them."

"I trust all of you guys," Trent said. "At least we'll be doing something. Standing here waiting is driving me crazy."

"I think he speaks for all of us," Captain Thorpe said. "I say go ahead and get the ball rolling. Keep us informed."

"I will," Captain Fritz promised. "We already have an officer at a judge's office to get the search warrant."

"Are you planning on searching his office?" Sheriff Wilson asked.

"No, at least not yet. I'm afraid that would shut everything down. We want the search warrant to be able to trace any phone calls made right after our visit to him. Hopefully there'll be one right after we leave that will go to Tennessee."

"I think that's a good call," Captain Thorpe said.

"We may search his office and home later if we don't find the girls, but we want to give him a chance to lead us to them first. If that doesn't work, then we'll do a search. I think he's too smart to keep anything in his office that would implicate him directly."

"I agree," Sheriff Wilson said.

"We've got extra men out looking for the SUV now," Captain Thorpe said, "and if we get a trace to a call somewhere out here, we'll move most of them to that area. Good luck, Captain Fritz, and be safe."

"Same to you. We'll keep you informed."

After the call ended the men got busy making plans so they would be ready to move the minute they got any information.

"I've got an idea," Jasmine said quietly as they sat far away from the vent. "It may not be great, but it's something. Maybe if we talk about it we can tweak it into something that might at least give us a chance of getting out of here."

"I've thought and thought and come up with nothing, so let's hear yours."

"As I look around here, the only thing I've found that we might be able to use is the window."

Sheila's eyes grew as she looked over and up at the window. "Jasmine, there's no way we can get up to that window, let alone crawl out. Even if we could, we'd probably get hurt jumping out. Look how high up it is."

"I think this room is partially underground, though, so it wouldn't be as far a drop as you think. Besides, I'm not planning on crawling through it anyway. All we have to do is make them think we did."

"I'm not following you."

"Well, if you look around, there's only one chair in this room. My thinking is if we put that chair underneath the window –"

"We still wouldn't be able to reach it," Sheila said, shaking her head as she looked again at the window.

"No, we wouldn't. But if we put everything we can find on the chair it would put us up higher."

"It would also be super dangerous."

"I know, but remember, we're two desperate ladies. Besides, like I said, I'm not planning on going out the window. All we have to do is make them think we did. My idea is to pile everything up on the chair to make it look as safe as possible. The hardest part is we'll have to find a way to open the window. Then we wait until one of them goes to get food and only one's left. We quickly stack things up, then make a loud noise, and hide in these cabinets. They're about empty so I'm sure we'd fit. When the one man remaining comes in to see what the noise was he'll see everything stacked up on the chair under the window, the window's open, and we're not here. What will he think?"

Sheila smiled. "That might work. He'll think we found a

way to get out the window, and run outside to look for us. But then what? Where will we go?"

"We have to hope he leaves the door open when he runs out, which he probably will since he'll be in a hurry to go look for us. Then we get out of the cabinets and go out in the house and look for a phone. If we find one, call for help. If we don't, there are two options I'm mulling over."

"What are they?"

"One is we see which way he goes, and we go the other, and try to find a house or someone that can help us."

"But he could turn around and see us before we get out of sight."

"I know, it's kind of risky, but it's a possibility. Hopefully we'll find a phone in the house and can call for help."

"What's your other option?"

"We hide in the house. If there's an attic, we go there. If they think we escaped, they won't look in the house, especially in the attic."

"Why will they especially not look in the attic; because attics are creepy?"

"Yeah, and that's one of the bad parts of that plan. But he wouldn't see us running away from the house that way. And we don't know where we are, so we wouldn't know where to go outside, even if he didn't see us. When they were bringing us here it seemed to me we left the city because it got quieter, no horns honking, and we didn't stop for traffic lights or stop signs. The road got rougher, too. So if we're out in the country, there may not be any houses around. Even if there's a woods we could run to so he wouldn't see us, where do we go from there?"

"And what if our only opportunity to do this is at night? It's creepy in the woods, and we'd be out there roaming around, with two men possibly out there looking for us. Yeah,

I think I'm liking the idea of hiding in the attic better. At least we'll have a roof over our heads."

"Hopefully we'll be able to hear them, so we'll know what they're doing. Then we can decide what we do from there. If there's a window in the attic we can get a feel for the area around us so we'll know where we want to go when we get a chance to escape."

"I like that idea," Sheila said. "We'll still be stuck in this house, but they won't know we're here. We can wait for our chance to make our escape. Maybe if they think we're gone they'll leave. Once they do, if we see them drive off, it'll give us a chance to go out and find another house or someone that can help."

"That's what I thought," Jasmine agreed. "I think if they think we escaped, they'll have to let their boss, whoever that is, know. Once that happens, I would think they would be out looking for us, or leaving the area so they won't get caught. We can identify them, so maybe they'll go out of state and lay low."

"Maybe, and that would be okay with me. It would give us a chance to escape."

"Exactly. So, do you think this idea will work? Is it worth trying?"

"I think it might. I certainly think it's worth trying, because what do we have to lose?"

"Well, the whole thing could go wrong," Jasmine warned. "He may come in here and not buy that we climbed out the window. He could look in the cabinet and find us. Or even if we make it to the attic, what if they find us there? We'll have to be really quiet. But even at that, what if they hear a noise in the attic when we move around any? And there won't be a bathroom. That's another problem. There's also the possibility that they could look at that camera and see what we're doing as we're doing it."

"I don't think they ever check the camera except when they're going to come in, to make sure we're not hiding behind the door. They've never said anything about checking it, or mentioning what we're doing."

"That's right. Since they already said there's no film in them and they're just for real time, seeing what's happening at the time, I think we'll be okay. They won't be able to see what we did before."

"We're lucky about that, or this plan might not have worked. But even if they do happen to look at the camera and see what we're doing – I mean, all those things you just said are true, any of them could happen, but if we stay here, what's going to happen? I say we go for it."

"Okay, if you agree, then we need to make some plans. The first thing is we have to find things we can stack up on a chair to get us high enough to open that window. Then we have to find enough things to stack up there to make it look like we actually reached the window."

Sheila nodded, and they both started looking around the room and in the cabinets. It was discouraging because there wasn't much there, but they made a note of anything that might be useful. They made sure to take breaks and talk about other things frequently, in case they could be heard. They didn't want to give their captors any reason to think they had any kind of plan.

Captain Fritz kept Captain Thorpe updated, as he promised, but things were moving much too slowly for Trent. He was beside himself with worry, afraid this would push the senator and his men to do something desperate in an attempt to get the information from the girls they all knew they didn't have and couldn't give them. The lawmen tried explaining why they probably wouldn't hurt the girls, but at the same time, they all understood, and even shared much of his anxiety.

Captain Fritz brought up one concern he had so they could discuss it and make a group decision about it. He felt their county sheriff should be made aware of the situation, and brought into the investigation. In thinking over what all could happen, he realized if the senator or any of his aids who were generally close by become combative, they could possibly have to arrest them to keep them from interfering. If that happened, they could be taken to the city jail or the county jail. In this case Captain Fritz preferred they be put in the county jail, as they had more individual cells. He would prefer they be put in separate cells, not close together, so they couldn't talk and come up with a story they all agreed to. The county jail was run by the sheriff's department, and Captain Fritz felt it would be better for the sheriff to know about the operation now, rather than if they had people already under arrest.

When Captain Fritz assured the men in Tennessee that he had known the sheriff for several years and had faith in him, didn't think he would be on the senator's payroll, the Tennessee group agreed. He would move as quickly as possible to do this, so they wouldn't be holding things up.

He in fact made a call as soon as he finished talking with the Tennessee group, and asked the sheriff if he could come to the patrol post ASAP for an urgent consult. A mere ten minutes later the captain was filling Sheriff Mike Allen in on what they were dealing with. He told him what they knew about the senator, including the photo Captain Thorpe had faxed to him. He quickly brought him up to speed on the two kidnapped girls and the death of the previous owner of the car. Finally he explained their plan, including his intent to put anyone taken into custody in the county jail, and asked if he saw any problems or would suggest any changes.

Sheriff Allen took a couple of minutes to consider every-thing, and gave it all a thumbs up, before asking what he could do to help.

Captain Thorpe had gotten the search warrant and deliv-ered it to the phone company, who put taps on the senator's phones. They also made sure any outgoing phone calls would be traced, and they would let them know if any went to Tennessee. They had obtained the cell phone number for the senator's aid that owned the black SUV, and a tap had been put on his phone.

They were hopeful he was the person who kidnapped the girls and the senator would call him after the officers confronted him with the pictures. If the senator did call, thanks to the tap they would be able to hear the conversation, even if he called from a burner phone. That might tell them where the girls were.

They worked hard and quickly to get everything in place. They had an officer watching each of the senator's employees, especially his aids, and the phone taps were all in place. They were finally ready to confront the senator.

"Okay, I think we have enough things to stack up there to make it look like we could possibly have climbed up that high. I'd never trust it, but I think it's enough things that will make it look doable. Finding that heavy waste paper can was exactly what we needed. It's definitely strong and sturdy enough to stand on, so it will make a good base to start with. In fact, I'm hoping it will be strong enough that we can put that on the chair and use this broom to get the window open. I think our whole plan hinges on that. If we can't get it open so it looks like we went out that way, the rest of the plan won't matter."

"We better start working on that," Sheila said. "Let's make

sure we can get the latch open on the window. Then when we're ready all we'll have to do is push the window open, stack the stuff up on the chair, and we'll be ready to put it into motion."

They worked together and put the chair under the window and the waste can upside down on the chair. "It was my idea, so if one of us falls off this and gets hurt it should be me," Jasmine said. "Help me up onto this, and try to help steady me as I work on the latch."

"You came up with the idea, so I should be the one to try this. We're in this together. Besides, I'm a little bit taller than you, and that may be important. Help me up on this and guide me. Give me any suggestions you have to get this thing unlatched. I hope it's not locked."

"Me, too. I hate to see you climb up on this, but you are taller. I'll let you try it, but if you don't feel comfortable, tell me and I'll try it."

"Deal." Working together, Sheila climbed up onto the chair. She braced herself against the wall as she took a big step to get up on top of the waste can. Once up there, she tested it a bit and found it to be much steadier than they'd expected. "It actually isn't bad. I still don't think we'd fit out the window, but if we were desperate enough to get up there, I wouldn't say for sure we couldn't fit. It's actually bigger than it looked from down on the floor."

"Hopefully they'll think we were desperate enough to try it and made it."

"Exactly. Now that I'm up here, this is actually pretty steady, so it should be believable when they look at it. Now, give me the broom."

Jasmine handed Sheila the broom, and she reached the broom handle up and could easily reach the latch on the window. With Jasmine's help she maneuvered the broom handle so it hit the latch at an angle, and she could feel the latch give some. She repeated it several times, until she felt it give. "I think we got it," she whispered. "Let me try pushing it and see if it opens."

"Try to open it, but just a little. If they come in again before we do this I don't want them to notice the window's open."

"Okay, you're right." She nudged on the window, but it didn't move.

"Try a little harder. It probably hasn't been open in years."

Sheila tried nudging it harder and it felt like it gave a little. Another nudge and they both saw it open a crack. She quickly stopped and Jasmine helped her climb down. They put the chair and waste can back where they were, along with the broom.

"Now we just have to wait until one of them leaves," Jasmine said. "I'm getting anxious and nervous. We finally have a plan. I just hope it works."

They waited and listened for what seemed like hours, until one of them finally said something about going to pick up a meal. "I'll go this time," one of them said, "if you want. What do you feel like having?"

"No, I'll go. You're still worried about someone seeing our vehicle. I don't know why. It's not like anyone saw us take them. There wasn't anyone around, so how would anyone know what kind of vehicle to look for? But you're worried about that, and you drive real nervous-like. That will draw attention to you and you'll get a cop following you just to see what's going on. Then you'll do something stupid like go through a stop sign or hurry to get back here and go over the speeding limit. I'll go. Besides, there's already a dent at the front of my vehicle, which the boss better pay to have fixed. I don't want anything else to happen to it."

The other guy grunted his displeasure, but they listened as the door opened and closed. A couple of minutes later they heard a vehicle start up, back up, and head down the road.

"Okay, this is our chance," Jasmine said, shaking a bit. "Give him a minute to be sure he's gone, out of sight, then let's move."

"I'm going to use the time to go to the bathroom," Sheila said with a giggle. "It's hard telling when we'll get a chance again."

"Good idea."

By the time they had both used the restroom they figured it had been long enough and they got busy. They put the chair back in place with the waste can. They used the broom again to open the window wider. Then they quickly placed two big old telephone books on top of the waste can. "I'm not sure why someone kept these two old phone books, as outdated as they are, but I'm sure glad they did," Sheila said. "They're huge!"

"I know," Jasmine said in a whispered giggle. She looked at the stack and then at Sheila. "I sure hope this works. We may not have found enough things to stack on to actually reach the window if we tried, but I'm hoping if we throw this big flower pot down on the ground it'll make enough of a racket to get him in here, and it'll look like we had it on top, and it fell off when the last one of us climbed out."

"I hope so, too. I mean, it makes sense. Whoever climbed out last would hold things for the first one to make sure they didn't fall. Then once the second one was on top of all of them, when she took the final move to the window, the top thing or two could easily topple. I just hope he sees it that way, too."

"Well, open the cabinet doors and get ready to hide. Are you ready to do this?"

"Yes," Sheila said resolutely. They gave each other a hug in case something went wrong, and Sheila went to the cupboard and opened the doors to the bottom part. Jasmine threw the large flowerpot to the ground, where it broke. She ran to the open door and climbed in quickly. They barely got the doors closed and settled themselves in when they heard the man curse in the other room, followed by the sound of him running. Seconds later the door to their room flew open.

Chapter 13

J asmine and Sheila held their breath as they were hiding in the cabinet, waiting to see what happened. "What the hell!" Then they heard footsteps going toward the window. "Damn! I gotta find those bitches."

They listened as the man ran out of their room. A few seconds later they heard a door slam. They quickly climbed out and released their breath when they saw the door to their room wide open. They peeked out of their room, didn't see anyone, and made their escape. They looked through the house for a phone, but came up empty. "Let's find a place to hide before he comes back," Jasmine said.

They looked through the house quickly and found the entrance to the attic, and paused to look at each other. It was a door on the ceiling in the hall, with a rope hanging from it. "I used to live in a house that had an attic like this," Sheila said. "You pull the rope and a set of stairs comes down."

"But if the stairs are down, they'll know where we are," Jasmine said, dismayed. "We better find somewhere else to hide. Maybe we need to go outside after all."

"No, wait. Once you go up the stairs there's usually a way to pull it back up. I always wondered why that was there, because why would you want to bring the stairs back up? That would be in essence locking you in."

"Do we want to do that? What if we pull the steps back up, and then we can't get them back down after the men abandon the house?"

They both went to a window and looked out a few moments, contemplating. Finally Sheila pointed. "Look, the man apparently figured we ran to the woods, which would make sense. It would be the closest place to get out of sight. I see him at the edge of the woods. He's looking both in the woods, and keeps turning and looking back toward the house, probably watching for the other man to come back. I'm sure he'd see us if we tried to run. I say we go up in the attic and see if we can pull the steps back up. I think we'd be safer there than trying to run, with him watching the house."

"I think you're right. If we can't get the steps down after they leave we'll come up with something. There's probably a window. Maybe it will lead to a porch and we can climb out onto the porch and flag someone down as they're driving by."

"We're two smart ladies. We'll come up with something, I'm sure. Let's get up there and hope we can pull the stairs up behind us."

They pulled the rope and stairs came down. Luckily, not much residue accompanied them. They picked up what did fall and got rid of it, and hoped it didn't leave a noticeable mess when they pulled them back up. Ten minutes later they were safely ensconced in the attic with the stairs back up, as well. They walked around to see what their new home had to offer.

There was a window, and they considered themselves fortunate to find that it overlooked the driveway. They would have to stay back to the side so they wouldn't be seen from outside, but they would be able to see when anyone came or left.

They tried to remember how the house was laid out, so they would have an idea where the men might be most apt to be. They seemed to spend a lot of time in the kitchen, which was where they were every time they heard them through the vent. They figured out approximately where that would be, and found a spot where they were fairly comfortable and could see out the window. Once the men were there they knew they would have to be sure not to move much so the men wouldn't hear them.

Having found a suitable spot to sit and wait, they got up to look around more and see if they could find anything that might prove useful. They didn't find much, but they hoped what they did find might help. There were two pocketknives laying on a dresser, and they each put one in their back pocket. If they got caught and the men tied them up, the knives might prove very useful.

The only other thing they found was two registers in the floor, one at each end of the attic. They were both closed, which made sense. People didn't usually heat or air condition an attic unless it provided additional living space, which this one definitely did not. They opened both of them up, hoping they might be able to hear someone talking below them. They knew it might not help, but it was worth trying.

Their quick search of the area didn't produce anything else, and they were afraid one or both of the men could show up at any time. They didn't want them hearing footsteps in the attic, so they went back to the spot they'd chosen to sit. They sat down and took a deep breath, trying to calm themselves while they waited.

The minute everything was in place and ready, Captain Fritz took two fellow state patrol officers and Sheriff Allen to the senator's office. Two of the officers had a small bug in their pocket. While Captain Thorpe and the sheriff talked with the senator, they attached the small bugs in an inconspicuous place in his office. One was attached to the front of the senator's desk, and the other to a chair at the opposite end of his office.

As they expected, the senator denied knowing anything about two missing girls, or the death of the owner of the car. "I'm sorry to hear about the death of a man and two missing ladies, but I don't have anything to do with either of them. As far as that photo, it's of such poor quality it's clearly a fake. Everyone knows how easy it is these days to alter photos. That one's so bad I can't even make out who the man is, but it certainly wasn't me."

"Do you recognize the other man in the photo?" Captain Fritz asked.

"Again, it's so grainy it's hard to see him very clearly, but as far as I can tell, no, I've never seen him before."

"You're sure about that?"

"Like I said, it's a poor quality photo, but the man doesn't look at all familiar to me."

"And you know nothing of these two girls that have been kidnapped?"

"Of course not. Why would I?"

"Let me just say that if either of those young ladies is injured, whoever is responsible for them being kidnapped will be in a great deal of trouble. With that in mind, do you want to reconsider your answer?"

"I don't know anything about this. If I did I would certainly tell you."

"Certainly," the captain said. "Okay. Just so you know, we feel confident this is you in this photo taking a bribe. We also feel you're the person behind the owner of the car being killed and the new owner of the car and her friend being kidnapped. We hoped you would make it easier for all of us and tell us where we can find the ladies. Since you chose this route, though, we'll go get the evidence we need to prove all that, and we'll be back." They left without saying anything further. The senator seemed awfully fidgety, but didn't say a word.

Things happened quickly after that. They went back to the patrol post and and found out they'd barely left his office before the senator did in fact call one of his aids. A call went from an unknown phone in his office to Kyle Solzman, his aid that owned a black SUV, who was indeed in Tennessee. The phone company was going to narrow the location down closer and would let them know what they found shortly.

They checked the bugs the officers had placed in his office, and had a little luck, but not as much as they'd hoped. He apparently was standing at the end of his office near his desk, but facing away from it. The bug at the far end of the room didn't pick up much of the conversation at all. The one on the front of his desk got part of the conversation, but not a lot. They heard enough to know he warned them he'd been visited by the police and they had a bad photo. There was urgency in the senator's voice, but they couldn't make out much more than that.

The good news came a few minutes later when the phone company called. They had been able to identify the general area of the Solzman phone. They had it narrowed down to a roughly ten square mile area in Tennessee, and were working to narrow it down further. They had also been able to tap his phone. Although the senator and his aid didn't talk about any specific plans, the senator made it clear that they needed to get those photos quickly. The phone company told Captain Thorpe that Mr. Solzman's phone was moving, and they would let him know when it stopped.

"That's the best news we've had yet," Captain Fritz said enthusiastically. He called Captain Thorpe and relayed what they'd learned, including the ten square mile area. "When the phone company lets us know the phone has stopped, we'll let you know right away."

"Terrific," Captain Thorpe said. "I'll send several officers to that area now, so when you let us know we should have men in the area and will be able to move in quickly."

As soon as he ended the call with Captain Fritz, he pulled out a map to look up the ten square mile area they were talking about. Once he had it identified, they determined it was outside the city limits, so it would be the jurisdiction of the sheriff's department and the state patrol. He immediately sent four state patrol units to that area with instructions to simply drive around the area, but stand by for additional instructions.

With the approval of everyone in the room, he also called in four sheriff's deputies with the idea of bringing them to the patrol post and bringing them into the mix. He would bring them up to speed on what was going on, and they would go out to the area, as well. Once they found the man or men that were holding the ladies hostage, the deputies would be there to escort them to the county jail, in cells apart from each other.

Sheriff Wilson was still filling his officers in on what was happening when they got word that Kyle Solzman's phone had stopped moving. Captain Thorpe, Sheriff Wilson and his four deputies, John and Trent left immediately, headed for the address. The captain told all the vehicles in the area to stay put and wait for his orders.

Jasmine and Sheila had barely settled into their new home and were still catching their breath when they heard a racket outside. They looked out the window and watched a black SUV speeding down the road, sliding around the turn into the lane and come to a screeching halt. A man jumped out of it and ran into the house.

Their eyes were wide with fright as they sat motionless, waiting to see what happened. They heard him yelling, "Charlie?" They could tell he was moving through the house, and they heard what sounded like a curse, and a door slam. Maybe a minute later they heard another door slam and could tell he was back in the house. He must have been in the kitchen because it sounded like it was right beneath them.

The girls were scared, and one look at each other told them they both felt the same way. Something was happening. The man was obviously upset when he got there, and he had to have found the room empty and his partner gone. They sat frozen, waiting to see what happened.

They didn't have to wait long. Opening the vent at that end of the house proved quite useful, as they heard the man yelling, apparently into his phone. "Charlie, where the hell are you, and the broads? They what? Damn. Well, get your ass back here now. We got a big problem. No, not just that. We got two problems now. Get your ass back here quick. We gotta figure out what to do."

Jasmine wanted so badly to say something to Sheila, but she knew she better not. From the look Sheila was giving her, the feeling was mutual. They sat quietly, careful not to move, until the door slammed again. "Where the hell you been?"

"I told you I was out looking for them. I came back right away."

"How far away were you; halfway across the county?"

"I was in the woods. The way I figure it that's where they had to have gone."

"What happened; how did they get loose?"

"Didn't you look in that room?"

"Yes, of course I did, but how did you find out they were gone? Do you have any idea when they got out?"

"Yes, that's why I said I figure they had to have run to the woods. I heard a crash, and I ran into their room quick. All that stuff was stacked up on the chair, the window was open, and the bitches were gone. There was a big flowerpot on the floor, busted. It was apparently the top item they used to get to the window and it fell and broke. I ran outside right away, but I didn't see them, so I figure they had to go to the woods. That was the closest place they could have gone to hide. That's why I was in there looking."

"How do you know they just escaped then? That flower pot could have sat there for a while before it fell and broke."

"Oh, shit, I never thought of that."

"So we don't really know when they got loose. When was the last time you saw them?"

"When we took the food in to them this morning. That was probably what- about ten o'clock?"

"Yeah, probably. When did you go looking for them?"

"About half an hour ago."

"So we really have no idea where they are or how far they may have gotten by now."

"I guess not. So what's this problem you said we have?"

"The boss called. The cops were there talking to him about the old man and the girls. He said they had a bad copy of a photo."

"Oh, shit. I'm sure he's not happy. What did he tell them?"

"I'm not sure. He didn't want to talk much. All I know is he said we gotta get them pictures and do something with the girls."

"Do what with them?"

"That's all he said, was do something with them. He said he'd call back soon. I think he wanted to get another phone and get out of his office so he could talk more."

"So what are we gonna do? We don't have the pictures, and now we don't even have the girls."

"I don't know. What do you think?"

"I say we say the hell with all this shit and we get outta here. You know the boss is gonna be pissed, but if the cops have already been there, they must be onto him. If they got him, what about us? They may already figure we're involved in it since we aren't there. Even if they don't, if they arrest him he'll blame it on us."

"But we only did what he told us to."

"It don't matter. You don't think he's gonna take the fall, do you? Besides, I don't like how this is going."

"What do you mean?"

"I never signed up for nothing like this. We kidnapped them ladies. I mean, we actually kidnapped them. He can call it whatever he wants, but if we get caught, we'll be charged with kidnapping. You do real time for that. And what about the old man? He died."

"We didn't kill him."

"No, we didn't, but someone did."

"The boss said he probably had a heart attack."

"Yeah, well, the boss lied, too. The news said he was shot."

"He was shot? Who shot him?"

"I don't know, but I sure didn't like it when I heard that. I should have quit then."

There was a pause before the next response. "I thought about quitting then, too, and I didn't even know the old man was shot."

"Why didn't you say something? We could a both quit."

"I didn't figure the boss would let us."

"What do you mean he wouldn't have let us? How could he stop us?"

"Think about it. He told us this old man has pictures of him taking bribes. He had us break in his house to get the pictures back, and told us to rough him up if we need to. He isn't going to want anyone out there knowing all that."

"So what, are you saying he would have killed us?"

"No, he wouldn't himself, but I was afraid he'd hire someone else to. That's probably what happened to the old man."

"Then we better get out of here."

"He doesn't know where we are, other than somewhere in Tennessee. I never gave him the address."

"Okay, so we're safe for a little bit. What are we gonna do when he calls? I don't think we want to tell him we don't have the pictures or the girls."

"No, we don't, and we aren't necessarily safe here, either. Here's what we'll do. When he calls we'll just let him think we still have them, but they don't seem to know what we're after. He'll tell us what he wants us to do next, and we'll just agree, act like we're going to. But we need to get out of here. We don't know where the girls are, but if they get to a phone they'll call the cops. They'll be able to tell them where we are."

"You're right, we better leave quick. Let's go."

"Wait. I don't think it's safe to take my vehicle, though, or either of our phones. They'll be able to trace us."

"But if we don't take the SUV, where will we go and how will we get there?"

"I think we need to call Uber or Lyft and go to a bus station or something. We'll figure out where we want to go when we get to the station."

It was quiet again. "I guess we better. That means we're going to be on the run. For how long? Can we go see any family? Maybe we could stay with my brother for a while."

"If the cops are looking for us they'll check our families. We can't go there."

"For how long? We aren't ever gonna be able to live a normal life again, are we? Damn him, he ruined our lives.

He's probably got the cops looking for us, and all we did was what he told us to."

"I know, but it's too late to worry about it now. We better get outta here. Get your clothes and stuff together while I call Uber. Then we'll leave the vehicle and our phones here. They can trace them here, but they won't find us."

They heard mumbling and footsteps, and it got quiet. Jasmine leaned over a bit and whispered, "I don't know what all this means, but it could be good."

Sheila nodded, but before either of them could say anything else, she pointed to the window. Jasmine turned to look, and gasped. Six or seven law enforcement cruisers were pulling into the lane. They didn't have their lights or sirens on, but several officers got out, all with their guns drawn. Before anything else happened they heard one of the men again. "Charlie, hurry your ass up. We gotta get out of here. I called Uber and told them to meet us at the corner, down at the intersection, so come on."

"Okay, I'm coming. Damn, I hate this."

Just then there was a bang, followed by all kinds of commotion. "Police! Get your hands up, now! Don't run, we've got the house surrounded. Get your hands up now! Get down on the ground." There was more commotion, then it quieted down. "Where are Jasmine and Sheila?"

"Who?"

"The two ladies you kidnapped. Where are they?"

"I don't know what you're talking about."

"Look for them. I'll give you one more chance. If you want to help yourself any, tell us where they are."

"I don't know —"

"Charlie, you're right, he's ruined our life already. We may as well do whatever we can to help ourselves."

"Smart move," an officer said. "So tell us where they are."

"We don't know. They aren't here."

"Look for them," the officer told his men.

"You can look all you want, but I'm telling you, they aren't here. They were, but they escaped."

"They were here?"

"Yes, they were, but they climbed out a window earlier today. We don't know where they are."

"Why did you kidnap them?"

"Look, we want to help ourselves. We'll tell you anything we can. We work for Senator Kingsley from Arizona. He told us to take them. Well, he told us to take the one, but they were both together, so we took both of them."

There was more commotion, then the officer spoke again. "Trent, you were supposed to wait in the car."

"I couldn't. The lady I love is missing, has been missing and she might be in here. Is she?"

"Unfortunately, no."

Jasmine couldn't take it any longer and started pounding on the floor with her hand. "Trent! Trent, we're up here!" She and Sheila started stomping on the floor.

Chaos broke out below them, as several people started talking at once. Sheila heard, "What the hell?" and "They escaped, I'm telling you." There were a few other things she heard parts of as they all talked at once and they couldn't make out who said what.

The only thing Jasmine heard was, "Jasmine? Where are you?"

"We're in the attic, Trent. There's a rope in the hallway."

Two minutes later Trent had the stairs pulled down and was stepping into the attic when Jasmine flew into his arms. The impact knocked him over, but luckily he fell into John, who was right behind him coming up the steps, and although John wasn't able to quite catch him, he did manage to keep Trent and Jasmine from falling on him and down the steps.

John couldn't help but laugh as he watched the two of

them laying on the dirty attic floor, wrapped in each other's arms. He glanced over and saw another young lady he hadn't met yet, and went to her. "May I assume you're Sheila?"

"Yes. Thank you so much."

The poor girl was shaking, having been through what was obviously a horrible ordeal. He pulled her to him and wrapped his arms around her, hoping to stop the shaking. "I'm John, close friend of Trent, and boy, am I glad to meet you." He held her, rocking her a bit, and was glad to see the shivering stop. He pulled her back and they both watched Trent and Jasmine, who were back on their feet now, but still in each other's arms. Trent held out an arm toward them. "Come here, Sheila," he said, and she hurried over for a hug with both him and Jasmine.

Captain Thorpe made his way up the attic steps and took one look at Trent holding both ladies. "Well, that's certainly a good sight," he told John, who nodded. "I'm going back downstairs. Send them down when they're ready to tell us what happened."

"Will do," John said, "but I think they need a few minutes to assure themselves it's finally over."

"Understood," the captain answered with an understanding smile.

John stood off to the side watching, and thinking back to the first time he met Jasmine, when he pulled her over for speeding. His first impression of her was that of a sassy little firebrand. He still felt she was a sassy little firebrand, but was now glad she was. It was likely to have been what kept them going. He didn't know how they ended up in the attic when the two men downstairs insisted they'd escaped, but they were obviously hiding right under their noses. He felt sure the sassy little firebrand had something to do with that, and was eager to hear their story. He also knew now that this sassy little thing was exactly the woman Trent needed in his life.

Chapter 14

It took three hours back at the patrol post for them to sort out what happened. The girls gave statements, answered all the questions any of them had. They repeated what they'd heard while hiding in the attic while the two men were getting ready to run.

Captain Thorpe called Captain Fritz and let him listen and be part of the process, and even ask questions of the girls. He was able to get all the questions he had answered, and verified that he understood correctly. Now that he had enough information and evidence to make some serious charges against the senator stick, he thanked the girls and all the men for their part in the case. Before hanging up he promised to let them know what happened when he returned to the senator's office, which he planned to do right away.

He talked with the sheriff and together they reviewed what all they had against the senator to be sure they hadn't missed anything. Now that they had his two aids that had done the actual kidnapping and they gave them statements, they felt they had a solid case, so Captain Fritz and Sheriff Allen made a return trip to see Senator Kingsley. He continued to deny knowing anything about them until they told him they had arrested Kyle Solzman and Charles Fry for kidnapping the ladies, and breaking and entering, and theft at the original car owner's home. Right away he told them Kyle had killed that old man, which was a shame. The officers just shook their head as they put him in handcuffs, read him his rights, and led him out the door.

"You can't do this," he insisted. "Do you know who I am?"

"Of course we do," Captain Fritz answered calmly. "You're the man in all the photos we have."

"I'm a United States senator. You can't arrest me like this."

"Sure we can," Captain Thorpe said, "if we have solid evidence proving you did a crime. The laws apply to senators the same as anyone else."

"At least hide the handcuffs," he pleaded before they went outside. "I'm a public official, and if someone has a phone and snaps a picture of me in handcuffs it'll be horrible for my future."

"A picture of you in handcuffs will be the least of your problems in the future," the sheriff told him. "With all the pictures we have of you taking bribes, and sending your men to get those pictures back, you're looking at a long time in prison. I'm pretty sure that will end your days as a senator."

"Wait, you can't do that. Surely we can work this out."

"I don't think so this time," Captain Thorpe said. "The only working out you'll be doing is in the prison gym on the days you're allowed in there." They led him outside and down the sidewalk a little ways to the sheriff's cruiser, where they put him in the back, as people were snapping pictures. The senator tried to hide his face and the handcuffs the whole time, unsuccessfully.

Once Sheila, Jasmine and Trent were finally done at the patrol post, Trent took them back to the girls' condo. Now that things were starting to settle down, they all realized they hadn't eaten in quite a while. No one wanted to go out, and Trent had done nothing but help look for them the last few days, so they had no groceries. They ordered a pizza and sat back to talk, with Jasmine wrapped in Trent's arms. John had told Trent the more he could get the girls to talk about the ordeal, the easier it would be for them to get past it, and Trent wanted to hear what all they had been through, so they spent the night talking.

As much as he wanted to hear all about what had happened from their end, Jasmine and Sheila were just as curious about how they found them, and wanted details about that. Trent figured they deserved to know, so he described their search for them. Jasmine had thanked him numerous times for getting John and the law involved and finding them, but he could tell now, from watching their reactions to what he said, they were a little surprised at what all was taking place behind the scenes, and thankful.

While they were talking, Captain Thorpe called to let them know the senator had been arrested, and he was sure there would be something about it on the news. They talked about that some, and Trent was a little surprised that the girls felt some sympathy for the men that kidnapped them. They had no sympathy for the senator, but some for the men. After all, they had done what they were told to do. Sure, they should have said no, but they understood their hesitancy and fear in telling the senator no. As they pointed out, he was a senator, after all. Trent understood their feelings, but didn't share their sympathy. He felt they should have gone to the police, although he wasn't sure if they would have had enough of a case to bring against a senator.

The one thing that changed their mind was when they

thought about the original owner of the car. They weren't sure what happened and why, but if they were responsible for the man's death, that was unforgivable. If they weren't the ones that killed him, and they neither one felt they were, they needed to find out who did and punish them.

Trent agreed, but refused to spend any time thinking about that, however. He had his Jasmine and her best friend back, and that was all he cared about at the moment.

While they were eating their pizza, he suggested the girls take the next couple of days, Thursday and Friday, off work to get themselves settled again, but both girls objected at the same time. "No way," Jasmine said. "I want my life back, just like it was. The sooner I can get back to normal, the better. I have an economics class tomorrow that I don't want to miss. I already missed a couple of classes and I don't want to fall behind in it."

Trent had to chuckle a bit. "I know someone who can help you get caught up in it."

"I know, and I will appreciate it if you will, but I don't want to fall any further behind. I don't want to miss any more work, either. We've been busy lately."

"And Lisa's probably had her hands full doing that job all herself," Sheila added. "I want to get back to help her."

"I'm sure she'll appreciate it," Trent said, "but I'm not sure how much work you'll get done. I have a feeling people will want to welcome you back and have lots of questions for both of you. Try to prepare yourself for that."

"I hadn't thought of that," Sheila said. "I hate being the center of attention."

"I know," Trent said, "but you're both very well liked at work, so I'm sure that will happen, whether you want the attention or not. Just remember it's because they care about you."

Both ladies nodded, but he was sure they wouldn't like all

the attention they would no doubt be getting the next several days. He knew because he'd gone into the office a couple of times over the last few days to sign papers and whatnot, and he'd been pretty overwhelmed himself.

It took a few days, but things finally began to settle back down. Well, most things. The girls had much more attention than they wanted for several days, and that had them feeling awkward. The worst part, it wasn't just at work. Everywhere they went people recognized them from the news and spoke to them. They were friendly, saying they were glad they were back home and safe, but the girls just couldn't put the ordeal behind them like they desperately wanted to. Trent knew how they felt, so he went to their condo or took them to his house every evening after work and the three of them cooked dinner together and ate in so they could eat in peace.

He wanted some alone time with Jasmine, but the girls had been clinging to each other, which he understood, so he didn't want to split them up. Finally, once they had been back five days, he asked Sheila if he could steal Jasmine for a couple of hours after dinner. She graciously agreed, though he could tell she wasn't thrilled with the idea of being alone. He made sure to remind her to call if she needed anything at all, and she agreed.

Once he'd taken Jasmine to his home and they were snuggling on the couch, he leaned down to kiss her temple. "I've missed this," he murmured, giving her a little hug.

"Me, too. It's one thing that kept me going."

He turned to look at her. She hadn't talked too much about her ordeal, other than to tell him what exactly had happened. She'd told him the facts, but very little about her feelings, which concerned him. "Do you mean thinking about us cuddling helped?"

"Yes. I love when we do this. I feel so safe and content when I'm snuggled in against you, and I wanted that so badly. I kept thinking if I could just have ten minutes of it, I was sure I'd feel better."

"I'm glad you enjoy it, too, because I feel the same way. With you cuddled in against me I feel like everything's okay, my world is good."

"Mmm," she mumbled, laying her head against his chest. They spent over an hour right there, doing not much, talking very little, but soaking up what they'd both been missing. Although he would have preferred to stay there all night, just like they were, he didn't want to leave Sheila alone too long. When he sighed and moved back a bit, she must have been thinking the same thing. "Are you thinking we should get back to Sheila?" she asked.

"Should being the operative word there," he said, giving her another little squeeze. "I would prefer to stay right here and not move any, but yes, I was thinking of Sheila. I don't want her getting worried. Are you ready for me to take you home?"

"Yeah, I suppose. I feel sorry for Sheila. I wouldn't have wanted to leave her tonight, either, except that I was leaving with you and I've missed my time with you. She doesn't have anyone special like that to lean on."

"That's why you and I, especially you, have to be there for her. Once she's feeling safe and comfortable again we can have more time alone." He stood and offered his hand. She put her little hand in his and allowed him to help her up, and he pulled her straight in against him for a kiss. This was a kiss that showed just how much he'd missed her and their time alone, and she returned his kiss with a very similar one of her own. He smiled down at her when they separated. "I've missed that more than I can say."

"Me, too," she said, reaching up to meet his lips one more time.

From then on over the next week they gradually spent more time alone, as Sheila felt more comfortable with it. It seemed to Trent as though she was adjusting quite well, even suggesting a couple of times that he take Jasmine out for dinner, and assuring him she would be fine home alone. He'd heard comments from people at work, as well, saying they were glad she seemed to be back to herself.

Jasmine, however, had him a little concerned. Some days she seemed to be doing fine, getting back to herself again, but other days she seemed off somehow. He hadn't been able to put his finger on exactly what it was, but she was just off. One thing he did notice was she seemed to have lost some of her confidence. She was a very strong, very capable young lady, which was one thing that had impressed him from the day he'd met her. But lately she seemed to be faltering a bit, second-guessing herself.

Being concerned led him to watch her more carefully, both at work and at home. After a few days of watching her a little closer and listening to both what she said and what anyone else said about her, he came to the conclusion the faltering behavior was mostly just around him. Her co-workers made comments that they were glad to have her back and up to speed again, and her work there was as good as it had ever been. Her boss was extremely proud of her and happy with her work, and was sure she'd do fine running the department soon.

With that thought, Trent focused his attention on time they spent together, both alone and with Sheila. It was actually Sheila that shed the first ray of light on what the problem might be. One thing he had picked up on was a stray comment she would make here and there that wasn't like her. They always caused him to pause a moment, but he let them slide, trying to give her all the time she needed to feel totally safe and secure again, since he felt that was her underlying problem.

One evening when the three of them were having dinner together they started talking about a new hire at work that wasn't working out real well. "It's probably none of my business," Sheila said, looking at Trent, "but how do you normally deal with someone like that? I mean, it's been long enough now and he obviously hasn't caught on to his job. I haven't heard of you actually firing anyone, except one or two people that didn't show up for work."

"I don't like to fire people if I can keep from it," Trent answered. "I've been thinking I'm going to have to do something with him, though. What I usually do is move them to a different job and see how they work out there. I've been giving this some thought, though, and I'm not sure where I could move him to."

"I wouldn't know, either," Jasmine said. "He's such a dumbass, I don't know where you could put him."

Trent was surprised by her comment, but it was Sheila's reaction that got him thinking. She dropped her fork and turned to look at Jasmine, her eyebrows raised. "Jazz, what is wrong with you?"

"What? He is." She finished chewing her bite and added, "Okay, I probably shouldn't have said that, but you can't deny it's true."

Sheila frowned at Jasmine, shook her head, and turned back to Trent. "What about out in the factory? I know he didn't want to work in the factory, on the line, but aren't there some jobs out there that are technically office jobs, kind of a go between with the factory and the main office? I mean, when I deliver memos it's mostly in the main office, but there's a section of offices, or actually cubicles out there that I deliver to, also. They always seem to work in the cubicles, not on the line."

Trent's eyebrows raised as he considered her words. "You're right, Sheila. They do paperwork, not line work, but they get the information they need from the factory foremen and managers, which is why they work out there. It's more basic work, gathering information and recording it for the main office. That might be an idea. Thank you, Sheila, for the suggestion. I'll give it some thought."

They changed the subject and finished their dinner, but Sheila's reaction to Jasmine's comment lingered in his mind. By the time he went to bed that night he was beginning to formulate a possible explanation. If his hypothesis proved correct, now he just had to figure out what to do about it.

His opportunity to confront the problem arose the next evening. In fact, it became crystal clear to him that not only was he right, but there was only one way to handle it. They were at his house working on her economics. He asked her a question about a new concept they were studying, and she shrugged her shoulders. "Jasmine, that's not an answer. You know what I think of people shrugging their shoulders. I thought we'd gotten past that."

"Well, I'm sorry, but I can't help it. I don't understand this shit and don't see why I'll ever need to know it."

That was all he needed, and seconds later she found herself over his knees. He unfastened her jeans and pulled them and her panties down to her knees. Just as he'd suspected, she wasn't arguing or squirming nearly as much as she normally would. He laid his hand on her bare bottom as he pulled her in a bit tighter, then began the spanking as he talked to her. "Jasmine, I know you've been through a horrible ordeal, but that's over. Thankfully you're back and you're fine, so we can get back to our normal. And in case you'd forgotten, our normal includes me watching out for you. That means I won't allow you to do things that might be harmful, things you'll regret later, or things that may harm our relationship. You know better than to shrug your shoulders when I ask you a question. You also know better than to use that kind of language. You know I don't approve, and it's not a good habit to get into. I especially don't want to hear you using language like that at work."

"I'm sorry, Trent," she said as tears rolled down her cheeks.

He watched her closely as he continued to spank her. He had to wonder what exactly the tears were from. He didn't think it was from pain because he wasn't spanking hard. He didn't think she realized that, though. He was pretty sure her problem lately, which culminated in her shrugging her shoulders, like she did when they first met and he scolded her the first time, and swearing, was because she was feeling unsure of herself. She would probably never admit it to herself, but she needed to know he still cared enough to watch her closely. She needed to know he would still give her a spanking if she did something that could harm her or their relationship.

He continued the spanking, but still not hard. She probably wouldn't even feel this in an hour or so, and that was okay with him. She didn't need to be sore today, just know he was still here for her. He had a feeling her tears represented that, and were tears of relief as much as anything else. "Jasmine, I love you too much to sit back and watch you do things like that. You're always disappointed in yourself afterwards, and I don't like seeing that. I won't allow it. You need to remember that."

She lay slumped over his lap, and to him she looked more relieved than sore or contrite, but that was okay this time. Eventually, he would encourage her to tell him if she was feeling unsure and needed a spanking to assure her he was still there for her, but he knew she wasn't ready for that yet. For now, he would just watch her closely after any traumatic event and make sure she felt safe and secure. If she seemed to be fidgety or off a little bit, like she had been now, he would repeat this if it was what she needed to feel his presence and protection again.

He ended the spanking and brought her up to sit on his lap. He hadn't even gotten his arms wrapped around her yet before she had her arms around him and her head laying on his chest. He leaned down and kissed the top of her head. "Are you okay, sweetheart?"

"Yes."

"I'm still here, honey, and I'm not going anywhere. I'm still keeping a close eye on you."

"Thank you."

He smiled, happy that his guess was right. He would always be happy to let her know he was still here and still cared. They sat there, neither one talking a lot, but neither one needing to. They were happy in each other's arms. They stayed that way for half an hour, until he finally sighed. "As much as I hate to change a thing, we really should go over your economics. After missing a couple of classes we have some catching up to do."

"You're right," she said with a sigh of her own. "Is there any chance I could stay here while we go over it, though?"

He grinned at her and nodded. "There's a good chance of it, as long as you're paying attention to what I'm explaining."

"I will," she promised. "I feel safe and content, and I'm not ready to give that up yet. You're right, though, I've got some catching up to do in this class."

An hour later he felt confident she had in fact paid attention and understood what they'd gone over, and as much as he hated to, he knew it was time for him to take her home. He felt sure she would sleep better tonight. In fact, he was pretty sure they both would.

Chapter 15

Jasmine and Sheila had wanted to show Trent how much they appreciated all he'd done to help find and rescue them. He insisted he hadn't done much other than call John, and he did that because he was going out of his mind with worry, but they insisted they wanted to do something special. After much debate, they decided to cook a special dinner for him on Saturday.

It actually worked out rather well, since he had to go into the office to get caught up on some paperwork he'd gotten behind on while the girls were missing. He worked all day, and when he got to their house he was surprised to see them so excited. He wasn't sure what, but he knew right away something had happened.

Jasmine met him at the door, bouncing on her toes. He placed his hands on her shoulders to hold her still long enough to give her a kiss. "What's got you two so excited?"

"You know that unmarried hot hunk of man flesh that works in research and development?"

Trent's eyes grew huge as he stood back far enough to look

into her eyes. "The unmarried hot hunk of man flesh? In our research and development department at work?"

"Yes, of course at work. Where else would we know about a hot hunk that works in research and development?"

He couldn't help but frown, but stopped to think a minute. "I didn't know we had any hot hunks of man flesh working at Douglas Manufacturing, but are you talking about Hunter Grenell?"

Now Jasmine's eyes grew. "What do you mean you didn't know there were any hot hunks working there? You had a major one there until I put my 'Sorry, Ladies, He's Spoken For' sign on him, but you weren't the only one roaming the halls of Douglas Manufacturing." She paused a moment before adding, "You were the best looking one, but you weren't the only one. And yes, of course we're talking about Hunter Grenell. What do you know about him?"

"He seems like a nice guy. I've been very happy with his work. He's a smart young man with good work ethics. When you two were missing he sought me out to ask if there was anything he could do to help. He said he knew I had to be worried sick, and he sure missed talking with Sheila, so he was willing to do anything that might help. I could tell he was sincere, and that impressed me. Why are you so interested in Hunter?"

Jasmine was surprised to see a look on his face that looked a lot like jealousy, and instantly felt bad. "Not for me, silly. You've got my heart and I'm not interested in anyone else, but he asked Sheila out."

He looked over at Sheila, who was beaming ear to ear and bouncing on her toes much like Jasmine was. "I take it you said yes?" he asked with a grin as he held out the arm that wasn't hugging Jasmine so he could bring her in on their hug.

"Yes, of course I did," she assured him as she hurried into his arms.

"I hope it works out well for you, Sheila. Hunter seems like a very nice, down to earth man. I could see the two of you getting together nicely. When are you going out?"

"He asked if I was free this evening, but I told him Jazz and I were making a special dinner for you to say thank you for all you did in bringing us back. I asked if he would consider another night, and we settled on Tuesday."

"I'm glad it worked out, but you could have gone tonight, Sheila. You didn't need to miss it just to cook dinner for me."

"I told her I could do it myself," Jasmine said.

"I know, and I appreciate it, both of you," Sheila said, "but you've both done so much for me, helping fix this meal was important to me. I appreciate what both of you have done for me, and in my mind this was one little way I could say thank you."

He hugged both of them close for a moment. "Sheila, I know you think I've done a lot to help you, but it's really all been Jasmine. She stole my heart, but she did that partly because of her big heart. That big heart is what brought you here. When I heard her plan, and how long she's been working toward her goal of getting you here and in college, I was touched. I may have hurried things up a bit, but it was all her plan and determination."

"I appreciate everything she did, but I also very much appreciate your hurrying things up a bit, as you put it," she said with a grin. "My life is totally different since I've been here."

"You mean you weren't kidnapped back in Arizona?" he asked with a laugh.

"No, actually, I wasn't, but that's not what I was referring to," she said with a laugh of her own. "Back there my life was going to work, which was hard and barely paid enough to cover my half of the rent for the apartment I shared with a lady who was nice, but I didn't even know her until I answered her ad looking for someone to share expenses with for an apartment. That was my life. Now there's so much more. Not only is it fun living with Jasmine, in an apartment that is way, way nicer, but I have so much to look forward to. I absolutely love my job, look forward to going every day, and I still can hardly believe I'm going to start college classes soon. It's a little overwhelming."

"And now there's an upcoming date with Hunter," Jasmine added. "But I totally get what you're saying, Sheila. I feel like I went through almost the same thing when I met Trent. I was jobless again, didn't know how I was going to pay the rent on my small apartment, and my cupboards were pretty bare. Trent gave me a job that paid more than I'd been making, and it's been all uphill since."

"Well, you're right that your cupboards were pretty bare," he said with a chuckle and a hug for her. "Your eating habits were upsetting to me, but I realized much of it was from lack of funds to buy healthier food. That's part of the reason I was touched by your determination to help Sheila. Now I'm glad we did bring her here a little earlier than planned, because she's a wonderful person and it's meant a lot to me to watch you two renew your friendship. Now, enough of this sappy stuff. Something smells delicious and I'm starving. What's for dinner?"

Dinner was filled with happy and excited conversation, and delicious food. Trent was impressed with the dinner the ladies made for him, and made sure they knew it. They both brushed it off, which didn't surprise him any. They all enjoyed their evening, which in each of their minds was a celebration of life getting back to normal.

Tuesday night found Jasmine and Sheila both getting ready for their dates. Jasmine helped Sheila pick out what they both deemed would be the perfect outfit for Sheila's first date with Hunter.

Since the girls' terrible experience, Trent hadn't felt right about leaving Sheila alone in the evening, so they generally all cooked together and stayed in, or the three of them went out together. He wasn't about to pass up this opportunity to take Jasmine out without having to worry about leaving Sheila home alone, so he made reservations for them at a new swanky restaurant they hadn't tried yet.

Jasmine was excited to get all dressed up and go out. Not only was it fun, but she always felt Trent was the sexiest man in a restaurant full of men in suits, and felt lucky to be the lady on his arm. Once they were happy that Sheila looked absolutely perfect, they did the same for Jasmine, giggling and totally enjoying themselves as they did so.

"I still can't believe how much my life has changed," Sheila said, standing back and looking at the two of them in the mirror. "I feel like for the first time I have a future, with so much to look forward to."

"I know," Jasmine said, giving her friend a hug. "I still feel that way a lot of times. But now we get to go through it together. I can't wait to compare notes later tonight."

They giggled again and were taking one last look in the mirror when the doorbell rang. "Who do you think it is?" Sheila asked.

Jasmine glanced at her watch and said, "Whoever it is, they're eight minutes early, so it's probably Hunter. I talked to him a few minutes today and he seemed awfully anxious for this evening. Trent is a stickler for showing up exactly when he says he'll be here."

"Maybe," Sheila said as they both went through the living room toward the door.

"I'll answer it, so you can make a grand entrance," Jasmine said with a gesture of grandeur and a chuckle.

"Yeah, right," Sheila said.

Jasmine had a big smile on her face as she opened the door. "Hi, Hunter. Come on in."

"Hi, Jasmine. Am I too early?"

"Not at all," she assured him. "We just came out to wait on our guys."

He came into the apartment, saw Sheila and smiled. "You ladies both look lovely this evening."

"Thank you," they parroted. They smiled at each other as Sheila moved closer to Hunter as he held out the flowers he'd been holding. For you, Sheila."

"Thank you," she said as her face blushed. "Let me go get a vase."

While she went to the kitchen, Hunter turned back to Jasmine. "Do you have special plans with Mr. Douglas this evening, Jasmine?"

"Yes, we do. We're trying out that new restaurant. Trent likes to have a nice restaurant to take potential clients now and then, and we haven't been to try it out yet. Have you?"

"No, but I was hoping maybe Sheila and I can try it out one day soon."

"Maybe we can all go together sometime, if we like it," she suggested.

Sheila came back to the living room and Hunter went to meet her. "Are you ready to go, Sheila?"

"Yes, of course. Is it warm out tonight?"

"It's not bad, but I'd bring a jacket. It was rather cool last evening." He helped her into her jacket and they were about to the door when the doorbell rang again.

Jasmine looked up at the clock just as it was striking seven o'clock and both ladies chuckled. "There's Trent," she said.

She opened the door and Trent leaned in to give her a kiss

on her cheek. "You look gorgeous, Jasmine." He saw the other two heading for the door and smiled. "Good evening, Sheila, Hunter."

"Good evening, Mr. Douglas," Hunter said.

"Please, we're not at the office, Hunter. Call me Trent."

"Thank you. If you'll excuse us, we'll be on our way. You two have a good evening."

"Thank you. You take care of her, and have a good evening yourselves."

Hunter smiled and shook Trent's hand before they left.

"They make a good-looking couple of," Trent said after they left.

"I thought the same thing," Jasmine agreed. "I hope it works out for them and they're as happy as us."

"Well, that's setting the bar pretty high," he said with a big smile. "But it would be nice. They're both good people. Are you ready?"

"Yep. I'm anxious to see what this place is like. I've heard it's pretty nice. Swanky, but nice."

Trent laughed as he shut the door behind them. "What exactly does swanky mean to you?"

"Ooh-la-la," she said with a giggle. "You know, fancy, nice, and expensive."

He was laughing as he held the car door for her. "Then let's go try this ooh-la-la place out."

They were both very impressed with the new restaurant, and felt it would become one of their main go-to places when they had something to celebrate. Afterwards he took her back to his place for a little much-missed time to themselves.

Hunter helped Sheila into his car, then went around to the driver's door. The awkwardness they both feared never materialized, as Hunter's question as to how Trent and Jasmine were doing proved to be the perfect opening for them. They were soon talking like old friends. Once they were seated at the restaurant the easy conversation continued, and by the time their food arrived they'd begun learning about each other.

Sheila was touched by Hunter's attention. She could tell when he asked a question he was genuinely interested in her answer, and not just asking to keep the conversation going. He listened carefully to everything she said, often asking follow-up questions. She wasn't used to having a man's undivided attention like that, and it meant a great deal to her.

As they told each other more about themselves and their past, they realized that although they had very different backgrounds, they shared a lot of the same ideals and beliefs. They decided they were awfully full after their meal, but Hunter ordered one dessert with two forks and some coffee, more to buy them a little more time together. Once that was done, he laid his hand gently over hers. "Sheila, I know etiquette says on a first date a gentleman should take the lady out to dinner, then take her home. If that's what you want me to do, I will, but I've really been enjoying this evening and I hate to see it end quite yet. Would you like to go for a walk in the park? It's warmer than it was last evening, so it's probably pretty nice out with a jacket. If you'd rather I take you home, I'll do that."

"No, a walk in the park sounds nice, Hunter. I've enjoyed talking with you this evening, too."

"Good." He paid the bill and tentatively reached for her hand as they left the restaurant. She smiled at him and moved a little closer so it was easier to hold hands as they walked to his car. Their easy banter continued as he drove them to the park. By the time it was getting dark they were laughing and talking like old friends.

"Well, thank you for extending our night with this walk, but I really do need to get you home. I'd hate to be responsible for you being tired at work tomorrow. Mr. Douglas might not be too impressed with me if I did that."

They both laughed a little and their conversation turned to Trent and Jasmine as they walked back to his car. When they got back to the girls' condo, Hunter walked her to the front door. Once she was inside and he knew she was safe, he took her hand in his. "Sheila, I had a wonderful time getting to know you, and I would very much like to see you again. Would you like to have dinner with me again, and maybe we could go see a movie?"

"I'd like that. I had a good time tonight, too."

"Good. How about this weekend? Do you have plans for Friday or Saturday evening?"

"Either night is good for me."

"Good. I'll see you at work the next few days, and we'll make some arrangements."

"Sounds good to me."

He leaned down and gave her cheek a quick kiss. "Good night, Sheila. Lock the door when I leave, and sleep well tonight."

"Thank you for this evening, Hunter."

She watched out the window until he turned onto the road and his lights disappeared. Then she turned around and went into the kitchen to look again at the flowers he'd brought. She picked them up and inhaled, loving the scent of the fresh carnations. She took the vase into the living room and set them down on the coffee table and sat down on the couch. She was thinking back on her wonderful evening and still staring at her flowers fifteen minutes later when Trent opened the door with Jasmine.

Seeing the dreamy look on Sheila's face, Jasmine ran over to her friend. "Well, how was it? Did you have a good time? Are you going to see him again?"

"It was wonderful," she said quietly as she hugged a pillow, "and yes, we're going to see each other again this weekend."

"Oh, good," Jasmine said, throwing her arms around her best friend. "I need details."

"I need a kiss first," Trent said. "It's obvious you two have some talking to do, so I'll get out of here. Just make sure you get to bed before too late. Tomorrow's a work day, you know."

Sheila giggled. "Hunter said he had to get me home so I could get a good night's sleep. He said you might not be too happy with him if he kept me out too late on a work night."

"I knew I liked that man," Trent said with a smile. He pulled Jasmine in for a goodnight kiss. "You two have a nice talk, but then get some sleep," he tried to say in his stern voice, but even he had to admit it didn't sound very convincing.

Jasmine was so concerned, she laughed. "Okay, I hear you, boss. I'll get some sleep tonight."

"You better get more than just some," he said with a chuckle. "Eight hours would be preferred. That gives you girls an hour or so to talk. Surely that should be long enough."

The girls looked at each other in a way that made Trent sigh. "Oh, my. Well, at least try for seven hours," he said as he leaned down to give her a kiss. "I love you," he whispered into her ear. "Talk fast, then both of you get a good night's sleep." He headed for the door, but turned back toward them as he got to the door and said, "Sleep well."

Jasmine locked the door, knowing Trent was more than likely still outside the door, waiting until he heard her lock it before going to his car. The two started talking, and never stopped as they got ready for bed. Sheila sat down on Jasmine's bed, where they finished their talk an hour and a half later.

Things started to settle down gradually. There were still stories on the news about the senator, which kept the girls from putting the whole ordeal completely behind them, but they were mentioning his role in the girls' kidnapping less and less, which helped. Still, there was another mention of it on the news every time he had another court appearance or more information leaked out about what all happened.

The girls got better at brushing off the extra unwanted attention, and their co-workers knew they were trying to get past it all, so at least it wasn't mentioned at work much. That was a relief to the girls.

They were both more interested in their men. Sheila and Hunter hit it off, and started seeing each other two or three evenings a week. Trent was happy to see that relationship blossom. Not only did he like both Sheila and Hunter and think they made a fine couple of, but it also gave him and Jasmine more alone time.

After Jasmine's spanking to remind her that he was still watching over her, she went back to being the old Jasmine he'd fallen in love with. She was doing great in her final college classes, and her boss felt she was ready to step into his shoes when he retired. She would still have several months of working full-time with him after she graduated before he retired, but with Trent's permission, he was planning on having her run the department from her graduation until he retired. He felt that would give her time to step into the position and take over while he was still around if she needed a little extra help. By the time he retired he felt she would have not only the knowledge, but also the confidence to step in as head of the department.

Six months after the kidnapping Trent couldn't be any happier with his life. His company was doing well. He and Jasmine were doing great. He'd gotten Sheila and Jasmine together, and watching their relationship grow had been a true blessing. Jasmine had graduated from college and was now running the purchasing department and doing a fine job. Sheila was still working at the same job by her choice, but part time now, as she had started taking college classes.

There was only one thing worrying him. He wanted to make Jasmine his wife. He felt they loved each other and were ready to be married and share their lives. The one concern he had was when.

When he helped Jasmine bring Sheila here, the plan was for the two of them to share the apartment. Jasmine would be able to pay the rent and utilities while Sheila went to college and worked part-time only, earning enough for her personal expenses. Jasmine had been working toward that goal for years, and was proud when she was finally able to put her plan into effect.

If he asked Jasmine to marry him now, what would that do to that plan? He was more than willing to continue paying the rent and utilities at the condo the girls were living in, and an apartment if the owner of the condo returned, but he wasn't sure the girls would be comfortable with that arrangement. In fact, he was pretty sure they wouldn't be. They were both independent enough that they wouldn't want a handout, as they would see it.

That would put Jasmine on the spot. She would have to choose between accepting his proposal and marrying him, which he thought she would be happy with, but then it would mean they would also have to accept his offer to pay for Sheila's apartment. Or she could turn down his proposal and continue working and paying for the apartment while Sheila went to college.

The more he thought about those two choices, the worse he felt. It basically boiled down to a choice between marrying him or honoring the promise she'd made to Sheila. That wouldn't be fair to Jasmine. She shouldn't have to make a choice like that. But he had no idea what else to do. For the time being, he didn't see that he had any choice but to leave things as they were, and keep thinking.

One evening the two couples were having dinner together, as they'd begun doing on a somewhat regular basis. Hunter mentioned he might be looking for a different apartment soon.

"Why?" Jasmine asked. "I thought you loved your apartment."

"I do, but I'm afraid it's about to change."

He had Trevor's attention. "How? When we were over at your apartment a few weeks ago I was really impressed with it. How is it changing?"

"Well, the building only has eight apartments, so it's not a huge building. They're nice apartments, though, mostly two bedroom, with nice finishes. They're not real cheap, but I was willing to pay a little more for it because it is very nice and comfortable, but also because I love the outdoor space."

"So do I," Sheila said. "There's land around it that's land-scaped really nice. It looks like a park."

"The first time I was there I said it was like you guys had your own private park in your backyard," Jasmine said. "I love the walking paths between the flower gardens, and the benches setting under the pretty shade trees."

"I know," Hunter said. "The far end also has spaces so any tenant who wants can plant a garden. I don't use mine, but I let my neighbor use it. She's into fresh vegetables and herbs, and she uses her space and mine together. Every now and then she gives me some fresh tomatoes from it, so it works out well for both of us."

"So how is it going to change?" Trent asked.

"The guy that owns it is moving away and doesn't want to have to worry about it, so he's selling it. There's a one-bedroom apartment that he lived in, and the rest are all two bedrooms. He bought it as an investment. He's single and didn't need two bedrooms, so he lived in the smaller one and everyone knew to go down to his apartment to pay their rent monthly and report any problems, any repairs that needed done. I talked to him yesterday and asked if he had any offers yet, and he's only had one. The guy that wants to buy it wants to take out all that beautiful landscaping and gardens and build another building there. He says it's going to be two and three bedroom apartments, but not as high end so that families will be able to afford to rent there. They'll have smaller rooms and use cheaper materials so he can get more apartments in the same space, with less money."

"But he can't take that space out," Jasmine said.

Trent thought about the situation a few moments. "That doesn't seem to me like it makes much sense from a business sense."

"I thought the same thing," Hunter said. "I could find another comparable apartment someplace else in town for a little less rent, but I'm willing to pay extra for the space out back. It's relaxing for me. Plus I appreciate the other tenants in the building. I'm not saying I'm better than other people that may not be able to afford that much for an apartment, but at this point in my life I enjoy the quiet. If he builds that other building, instead of coming home to a quiet place to enjoy out back, I'll be coming home to a bunch of families with kids."

"Not what you're willing to pay extra for," Trent said.

"Exactly. Without the peaceful backyard, I'll go somewhere else and pay less for the same quality apartment with no outside space."

"That's a shame," Jasmine said. "Maybe he'll find someone else willing to buy it and keep it as it is."

"I hope so, and so does he," Hunter said. "He said it's not a bad offer, but he's holding out a while longer, hoping to find someone who wants to keep it as is. He feels like he'd be letting all of us down if he sells it to this guy. He said he figured several of us would move if he does that."

"I think most would," Sheila said. "Everyone there is like you, young professionals who like the quiet. If that goes, I would say they will, also. Plus, just think how noisy it will be while the building is going up right there in your backyard."

"Yeah, not something I'd be looking forward to," Hunter agreed.

"I hate to hear that," Trent said, "but if you decide to leave, let us know. We'll help you move once you find a new place."

"Thanks."

Their conversation turned to something else, but Trent kept thinking about what he'd learned. Over the next few days he came up with a plan. This could possibly be the solution to his problem. Eager to see if it would work, he rearranged a couple of meetings the next day, called the man that owned the apartment building and set up a time to meet with him. When he got back to the office he got out his calculator and did some serious figuring and thinking. Happy with what he saw, he called the bank.

Chapter 16

Trent did a lot of thinking and planning over the next few days, and decided to take Jasmine out for a special dinner Saturday evening and have a talk with her. If the talk went well, he would propose. However, as anxious as he was for their special dinner, John called him Friday afternoon and the news he had put a wrench in his plans.

He had an update for them on Senator Kingsley's case. He filled Trent in, and warned him it was going to be on the evening news again, probably yet today. Trent thanked him and sat back in his chair, rethinking everything he'd just spent the last several days thinking through and planning.

The first thing he did was call Hunter and pass the information he'd learned onto him. They both felt sure the girls would want to be home when they heard the news. They decided to all go to Trent's house and spend the evening there. After sharing the information with them, they would all watch the news together.

The men told their ladies something had come up they all needed to talk about, and they would be spending the evening at Trent's. They told them to go home after work and change into something comfortable and Hunter was going to stop and get both of them and take them to Trent's. Trent was going to order meals to go from one of their favorite restaurants and would pick that up on his way home so they could enjoy a good dinner and still be able to talk about the situation privately, without having to worry about anyone approaching them after hearing something about the senator.

Trent stopped and picked up their food and had time after he got home to change into some comfortable jeans and a tee shirt before Hunter got there with both ladies. He was glad to see they'd all done the same. He suggested they sit down and eat their meal while it was warm, and he could explain why he'd called them together. Once they started their meal, all eyes turned to Trent, eager to hear what he had to tell them.

He took a deep breath, exhaled slowly, and began. "Captain Fritz called from Arizona to give me a little warning."

"Something's happened with Senator Kingsley," Jasmine said, putting her fork down and giving him her full attention.

"It has," Trent confirmed, "and it will more than likely be on the evening news. He thought we might appreciate a heads up, and I'm glad he called. Kyle Solzman, the one of your kidnappers that had the SUV —"

"He was the one of the two that seemed to be in charge," Jasmine said. "Whoever they called the boss always called him, not the other guy, and he seemed to make the decisions." Sheila nodded in agreement.

"That would go along with what Captain Fritz said. He said they got more information from him. They asked both of them about the man that owned the car before you, Sheila, and how he died, and apparently they both told them pretty much the same thing. They said that they were told the man had pictures that showed the senator taking bribes, and they had to get those pictures back, no matter what it took. They said on the senator's instructions they broke into his house and looked for them, but found nothing. They could tell the senator was extremely upset with them for not finding the photos, and threatened them if they didn't find them. That's when they broke into his house again and ransacked the place, searching everywhere."

"So why or how did they kill him?" Sheila asked. "Did he walk in on them while they were doing it, or was it because he wouldn't give them the pictures?"

"According to them, they didn't kill him. They swore he wasn't home at the time and never came home while they were there."

Sheila looked skeptical. "Then who did shoot him? My friend I bought the car from and her mom deserve to at least know who shot him."

"I agree," Trent said, "and so do the police. "They pushed the men for anything else that might help, and Kyle thought of something, though he didn't know if it meant anything. They asked about the phone calls he would get from the senator, and he said they generally all came at about the same time of day, and always from the same phone, which was a cell phone, but not the one he normally used. He said there was one time a call came from a different phone. He remembered it because he didn't answer it, not knowing who it was, and the senator called a couple of hours later from his normal phone and chewed him out for not answering the call a couple of hours earlier."

Hunter's eyebrows raised. "Another burner phone?"

"As it turned out, yes. The police went through all Kyle's calls, and he pointed out the one that was from a different phone. It turned out to be a burner phone, not listed to anyone, with prepaid minutes. They got a search warrant for it and found several calls, all to the same number. They traced that number and it was a man local police in Arizona had suspected was a hit man, but they'd never been able to find the evidence they needed to convict him."

Jasmine dropped her fork. "A hit man? I thought they only existed in movies and cop shows. Was he the one that killed him?"

"Yes," Trent confirmed. "The police looked into him and found out he had an outstanding warrant in another state for a probation violation. They got a search warrant for his house and arrested him. When they searched his house they found a gun that could have been the one used for the murder. It was the right kind, and when they ran a check on the gun it came back as being stolen. They told him they now had all the proof they needed to prove that he killed the man. They could now also charge him with stealing that gun, and the four other guns that were taken at the same time. With all the things they could charge him with now, he was definitely looking at life in prison."

"And he deserves it," Hunter said.

"But after three days in jail, the man wanted to talk to the police. It turns out he wanted to reduce his time in prison however he could, and offered to give them proof that someone big and important was behind it all, in exchange for a lighter sentence. They assumed he was talking about the senator, and agreed to listen. If he had good, useful information they would offer a plea deal of some sort."

"I'm not sure how I feel about that," Jasmine said. "I mean, I want the senator to be charged and brought to justice, but if this guy shot someone, they can't just let him off."

"They're not letting him off with nothing, but they did agree to reduce his time in prison if he gives them the proof they need to convict the senator," Trent said.

"I'm good with that," Sheila said after a moment of silence, while everyone considered the situation. "I mean, it was actually the senator that killed him. He may not have pulled the trigger, but if it was on his order, he was actually the man that killed him. The hit man wouldn't have killed him if he wasn't being paid to."

"That's true," Jasmine said. "It was actually his order that got him killed. He is the main person responsible for his death. So what did they do?"

All eyes turned back to Trent and he continued the story. "The police agreed with you and feel he's the main person responsible for the poor man's death, so they agreed to lessen the prison sentence if he had enough information to get the senator charged and convicted. He said he told the senator how much his fee would be, but that he also would need a gun that couldn't be traced back to him. The senator refused to give him one, but did agree to send enough money that could be used to purchase one. He told the officers whom he purchased it from. He admitted when he bought the gun the numbers had been filed off, so he thought it might have been stolen, but he didn't know for sure. The numbers on the gun had been filed off, but it turned out it hadn't been done good enough. An expert was able to find indentations in the metal where the numbers had been, and when they traced the numbers they felt had been there, it came back to that exact type and model, and it had been stolen."

"So the thief was a bad thief," Hunter said with a chuckle.

"Apparently, and that was a good thing," Trent said. "They arrested the man he bought the gun from, and he had three other stolen guns at his house. The numbers had all been filed off, but not deep enough. Although you couldn't see the numbers, the experts were still able to use super magnification to find the impressions. Anyway, so that part of his story proved true. They were also able to trace the money sent to him for both the purchase of the gun and the amount he charged for the hit back to similar withdrawals from an account the senator kept in his name only. They were even able to trace the burner phone to an extent. They have the security tape from a store close to the restaurant the senator eats breakfast at every morning, and it shows the senator purchasing a phone just like the burner phone used to call this guy. It's the same day the phone was activated and the first call was made to the hit man. It also shows the call made to Kyle."

"So it sounds like they have the senator," Hunter said.

"Captain Fritz feels confident they have enough for a guilty verdict on a number of charges, including ordering the murder and having you ladies kidnapped."

"Good," Jasmine said, and was echoed by Sheila.

"Yes, but now for the bad news," Trent went on, again drawing everyone's eyes and attention. "They filed additional charges against the senator today, serious charges, and that's going to be a main story on the news, both tonight and probably for the next little while."

"And probably from now on until the trial is over," Jasmine said with a long sigh.

"Probably," Trent confirmed. "Captain Fritz wanted us to know all of this in advance so we could at least be ready for the onslaught of publicity again."

"I'm glad he gave us the heads up," Hunter said, looking at Sheila. "It's not going to be fun or easy for you, but at least you've had a little warning."

"Yes," Sheila agreed. "It would have been awful to hear about it on the news tonight, or even worse, from people tomorrow."

"True," Jasmine agreed. She reached over and took Trent's hand. "Do you know what all they're going to say? I mean, are our names and pictures going to be splashed all over the news again?"

"I don't honestly know," Trent said, "but it wouldn't surprise me any. That was a big story when it happened. They showed your pictures nightly, hoping someone would have seen you and could help the police find you. Since this is related to that, I'm guessing they'll review your case, then go into how he was arrested. I'm not sure what all they know and will report, but I'm afraid you two are apt to be part of the story. I'm sorry. I wish there was something Hunter and I could do."

"I've been thinking about that, Trent, and there may be," Hunter said. "I'm not sure how much it will help, but it may be worth trying."

"I'll try anything and appreciate any help I can get," Sheila said. "What are you thinking?"

Hunter turned to Sheila and took her hand in his. "If someone at work says something, tell them you're glad we're seeing each other now and I'm helping you through it this time. If they know both of us it will switch the attention off of just you and onto both of us. Then if you want, I'll stay with you anytime you're out in public," he offered. "Then if someone recognizes you and stops you to mention it, just say something like you're glad you have someone to help you through it now. I'll give you a little squeeze, and that might turn the attention to us. They may wish us well, but it will at least get the attention off the awful thing that happened to you."

"You would do that for me?"

"Of course I would. In fact," he said, looking a bit sheepish, "I'd be proud to announce to the world that you've agreed to spend time with me. I'm not sure how much it will help you, but it might help a little bit."

"I love the idea," Sheila said, "and I appreciate it. Especially the part about you being with me if we go anywhere other than at work. Having you there with me for moral support will be a big help. Thank you."

"That's a good idea," Trent said. "We were together the first time all this publicity hit, but we didn't approach it that way. I think it's a good idea, though." He turned to Jasmine. "I'll accompany you anywhere you go other than at work, and if someone stops you, tell them you're glad you can lean on me for support, or something like that. Hunter's right, that should change people's view of the situation a bit and shift some of the attention onto us instead of just you." He turned to Hunter. "Thank you for the idea."

"Yes, thank you," Jasmine said. "And like Sheila, I like the idea of being with you everywhere I go for a while. The support, feeling your arm around me makes a big difference."

"Then it's settled," Trent said. "I suggest we spend a lot of time at home, or out of the public eye, but when we go out we'll go either in pairs, or the four of us together."

They all agreed, and went to the living room to turn the television on since it was about time for the news. They were nervous as the news came on and their leading story started with a picture of the senator. As they feared, the story of their kidnapping was reviewed, with pictures of them appearing on the screen. Then they took the story forward, saying Arizona police, who had previously arrested Senator Kingsley in connection with bribery, filed additional charges today having to do with the kidnapping of the girls and the death of the man that had owned the car Sheila purchased.

Trent had set his television to record another station's evening news, so once the channel they were watching was over they watched the one he'd recorded. As they'd feared, it was very similar, telling the same story. Trent told Jasmine he would pick her up in the morning and take her to work so she wouldn't be walking in alone. He offered to take Sheila, as well, but Hunter stepped in. He thanked him for the offer, but assured him he'd planned on taking Sheila to and from work the next few days, as well.

When the men took their ladies home that evening, they assured them they would be there for them. Their kiss goodnight was more passionate and reassuring, and they held them in their arms a little longer than normal.

The following day Trent checked with Hunter to be sure he planned on spending the evening with Sheila. Once he was assured she wouldn't be alone, he took Jasmine to his house. They worked together to make dinner, and settled on the couch afterward, where he said he had something important he needed to talk to her about.

"Is this something to do with the senator?" she asked as she leaned in against him, enjoying the feel of his arm around her.

"Nope. It has nothing to do with any of that."

"Good. That's all I've heard about all day, and I'd like to be able to get my mind off that for a while."

"I guarantee this should do that. I've set a plan in motion that I think you'll like, but I want to be sure you're in agreement with it before I give the final go ahead."

"What kind of plan?"

"A plan to buy the apartment complex where Hunter lives."

Jasmine's eyes widened. "Wow. You're going to buy the whole complex?"

"That's my plan. My financial planner has been suggesting I invest in something like real estate, so when Hunter was telling us he may have to move because that complex is for sale, it got me thinking. That may be the answer to a couple of concerns I've had. It would be an investment, and I think a good one. I always liked where he lives, for the reasons he mentioned. It's a nice place for young professionals. If they sell it and add another building of apartments that aren't as nice and a little bigger, good for families, that changes the whole feel of the complex. It eliminates the quiet, park setting that many of the people living there now pay to have. They're willing to pay more to have that."

"That's true. Hunter said he would probably move, and I doubt he would be the only one."

"I agree."

"I'm sure Hunter will be happy to hear that." She was quiet a few moments. "But he said the person who owns it now lives in a smaller unit. If he moves out, won't it be a problem, not having the owner on site so he can collect rent and people can tell him when they have a problem that needs fixed?"

"That's part of my plan, and the part I want to hear your opinion on. I thought Sheila might be interested in doing it. She could live in the small unit he lived in. She could do what he did in exchange for no rent. It would require her to collect and deposit the rents, and call repairmen to take care of any problems that came up and then pay them. Doing that would be worth free rent, and hopefully it would still give her enough time to work part-time and do her school work. I thought –"

"You're going to give her free rent?"

"If she wants to do those things, yes. I won't make her, but I thought since she'll be working part-time and going to college, that might be a good solution. I'm hoping –"

Jasmine stood up and turned to look at him. "But what about me?"

"That's the other part of what I wanted to talk to you about."

"That's fine for her, but it leaves me kind of stranded."

"Jasmine, calm down and let me finish."

"That means I have to pay the rent myself, which I should be able to do since I'm working full-time now, but I told Sheila I'd pay her college tuition this semester, too. Did you forget about that?"

"No, I didn't. If you'll let me continue —"

"I mean, I know I make more now since I'm full time, but to pay the rent myself, plus pay her tuition, I mean, that's going to make things pretty tight." She turned to glare at him. "It would have been nice if you would have been considerate enough to talk to me about it first, before you made all these plans."

Trent stood now, as well, and put his hands on her arms, holding her in place to get her attention. "Jasmine, speaking of being considerate, I might suggest you do the same thing. Be considerate enough to let me explain —"

She pulled her arms free and stomped a few feet away from Trent, obviously upset. "Don't talk to me right now about being considerate. You should have talked to me first."

"Jasmine, I am talking to you. Or at least I'm trying to. Listen, I know you've had a rather rough day, but you need to trust me and calm down."

"You're right, I have had a hell of a day. And it's getting worse. Instead of helping me, you're springing this on me, and it's not helping any. I can't believe you would do this, and then have the gall to lecture me about being considerate!"

"Oh, Jasmine, this isn't the way this was supposed to go, but you leave me no choice at this point." Before she had a chance to even try to understand what he meant, she found herself being lifted off her feet. He sat down and laid her over his knees, easily reaching beneath her to unfasten her pants and pull them and her panties down.

"Not again," she muttered as she realized what was about to happen.

"Jasmine, as much as I hate to do this right now, you know I will not allow you to have that kind of attitude. You wouldn't even let me finish telling you about my plans."

"But your plan sucks."

He immediately started the spanking, but before he could

say a word, she continued with her rant. "It leaves me stuck without a roommate." Tears started running down her cheeks as she added, "It leaves me out altogether."

It almost broke his heart to know she felt that way, but she needed to know he was always looking out for her, and she needed to always be respectful to him. He continued spanking, though not very hard. His concern at this point was simply to get her to realize she was being less than polite, and to calm down. "Jasmine, if you would have stopped interrupting me long enough to allow me to finish explaining my plan you would have realized my plan does not ignore you at all. In fact, the whole plan is centered around you."

"How can you say that? It leaves me living alone in our apartment, paying the expenses myself."

Trent was getting frustrated with her now. "No, it doesn't. The owner of your condo called the other day to let me know he'll be coming back in three or four months."

"Oh, great," she said as she started wriggling more, trying to escape his hand. "Now I don't even have an apartment."

"But hopefully you'll accept my proposal and you won't need one. I was trying to get to that, but you wouldn't give me the courtesy of listening to what I was trying to say. So now we're here, where I have to remind you how important it is to be courteous. Once we've gotten past that, hopefully you'll be ready to listen to my plan."

"Wait. What did you just say?"

"I said since you decided not to give me the common courtesy of allowing me to finish telling you my plan, we have to see if we can't remind you how to be respectful."

"No, not that part."

Continuing the spanking, but still not in a harsh or severe way, he asked, "Do you mean the part where I said that hopefully once I'm convinced you're ready to be respectful again, you'll be ready to listen to my plan?"

"No, not that part, either. The first part."

"Before I repeat that part," he said as he gave her a few harder swats, "have I succeeded in reminding you the importance of respect?"

He gave her four more harder swats, and she nodded vigorously. "You have, and I'm sorry."

"Good," he said as he helped her up and onto his lap. Once they were cuddled together comfortably, with his arms wrapped around her and her leaning against his chest, he rubbed her arm. It didn't take long for her to stop crying, which didn't surprise him since he never did spank her as hard as normal. "Are you ready to listen to me now?"

"Yes," she answered in a meek voice. "I'm sorry, Trent. I didn't like all the attention I got from everyone again today and I let it get to me. I know that wasn't fair to you and I'm sorry. I know I've said that before, but I really am sorry."

"I know you are, baby." He chuckled a bit as he said, "I know you're truly sorry every time you say it. You still do it, and I still spank you for it every time, but I know you're sincere every time you tell me you're sorry. Which, by the way, is happening less frequently than it used to, which means these spankings are helping. You have a little ways to go yet, but you're making progress over the last ten months. Hopefully a year from now you'll be controlling your temper better and you won't be forgetting to be respectful."

"I hope so, too," she said, reaching back to rub her bottom, even though it really wasn't very sore.

He smiled as he pulled her hands around in front of her. Instead of letting them go, he held onto them, bringing one of them up to kiss. He met her eyes as he kissed the other one. "Hopefully there will be another major change a year from now."

She looked at him, confusion written on her face. "What do you mean?"

"Again, this wasn't exactly the way I planned this, but Jasmine, I love you and want to spend the rest of my life with you next to me. Would you allow me to do that by marrying me? Would you please agree to become Mrs. Trent Douglas?"

Her eyes were huge, and full of unshed tears as she searched his eyes. "You were serious about proposing to me? You really mean it?"

"You still haven't learned that I don't say things I don't mean? Yes, Jasmine, I'm completely serious. I want to marry you, and I'm hoping you will agree to it. In fact, I'm hoping you agree to it soon, because the longer you make me sit here without an answer, not knowing if you're going to tell me yes or no, the more nervous I'm getting."

She stared at him another two minutes without saying a word. Trent was beginning to seriously worry. She was going to turn him down, and he wasn't sure what he should do. Did she simply need more time? Was she having second thoughts about him? How should he handle this?

Finally, after what he was sure must have been at least two hours, Jasmine smiled as she threw herself into him. "Yes! Oh, yes! Yes, of course I'll marry you!"

Trent was a little overwhelmed, which normally didn't happen to him. He reached out his arms and caught her as she was talking, and it took a moment for her words to sink in. He was so sure she was going to turn him down, it took a moment to wrap his head around the fact that she'd just told him yes. His arms tightened around her as the news reached his brain and he processed it. His little minx had agreed to become his wife!

Their lips met in a kiss that proved to themselves and each other that they were in fact about to become man and wife, share their lives, and neither could be any happier about it. When they finally pulled back, she looked into his eyes. "I feel like I have to be dreaming. You really just asked me to marry you?"

"I did. And you really said yes?"

"I did," she said, laughing. "So does that mean no backing out now, we're stuck with each other?"

"I'd say it does," he said with a big grin. "We have a lot to talk about, but I need another kiss first."

"Oh, good, because so do I." Their second kiss lasted even longer than the first, but was just as full of compassion and promise.

This kiss eventually ended, with both of them needing a moment to breathe. He stood her up, pulled her panties and pants back up, and settled her in next to him, with his arm pulling her in tightly against him. "Now, we've got some talking to do. Any chance you can let me finish telling you about my plans now? I really do want to know if you like them, or how we can change them to be better."

Her face red, she nodded. "Now that I know I'm in your plans, yes, I'm ready to listen." She took a breath and continued, before he had a chance to say a word. "So, we're about to lose our condo, and since you watch out for me and Sheila, you came up with a solution for us before we even knew we had a problem. You decided to buy Hunter's apartment complex so it can stay as is. In order to do that, you need someone to be sort of a manager, and you thought you could offer that job to Sheila in exchange for a free apartment, which I think is a wonderful and very generous idea. It will help her a lot so she can work part-time while going to school, without having to worry about rent."

"Right."

He took a breath to explain more, but once again, she jumped in before he had a chance. "Hunter will love the idea because he'll be able to keep his apartment, just the way it is, the way he and the others that live there are willing to pay a little extra for. I'm guessing they'll both be happy to find out they'll be living in the same apartment building."

Trent nodded, but again, before he could say a word, she continued. "And the best part of the plan is that I won't need to find a new apartment because I get to marry the man I love." She had a big smile on her face, which he was glad to see. "So it sounds to me like you fixed the problem perfectly for everybody, especially me, before any of us even knew there was a problem."

He leaned down and kissed the top of her head and tried to use his stern voice. "So it seems now I just have one problem left."

"What's that?"

"My fiancée still doesn't seem to want to let me finish explaining my plan. I'm not sure what I'm going to have to do to her."

She looked up at him with a look of alarm. "What do you mean? You just explained it. It all sounds wonderful to me."

He saw the look of sincerity in her eyes and knew that in her mind, he had explained it. He laughed out loud, and when she gave him a look of confusion he couldn't help but to laugh a little harder. "Okay. I must have done a good job explaining it then if it all sounds good to you."

"You did, and like I said, it all sounds wonderful. I have a couple of questions, but everything I've heard so far sounds fantastic."

"Good. What are your questions?"

"First, how soon can we get married?"

He couldn't hold back a smile, loving her enthusiasm. He hoped she wouldn't want a long engagement, but was prepared to give her as long as she wanted. Apparently, he wouldn't have to worry too much about that. "How soon do you want to get married?"

"I'm free tomorrow."

"Tomorrow?"

"Is that rushing you a little too much? I suppose you want a long engagement?"

He laughed again as he rubbed her arm. "No, I don't want a long engagement unless you do, but I think tomorrow is rushing it just a bit. We have to get a marriage license first, and I don't know how long that takes. Then we should make a few plans. I assume you'd like to take a honeymoon after we get married, and to do that we have to decide where we want to go, make reservations, and arrange for someone at work to cover for us. Would you like to try to find your parents and have them here?"

She was quiet for several moments, and he was afraid mentioning her parents might have hit on a tender subject. He was about to tell her it was her choice, she didn't have to try to invite them, when she turned to face him. "I never thought of that. Is that going to be a problem? I mean, George is still at the company, so I'm sure he and Beth can handle the purchasing department, but how does the president of the company get away? Who do you have cover for you?"

Again it took a moment for him to realize her concern had been for work, not her parents. "That's why I have vice-presidents," he answered smoothly. "I'll take care of anything major I know of that will be coming up, then let them handle everything else on a day to day basis. We just have to plan ahead so they know we'll be gone and for how long."

"Okay, we should be able to do that. So, how long will it take to make all these plans?"

"It depends. How big a wedding do you want? How long will it take you to find a dress you like? Do you want your parents to be here? Do you want a dinner after the wedding? We'll have to find a caterer and plan the meal. Where do you want to have the wedding? We'll have to book that location."

Again she was quiet for several minutes. "Oh, wow. Marrying you is more complicated than I thought."

"Why is marrying me complicated?"

"I know a lot of ladies plan a big dream wedding in their head, and some of them dream about it for a long time, but I never did that. I never really gave it a lot of thought. I always hoped one day I would get married to someone I loved, and I knew he loved me. That part is all that ever seemed important to me. I've heard of ladies marrying someone because they had money, or because they were afraid no one else would ask them and they didn't want to be alone. I always thought that was sad. I never planned on getting married unless and until I found the one man that I loved and I knew he loved me."

"Well, you've found that man, so now you can plan whatever kind of wedding you want."

"But don't you see? The wedding isn't important to me. The marriage is, but not the wedding. I really never gave it much thought. I honestly would be fine with going to the mayor or the judge or whoever is qualified to marry people. I don't need a new dress or a fancy meal or any of that. What I care about is the wonderful life together with the man I love, which starts after the wedding."

It was Trent's turn to be quiet for a few moments while he absorbed the information she'd just given him. As he thought about it, he shouldn't have been at all surprised by it. Since he'd known her he'd come to realize that material things truly didn't mean much to her. She'd had them at one time and now knew that they were nothing compared with knowing that someone loved you and cared about you. He would certainly make sure she always knew he loves her and cares about her, but he'd like her to have a special day to remember, as well.

He was thinking about how best to approach it, when once again, she took care of it for him. "I may not need a big wedding, but that's one of the things that's complicated about marrying you. Since you're the president of the company, we probably need to have a wedding big enough so any of your employees that want to can go to it, don't we? Then have a dinner afterwards. So we better start planning this thing. When do you want to have it? Do you have anyplace in mind for it?"

"As much as I'd be willing to go to a judge or mayor, too, you're probably right. Some people feel hurt if they aren't invited to a wedding. The people at work have been good to us and I don't want to hurt anyone's feelings. Let's talk about it and see if we can come up with a way to have a nice wedding, but nothing huge or extravagant. A meal afterwards would be a nice way to visit with them and thank them for caring enough to come share the day with us. Again, I would prefer we keep it rather simple, nothing too formal. How about you?"

"I'm with you there."

They spent the rest of the evening trying to come up with ideas and plans for a simple, although they both admitted it may be rather large, wedding. When it was time to take her home, he asked one last question. "Well, did I manage to get your mind off the senator and that whole mess this evening?"

"Yes, you certainly did," she said with a big grin, "and thank you."

"You're welcome. Hopefully this might help the next few days, too. Now when somebody brings it up you can tell them you have a future husband to help you through it now. That should certainly change the topic to something you're more willing to talk about."

"It certainly should, and I'm glad. Thank you for that, too."

"See, I try to take care of you." He grinned and added, "Even when you're disrespectful and won't allow me to propose to you."

He watched her face turn red again and she looked down. "I know."

"Well, the way I see things, we have an interesting story to tell our grandchildren some day about how we met. You thought I gave you a fifty-dollar bill when I gave you a hundred. I still remember when I asked you to look at the bill I gave you one more time, and you said 'once again, you're wrong.' Then when that ill-behaved young boy ran into you at the restaurant and you spilled iced tea on me, you looked at me to apologize and said 'you again'? I believe I heard the phrase 'once again, I did nothing wrong' a few times when I pulled you over my knee. There were other times you found yourself in the same position and told me, 'not again.' Now when they ask how I proposed to you —"

Her head flew up to meet his eyes. "You wouldn't tell them that, would you?"

He laughed, and raised his eyebrows. "I don't know. Would I?"

"Please don't."

"But this time you were much more polite. You said 'please not again'." He saw the worry in her eyes and pulled her in against him again. "No, Jasmine, like always, I will never tell anyone else about that. Any spanking you get is between us, and if you want anyone else to know, it's your story to tell. You might want to give it some thought, though. You have a fair amount of time yet to come up with what you want to tell our grandkids some day if they do ask you about the night we got engaged."

She thought a few moments, and looked up at him with the adorable, mischievous look he'd grown to love. "I know what I'm going to tell them. I'll tell them once again, their grandfather swept me off my feet and made me the happiest lady alive. Every word of that will be the truth. You did sweep me off my feet. I won't mention that you swept me off my feet and over your knees. It's also true you've made me the happiest lady alive tonight, so I can be completely honest with them when I tell them that."

He laughed again and gave her a squeeze. "And once again, you've made me realize how lucky I am, and that life will always be fun and exciting with you at my side."

"And once again, I agree with you completely. Life is always going to be exciting for us."

Misty Malone

Writing has been a dream of Misty's for several years. She's finally following that dream, and began writing in 2013. She enjoys writing romance stories, with a handsome man who falls in love with a lovely lady in need of a strong man who can take her in hand. Having grown up on a farm, she especially enjoys writing about strong cowboys. She lives in the Midwest with her husband and son, not far from where she grew up. Misty hopes you enjoy reading her books as much as she enjoys writing them. Reviews to her books are very much appreciated, and she would like to thank you for each one of them. She invites you to leave a message for her at authormistymalone@gmail.com.

Don't miss these exciting titles by Misty Malone and Blushing Books!

Pine Falls Series
The Town's Inheritance
Say Something
Nothing Average

Western Camping series
The Camping Cowgirl, Book 1
The Camping Cowboy, Book 2

Holiday House Series
Finding Holly

Warning Merry
Convincing Sarah

Wyoming Ranch Life series
Mail Order Surprise, Book 1
Ranch Life is Great, Book 2
Ranch Life Surprise, Book 3
Wyoming Ranch Live Collection

Life at the Ranch series
Life at the Ranch, Book 1
Christmas at the Ranch, Book 2

Last Chance Program series
Cheyenne and Jason, Book 1
Gina and Paul, Book 2

Single Titles
Again and Again
I Guess I Love You
The Bridge Repair
Back to the Ranch
Whoops! Wrong Ranch
How to Stir Up a Ranch
The Real Prize
That Beautiful Orange Gown
Not Just a House
I'm on a Ranch?
It's My Ranch?
My Ranch, My Way
Learning to Drive… Him Crazy
The Strange Healing
Count This Cowboy In

Cowboy Motel
A Quiet Christmas Alone…Kinda
On Probation
One Smart Cowboy
It's Just A Ranch
A Beautiful Ranch
Being Schooled
Nice to Meet You
Stealing Her Breath
Mail Order Mystery
The Best Accident Ever
She Did What?
Never Again
Not Lonely Now
Top Cop
Darn Noisy Neighbors
Listen Here, Cowboy
Can't Argue with That
Hidden Talents
It'll Work Out
Work and Play

Anthologies
Tamed By The Cowboy
12 Naughty Days of Christmas 2018
Love of a Cowboy, Two
Sweet Town Love

Audio Books
The Real Prize
It's My Ranch?
Mail Order Surprise

Connect with Misty Malone
authormistymalone@gmail.com

Blushing Books

Blushing Books is the oldest eBook publisher on the web. We've been running websites that publish steamy romance and erotica since 1999, and we have been selling eBooks since 2003. We have free and promotional offerings that change weekly, so please do visit us at http://www.blushingbooks.com/free.

Blushing Books Newsletter

Please join the Blushing Books newsletter
to receive updates & special promotional offers.
You can also join by using your mobile phone:
Just text BLUSHING to 22828.

Every month, one new sign up via text messaging will receive
a $25.00 Amazon gift card, so sign up today!